CHARON'S LAST CALL

BY

GINA LYNELLE SCHAEFER

CHARON'S LAST CALL

BY

GINA LYNELLE SCHAEFER

Ginalynelle.com

TEXAS

Charon's Last Call
Copyright 2021 by Gina Lynelle Schaefer
All rights reserved

Second Edition

13   12   11   10   9   8   7   6   5   4   3   2   1

ISBN 978-1-946182-20-3 (trade paper)
ISBN 978-1-946182-21-0 (ePub)

Houston, Texas

This novel's story and characters are fictitious.
Certain long-standing institutions, agencies, and
public offices are mentioned, but the characters
involved are wholly imaginary.

Ginalynelle.com

HOUSTON, TEXAS

Dedicated To

my loving husband and son.

Introduction

The events in this book are not a guide for the afterlife and offer no guarantees to help your bad habits in a particular way. The cases on the following pages will make you uncomfortable and possibly disturb the boldest of us. Life is not for the faint of heart, and in Coma, the Last Chance Casino has no rubber room but instead suggests a compelling sip of reality with a twist of free will. Without numbers, lines, and all the time in the world, the only way to get out of this pinch is with a spin of chance. So, whatever your theory of immanence may be, this place doesn't apologize for its rules and is never on break. Kiss your loved ones, pour a drink, and enjoy a robust set of individuals that have loved and lost, hated, and tormented, served their god of choice, and are ready to risk salvation.

Patrick Beck

TABLE OF CONTENTS:

Purgatory

Damn bowtie! I can't believe I'm forced to wear this stupid debacle of an outfit!

Gary looked at his reflection in the narrow mirror lined with an assortment of old-time liquor bottles. His baby thin dirty-blonde hair was short, not the buzz cut he preferred, but it was not like it ever got dirty, so it was manageable. His long white shirt ballooned up at the sleeves and was held down by a narrow ribbon that reminded him of his wife's garters she wore before age withered her body, and his conscience became clouded with neglect. His straight black pants fit him perfectly. But thin black suspenders were part of the attire, so he wore them along with the black silk bowtie, the final shackle of his costume.

His bar always immaculate with its nicely organized spirits that came from all eras of life as well as the cigars that stayed neatly stacked in the dispenser next to a glass rack. A tray of every type of cigarette imaginable along with rolls of tobacco adorned the side of the tray that held colorful delicious fruit that never faded or rotted regardless of the passage of time or the condition of the environment, for the drinkers with a tropical taste. A small swing door resided in the middle of the bar to accommodate a pathway to a slot machine decorated with tacky gold leaves and a heavy large gold handle holding a gold globe of the world at the tip. A halo of colorful lights circled around it like mysterious sparklers.

"Well, I guess life really is a gamble," a high-pitch southern drawl announced from the left side of the bar.

"What is that?" An elderly lady quietly eased her way in, making herself comfortable in one of the barstools with a red cushion back. She was tall and slender with a curvy body however the footprints of time crept under her bluish green eyes and her nasolabial folds. She pushed her stool up a little closer to the bar and gently folded her arthritic hands to rest while flashing a gold band on her left hand, smiling gently at the barkeep.

"No solitaire?"

"Oh no, I gave that to the boy years ago. He met this wonderful girl in college, he just couldn't wait to propose and begin a life of marital bliss. So, I gave him my ring." Nudging her head at the slot machine, "am I to understand that there is gambling at the bar as well?"

Standing back to let her have a better view, "that my dear is the coveted slot machine of station three in purgatory." Walking over to it he spins the rotating mount it rested on so she could get a better view. "This determines fate."

"Fate? I don't follow. Fate as we make it or what the great lord has in store for us?"

"The fate of the sleeping soul's journey." He looks at her with a smile, "did you know that it has been said that often times a soul will fall before it even dies?"

"You don't say," she said with a half-hearted grin.

"Yep. Some believe that when that happens that a demon inhabits the body until the body's natural death."

"Like when you fall in your dreams?"

"Not exactly. Or at least I don't know. I am not what you would call a mastermind of one's dreams. But I can speak to those that are in such a deep sleep that the living world does not know what side the sleeper is closer to." Looking up at the beveled ceiling. "They just pray and hope that they are answered with the response desired."

"Response desired? You mean they pray that the sleeper wakes up and if they don't than the person praying response went unanswered."

"No. It's not like that when it comes to prayers. Our good father answers all prayers, its just at times, the answer is no, and that leaves the noble one praying to question themselves and often time their faith."

Nodding towards the casino in the distance. "So are you going to tell me that is what is happening with all those gamblers over there."

"Maybe it is. They all eventually end up here. No matter

how many chips they throw on the table out there, they end up with two gold coins in their pockets and restlessness on their mind and fear in their heart."

She rests her arms on the bar and pulls her body closer. "Now let me guess. Those are the coins that will pay their fare over these nasty waters." She looks around at the different rivers flowing in multiple directions. "And if I am understanding this right, they pay you and you take them across."

"Something like that, but I think you have more of a romantic version in mind. I am not some gondolier carrying these sinners up and down the streams here. No serenading here."

"And where is here may I ask. Hell?"

"God no, they wouldn't send you there even to visit me now, would they?"

"Well, I wouldn't think so, but this place seems, well…" she looks around, hesitant with her words and then whispers, "can anybody hear our conversation?"

"Probably but guess what. They don't care. Speak your mind. It's not like they can't figure out your thoughts."

"And is they God and Satan?"

Gary rolled his eyes. "Wow, people get too scared from their Sunday school lessons." He then looks around and notices a man at the side of one of the shores frantically scavenging for body pieces. "This is all a façade. A realistic one, but a façade, nevertheless. People sin, and they get joy from it, until they realize that this god thing is real and then they get scared shitless because they figured they pissed him off and lie to themselves that they were never really that bad in hopes to convince themselves as well as god that they are remorseful even though it is all a manipulation of emotions."

"God thing? For a believer, you are not very convincing."

"I don't mean it that way and despite the looks of this architectural nightmare of a waiting room, this isn't the real hell."

"Then what is it?"

"Purgatory. A form of it anyway. A long disgusting waste

of time for people to gather their thoughts before they find out exactly what fate has in store for them."

"And how do they find out?"

Gary relaxes on the slot machine, his inquisitor pulls herself in closer as he whispers, "it's magic."

"Oh, it is not." She pushers herself back from the bar, "you are full of it. Are you going to tell me or am I wasting my time?"

"Okay, okay, I'll tell you. Every person that is meant to be a passenger through this realm of ill-fated rest, arrives with two magic beans."

She leans back, pushes a loose gray strand of hair behind her ear and responds, "really, magic beans. Excuse me Jack but your beanstalk has been cut short."

"Oh, okay, you win. But they do come with two gold coins like the ones you asked about. Real old looking too if you ask me. Probably would be worth a fortune up there," as he spoke his eyes move up as if pointing to a world far beyond the ceiling.

"Anyway, the final gamble so to speak involves taking those two coins and putting them in this here slot machine." He gestures his arms making a modeling move to showcase the gadget. "When they pull the slot, they have three possibilities that they can land on. Life, which means they will wake up from their coma and live the rest of their life as it was meant to be, death which means, … well, you know." He then shrugged and lifted his arms each one pointing to a different direction. The left arm pointed to a glass smokey doorway covered with hideous faces and objects of torment, horrendous cries sound out from behind the doors coupled with wicked laughter. The door on the right made from a deep rich mahogany with gold handles and released a scent of roses and vanilla, lined with cherubs and a soft bright light streaming from underneath, with the faint sound of a choir singing.

He then takes a bow before the lady barfly and says, "I my dear, lead the gambler to their final destination."

She nodded, "okay, that seems simple enough. Dare I say

that you are pointing out the paths between heaven and hell?"

Gary smiles with smug satisfaction, "Yes, and I am your guide. But your observation is superficial."

"Really, I'm intrigued; explain."

"Well, I'm just a simple guide over the bridges and the pathways. From what I can tell, my customers have already perused the hallways of heaven and hell." The lady barfly knits her brow, but Gary ignores the concern and continues, "people have a way of creating their own happiness and their own torment. They embrace or reject spiritual values bestowed on them at an early age and choose whether to create a circle of their own making consisting of a peaceful utopia or, well they… they yield an appetite of violence, perfusion, malice and fraud."

"Well, I get that," she pauses as she determines how to manipulate her words, "if you can't have light without dark than you cannot have a heaven without a hell." Gary starts to respond but she holds up her right index finger, "and with that, comes an all-forgiving God. Isn't life simply a journey where one finds their way back to him. His love, his embrace?"

"I hear you, but what you are speaking of is faith. Not everyone who comes through those doors," Gary points to a set of sleek gold, elevator doors with a bronze clock on top reading three o'clock, "many find themselves lost, astray from their morals with little remorse and no thoughts of salvation."

As Gary spoke a frightful growl emerges from the left door, sparking flames spurt out from underneath while three hideous beasts with a wingspan of six feet flapped as gamblers tiptoed by, drinks in hand, fear in eyes. The lady shuddered.

"Don't mind them," Gary chuckles assuring, "they do that for dramatic effect. They want to induce fear and power. It is how they work. Don't listen to their growls or words, as they are lies and meant to instill fear in you if you don't follow their suggestions. They thrive on the souls that cannot resist, on incontinence, violence, malice. Sometimes they will go as far as to offer them life if they take their last drink in hopes to possess their souls when they wake up from their medical slumber. Kind of like a walk-in. The soul thinks they are getting their life back only to have their body occupied by the clever demon whom they made the arrangement with."

The lady barfly nods as in deep thought but then speaks up, "wait life? I'm confused. I thought the souls that find themselves here were too late for redemption."

"Ha, you would think so, but there is another option other than eternal life filled with damnation of hell or the embrace of love. Some unsuspecting individuals may be offered a third option, an olive branch in a way and that is choice."

"Interesting thought. Choice," she said thoughtfully, "so how does it work?"

"A person should never abandon all hope and if one is smart enough to recognize that, even an ounce of remorse, then they may lead to a cause that lands them here. In this vestibule of sin, you can say. Most of them never really took a side. Good or evil, white cowboy hat verses black cowboy hat, angel on the right shoulder, devil on the left, however you want to see it in the absurd fairy tales related by naïve Sunday school teachers."

"Sounds like heartless selfish people."

"Maybe, but think about it," Gary walks over to her and leans on the counter, "can you really feel compassion or distribute it if it you never experienced it. If a child never felt love, do they know how to express it as adults? Or even recognize it when they feel it. Emotions is a gift that individuals often take for granted. They are the building blocks of your soul that threads the humanity in all of us. Or at least should be. A building without windows is a lonely cell, a person without vision, is an empty shell going through the motions. When a patron comes to drink from my bar, they are allowed a glimpse into their life, and often it is the darkness that provokes the reflection." Moving towards the slot machine, "You see my fancy contraption?" The barfly nods, "Look out there," Gary looks out to the patrons in the casino area, "they are here just goofing around until they decide to come and get their final drink."

"Final drink?"

"Well yes, it is included in the fare." Looking out into the crowd again, "they are all gambling and drinking free Lotus drinks until they decide when they want to come up and share their story and play their game."

"What's a Lotus drink?"

"It is a delicious nectar, here I'll get you one." He whistles at a woman walking around with a tray of tall crystal flute glasses with stems set in a crystal flower holding a blush-colored liquid. She smiles at Gary when she walks up.

"Yes sir."

"Please offer this fine lady a drink." The waitress walks briskly to her and lowers the tray. Hesitantly, she looks at Gary and then accepts a drink, thanking the waitress as she walks away.

"Um, sweet. Is there a lot of alcohol in this?"

"Not at all, it is a recipe from the gods that allows the consumer to have time stand still in their world."

"Wait, their time? Their world?"

"Yes, you see," Gary waves his arm in a long stretch across the rooms. "These people are from different times running parallel to each other. They have had their incidents or accidents; however, you want to refer to it as that led them into a coma state. If they drink the Lotus drink which they all do because it is delicious, then their time will stand still while the parallel worlds or time continues to not disrupt the nature of the universe. This gives them the ability to rest their bodies and cleanse their soul. Some stay here for a long time, years on earth and others, want to get their decisions over with."

Gary smiles, "those are the ones that don't care for the anguish screams expelling from the door to the left or perhaps they are just anxious to meet their loved ones waiting for them behind the doors of the right. You see they make up stories out there, as to what it is really like behind the separate doors but they truth is, nobody really knows. They are the unclassified, unclear if hell or heaven is in their future. Each time they pull a slot, or place a bet out there, they are questioning every decision they made in their lives. Lives that have faded with each passing day on earth but, burns in their conscience here. The Lotus drink may make time stand still but anxiety runs rapid." Gary winks at her, "I think the demons get off on that. Feed on it actually. Anyway, that is where I come in."

"Well, I hardly doubt you are the one to make the decision."

Gary laughs, "no, I leave that up to fate."

The barfly notices that the words *Wheel of Fate* is stamped in the gold of the slot machine. Gary puts his hands up to it. "You see, when a patron comes and after they speak their story, they pull the lever, and the wheels display what is in store for them. Life, death, or choice. I in return lead them to their Final Destination."

"Do you cross them over in a boat?"

"Ah! I see you have been reading a little too much Dante."

The barfly looks around at the different bridges, "well then, what is the water surrounding us?"

"Again, for dramatic effect. We all have troubled waters that we cross in our lifetime, sometimes that carries on to death. Notice there are five main points streaming through the room. Each bridge that you see crosses a distributary that continues into the cycle of the main river." Looking seriously at her, "you must be careful over those as they are as much of the soul's story as the bar and the casino."

The barfly looks at him quizzically, "My bar is on the shore of the Acheron, which is rightfully fitting I suppose, however, I feel like I run a confessional more than a bar."

"So, if they get life then they get to go back and continuing living?"

"Sort of," Gary looks back out into the crowd. "Although, time creeped along there, they still have to recover from the situation that brought them to here to begin with. An alternate new life may begin as they have to recover."

"How so? I mean, will they go back will they have to deal with a disability or something like that."

"Perhaps, or the loss of a loved one they were not allowed to grieve, or perhaps a job or a home. It all gets complicated when one simple incident, an accident or even a crime happens in a mere moment and then life ripples resulting in being uprooted into a disarray of convulsing confusion." Gary takes a breath and then goes on. "my love, look." Gary points the second point of the arena where a cluster of noise from obnoxious gamblers that are circled by the Cocytus River. "A mysterious pathway will form, befitting for the traveler when one has built up the nerve to come across." He winks at her, "you see that river on the left?"

The lady nodded.

"That is the Phlegethon waters. They circle the area around the gates of hell, and let's just say the demons that dance around that place like to give them a hard time when they cross. Practically begging them to trespass. It's a game of cat and mouse for them." He looks down for a moment as he is interrupted by a shriek of a meow by an annoying feline. Then looking back up into her eyes he continues, "you know, many people don't acknowledge God until the moment they see the possibility of life being ceased from them. Then they beg for forgiveness for their sins, but their repentance is questionable. So, they linger there," Gary's eyes nod up towards the direction of the casino, "pretending to enjoy the freedom of gambling until, and mind my vulgarity please, but until they get the balls to cross the bridge of the Phlegethon and then that of the Acheron because if I might point out, there is no straight bridge across."

The woman is silent, as her memory of crossing the Styx from the elevator and taking the dreadful path to the bar completely escaped her. Finally, she speaks, "and if a gambler gets choice do, they know what lies ahead? What they will have to deal with if they go back."

"No ma'am. And trust me, that is a question that often

comes up. But I know nothing of their destiny except for what I can infer from the pieces of time that they share with me. This is good since I cannot in anyway influence the decision. I like to think of myself as a simple man. A ferryman that guides them to their long-term destination." He straightens up and shrugs his shoulders, "hell, I don't even know where to take them until the bridge opens up. Yet, so many times they see me as their savior to devour their guilt in hopes to use me as a portal for god's forgiveness." He shakes his head, "poor bastards. Poor stupid bastards."

Looking at the two doors at the ends of the room. "Doesn't seem like to far of a walk to me."

Gary chuckled, "well, I like to think that my job is important so maybe I embellished a little." As he spoke, a black and white tuxedo cat jumped up on the bar. "Hey Kitty Kat, come to see your daddy?" The cat purred and nuzzled up against him as he pulled out a small jar of cat treats from under the bar.

The lady squealed, "what on earth! I knew I heard a meow." Her eyes lit up in excitement when she saw the pretty feline.

"This was part of my negotiation, I didn't want this job," Gary said thoughtfully as he scratched the cat below her chin, "and I don't think I really had a choice but for a consolation prize they let me keep her with me."

"Who are they?"

"The powers that be." He studied her again, she was immaculately dressed, her long gray hair was braided and placed over her right shoulder with a few loose curls that fell over her face on occasions, she looked at him and smiled, taking another sip of her Lotus flower.

"So, since you are sitting at the bar, are you interested in trying the one-armed-bandit?"

A moment of recollection fell over her, and she smiled, "No, not me. I, too made a negotiation. I am a storyteller you know, and lately, I feel like I have run out of stories." Throwing in a coy smile, "I was hoping, if you don't mind, that I can sit here for a while and listen to the tales that are told to you."

"Don't recall that ever being an option before, but then again, if nobody comes to a stop it, I don't see a problem with it."

Gary then hollers out, ""Last call."

Camilla

"Excuse me," a sweet soft voice said behind the storyteller.

"Oh my, you hardly seem like you belong here." She turns and arches an eyebrow at Gary while Kitty Kat jumps on the bar sending the tiny voice into a flutter of giggles. Gary got up and walked around the bar and picked up the tiny girl placing her on a bar stool, swiveling it a few times, sending her giggles into squeals of laughter.

"I think my lady friend is right, but we can't judge those that walk through the gold elevator doors. We can only listen." Winking at her, "now tell me, pretty one, what's your name?"

"Camilla, but mama calls me Cammy." Looking around, "is she here? I followed that man's directions, the one that told me to walk in the middle of the bridge and not look to the left." Tears began to weld up in her eyes, "the sounds, they were so scary, the fire was hot. Why am I here? I want my mommy. Where is she? Is she here?" Her small body began to shake so Gary stepped a little closer to her, softening his voice and calmly comforting the girl's urgent pleas.

"I'm afraid not, but you did good listening to Mr. Herman, and now you are safe, and you are not alone. Do you remember anything?"

"Ice-cream. Lots of ice cream."

"Ice-cream!"

"Well, raspberry sherbet, actually. I always get it right after my treatments."

"Treatments?"

"Yes, the nurses bring us a round to settle our stomachs, but well…sometimes it doesn't work." She looks up, "it's not that we don't appreciate it, it's just sometimes we aren't hungry, but we don't want to disappoint them. They are so nice. We never want to disappoint them."

"Oh, I'm sure they understand. Your body goes through a lot when you have those treatments."

"Mama says that I'm raging a war with the great "C"" Her voice perks up an optic louder as she places her arms on her waist in pride, "but I can handle it cause God made me strong." Looking around, "I don't recognize anyone yet. Where's my mama? She said that she would be there when I woke up." Blinking her eyes at Gary, "Am I awake. Mama says sometimes my imagination slips into my dreams and becomes real. I even talk in my sleep sometimes."

Gary brings Kitty Kat closer, and Cammy's soft pale hand reaches out as the cat raises her head so she could scratch under her chin. "Your cat sure is pretty."

"Yeah, I like to think of myself as her cat daddy."

Camilla lets out another giggle, "my daddy doesn't like cats. We have a dog. A Pit Bull named Hades. Mama don't like it, says that he had no business bringing that thing home. Around a sick child at that." Shifting in her seat, "I'm sick, you know."

"Really? How do you feel now?"

"Just fine, sir. Thank you for asking." Camilla's voice lifts as she lets out a big smile. "Daddy, he don't come to the hospital when I have my treatments, or they keep me for a few days. Says he don't like hospitals. Guess I don't either, but I don't have a choice. Mama though, she's always there." Getting anxious, "I don't understand why I can't see her."

"So, Camilla, or would you like me to call you Cammy?"

"Don't know, sir, only my family, and friends call me Cammy, and I don't even know your name."

"Smart girl knows about stranger danger. My name is Gary." He lets out a hand so that she can shake it.

"Pleased to meet you, Mr. Gary, sir."

"Likewise, I'm sure. Now tell me, Cammy, can I get you something to drink?"

"Well, I sure like a Shirley Temple."

"A Shirley Temple it is."

"And could I please have two cherries?"

"You can have as many cherries as you like," Gary says over his shoulder as he fills up a tall malt glass with Sprite and a splash of grenadine. He then plucked, out of the never-rotting fruit tray, five of the fattest juiciest cherries that Camilla had ever seen in her short seven years of life and dropped them into the Sprite, where they magnified against the light. Looking like large bombs in the drink.

"You drink up, my sweet girl." Camilla smiled and immediately began to slurp out of the bendy straw that Gary slid in her drink before making his own Shirley Temple and sat comfortably adjacent to her.

"Now, tell me whatever you want to tell me."

"Like what?"

"I don't know, whatever comes to mind."

The lady barfly watched curiously at the exchange in silence.

The little girl thought for a moment, wincing her eyebrows as she pondered the idea. "Wow, sir, I never really get to talk about what I want to. Hmmm" Knitting her eyebrows, she finally said, "I like school."

"Well, that is a fine start. Tell me why."

"Because Mrs. Ferguson says my pictures are beautiful even when I color outside of the lines. And when I am done with my work, I can listen to *Where the Sidewalk Ends* as much as I want. But…" she pauses and looks up at Gary, "sometimes the teachers whisper about me, and I don't like that."

Gary tilts his head slightly, "really, what do they whisper about?"

"I'm not sure, but it started when mama came up to the school last year and told them about my a-cute my-loide-look-at-me."

"I think you mean acute myeloid leukemia."

"I say it better."

"Yes, you do, so you think the teachers talk about you."

Stirring her drink with her straw. "I know they do. I'm young, but I see the looks on their faces. You know, they don't look directly at me, more like through me like I am some sort of doll. But they are really nice to me. Sometimes to the point where the other kids get mad and call me names under their breath. You know, soft enough to where the teachers can't hear, but they make sure I can."

"Now, why do you think that is?"

"Well, I always get called on when I raise my hand and left alone when I don't. I am always chosen to be the line leader, and if I don't want to participate in PE, then I don't have to. I get to go back to the room and be the teacher's little helper." She puffed out her chest and pulled back her arms as she spoke. The lady barfly smiled encourage but remained silent. Camilla then looks back and Gary and lowers her voice, "Mama says the other kids are jealous because I am so special, but I know that I'm not so special."

"What? With a grown-up mind like yours. I find that hard to believe. Now, what makes you think that you are not special?"

"Because I won't have as many birthday parties as the other kids at my school." Her head drops down.

"Now, who told you that?"

"Nobody directly but I heard Mrs. Ferguson whisper it to one of the boys who was being mean to me to make him stop and instead he told the whole class, and then they told me that I was bad. I started to cry, so the teacher sent me to Mrs. Thiess, the counselor who called my mama and told her that she needed to get me baptized or I will go to hell when I pass."

Large wet tears fell out of Camilla's big blue eyes, her shoulders shook again, Kitty Cat extended a white paw to her lap, and Gary placed his hands on her shoulders.

"You listen to me, Cammy. That mean old counselor shouldn't have said that to your mama or you. She ain't got no sense if you ask me."

Camilla looked out into the casino. "But why am I here? I mean, this doesn't look…" she hesitated, then looked up at him. "Mama says I shouldn't say that word. I shouldn't have said it to you."

"Oh, trust me, child. I've heard a lot worse. In fact, I've said a lot worse." Then bending in closer to her, "but not to anyone as sweet as you."

"Mama wanted to get me baptized," Camilla chirped, kicking her feet back and forth and taking another sip of her Shirley Temple. "Wow, sir, you sure gave me a big drink. I've never been allowed to have so much sugar. Mama gonna be mad when she finds out."

"Oh, I think she will forgive you just this once. So, she was going to get you baptized you say."

"Huh, Huh. She was gonna bring me to the church and have him do it right before…." Camilla squinted her eyes in confusion, looking up to Gary, "how did I get here?"

"Well, what do you remember last?"

"I was playing on the merry-go-round at school. Mrs. Ferguson called us in, but I did not want to go. Spinning around and looking up at the sky, it felt so good out, and I could hear birds singing. I got up, but I guess I stumbled and fell." Camilla becomes quiet, deep in thought.

Still on the bar, Kitty Kat creeps closer to her and nestles down near her, resting her head on the child's arm.

Camilla bends down and nuzzles the cat with her nose, comforted by her loud purr. "She sure, is a pretty cat."

Gary remained quiet, eyes focused on her, forgetting the silent observer at the end of the bar or the rowdy crowd squawking in the casino. "I don't really know why I didn't get baptized." Looking up, suddenly surprised, "I fell, but I woke up in the hospital. Mama was crying. She couldn't hear me tell her that I'm okay." Looking around. "Somebody should call her. She must be worried." Looking at Gary's face. "She worries, you know. People don't think she does, but I know she does. I hear her cry at night." Dropping her head down, "mostly about me."

"What people?"

"Huh?"

"You said that people don't think she cares. What people?"

"Aunt Stacy, for starters. She's nice to me, but she is always yelling at mama for something. Seems like most of the time, it is about me." Looking up at him, "she told mama that she had no business trying to take care of me and that it was her fault that I was sick on account of her drinking. She said that I should go live with her."

"Well, I bet that didn't sit well with your mama."

"No, Sir! She told my Aunt Stacy to go straight to hell!" Then sorrowful, "oops, I said it again."

Looking her right in the eye, "tell me, Cammy, do you believe in Jesus?"

"I sure do, and I accept him as my Lord and Savior." Giggling, I learned that in Vacation Bible School. I went with a friend one year.

"Well, sweetheart, you didn't have a choice so. Therefore, nobody, not even Jesus Christ himself, will hold that against you."

"But Aunt Stacy says that baptisms are the portal to heaven, and if you are not baptized, you are doomed with eternal damnation. Oops!" She quickly puts her hand over her mouth, "is that a bad word?'

"No, baby. Now tell me, what does your mama say when your aunt says these things?"

"Oh, my mama doesn't put up with it. She kicked her out of our home on Thanksgiving Day. Told her to mind her own dang business, pushing her out and slamming the door behind her. only she didn't say dang." Sitting back in the chair, crossing her arms. "Nobody messes with my mama." Reaching for her Shirley Temple, she whispers, "that's when Aunt Stacy called CPS on us. Mama said she was trying to sue for medical guardianship over me because she wasn't fit. But mama takes care of me just fine." Playing with her stray hairs, "you know, I don't really know how I got from the play yard to the hospital. I was just there. I didn't like it though, you know, nobody ever listened to me. That's all I ever wanted you to know... to be heard."

"Wow, you sound mighty adult-like for such a young thing."

Camilla smiles brightly, "grandpa says that I'm an old soul."

"That may be so, but I suspect that you want more than to be heard."

"Oh, I do. I want to grow up and marry royalty. Maybe Prince George or if Archie grows up to be cute, then maybe him accept; he will have to go back to being royalty."

"Really, and why them, you can find many nice American boys."

"That may be so, but I want to travel everywhere in a horse-drawn carriage and live in a great castle and talk about smart things while drinking tea and eating crumpets."

"Well, you are a fancy one."

Camilla's voice softens, a loud roar is heard in the distance, and she frowns at the crowd. "Do you think I ever will?"

"Ever will what?"

"Live in a castle and drink tea and eat crumpets."

Gary scratches the cat's neck, "What do you think, Kitty Kat?" She looks up at him and lets out a loud meow, "I think you're right," then turning to her, "wherever your fate leads you, I believe that there will be tea and crumpets waiting."

Camilla smiled. "My glass is almost emp…mama?" The bottom of the glass expanded and blended into the mirror bar top that served as a one-way-looking glass. Pointing to the bar, "look, my mama. Do you see, she's right there?"

Gary smiled, "it is for you to see. Your glimpse into the lives of those that you touched. And I have a feeling that you have touched many."

Camilla stopped listening, too mesmerized with what she was seeing.

"Mama, why are you crying? I'm okay. I'm right here. I'm safe, look mama, a kitty kat. You said I couldn't have a cat because it would upset my allergies, but I have been playing with her all this time, and look, I'm just fine. I haven't sneezed or nothing." Camilla watched as she saw her mom talking to her Aunt Stacy. Mrs. Ferguson was there too. She was looking in her living room, where her toy hamper was still overfilled with toys, and her shoes rested at the entryway.

"Oh, oh, I was supposed to pick those up. I'm sorry, mama.

I'll do it as soon as I get home." Looking up at Gary, "I need you to take me home, she's gonna be mad that I'm not there. Then she'll start crying. Look, "she points to the vision, "they're probably looking for me now."

"Look some more."

Camilla looked down again into the mirror, but this time, red and green lights bounced off her. "Christmas. I just love Christmas." She peered some more.

"What do you like about it."

"I get gifts and mamma, and daddy don't fight. They just hold each other on the couch while I open my presents. See, look, I got a Holly Hobby doll. Isn't she great? I sleep with her. She's not as good as a Kitty Kat, but I have allergies, you know." Snuggling against Kitty Kat, "well, I guess here I don't." Looking deeper, "what is happening?" Camilla notices that while she is opening her gifts, mama is sobbing into her father's arm. "What's wrong with her? Daddy gave her a nice present. A diamond necklace of an angel feather. Mama loves angels."

The image expanded, and Camilla sees her parents get off the couch and go into the kitchen while she is pulling out the pieces of a Barbie Fun House.

"We can't afford the treatments," Camilla hears her daddy telling her mama. "Besides that, it sounds monstrous."

"They are discovering that the treatments stop cancer from spreading. Isn't it worth a try? For our little girl?"

"And who are they? Doctors, researchers, and scientists, who know nothing of people except how to use them as lab rats. I'm not letting them do that to my little girl."

"It wouldn't have been suggested if it wasn't a sensible solution."

"Sensible solution. It wasn't even offered. You read a magazine article. Dr. Reynolds doesn't even practice it."

Camilla looked up, "they fight about me a lot. Mama always wants me to go to all these special doctors all over the place, but daddy says we don't have the means to get there. Then mama cries, and daddy leaves." In a whisper, "when he comes home, he is usually drunk. Mama drinks too but, she stays home and drinks from the big bottle behind the instant potatoes."

Camilla looks back down to see herself as a two-year-old standing next to her grandpa. "Look! Grandpa liked to take me fishing. I never had the heart to tell him I didn't like to go." She smiles at Gary. "Fish smell. Anyway, that day was fun." Camilla starts to giggle as a pelican comes up and takes part of her sandwich. Laughing harder, she tells Gary, "He wasn't even afraid of us. Just walked right up and took our food. Snatched it right away. When I told Mama about it, she said he was probably used to people feeding him, but Grandpa said that the pelican knew I was a good person and wouldn't hurt him. He says that God puts sense into living creatures that cannot converse with us so that they can know the difference between the good and the bad. I wonder if the janitor who doesn't speak English has that sense. He is always really nice to me."

"Seems like your grandpa really loves you."

"Yeah, he does. He misses Grandma something fierce, but he says that when we go, we get to all be together again."

Camilla puts her face in her hands and begins to sob. Her tiny body trembles as her sobs grow into loud cries.

Gary places a hand on her shoulder. "Why the tears?"

"I'm dead, aren't I? I'm not ever gonna see Mama and Grandpa or even Aunt Stacy. I won't return my library book. I'm supposed to return it on Tuesday. *Where the Red Fern Grows*. It is one of the most popular. If I don't return it, Mrs. Mitchel in the library will be so mad. I promised I would return it."

"I think that Mrs. Mitchell will understand. Look in your pocket."

Camilla drops a hand and reaches into her dress pocket. Through her sniffles, she rummages before pulling out two gold, silver-dollar-size coins.

"These look like the chocolate coins that I get in my Easter basket. Is it Easter? I thought it was May."

"No, sweetheart, those are real coins."

"They don't look real." She picks at the edges of the coins. "What are they for?"

"Well, in most cases, it is to pay your fare. But here," Gary looks around, "it's a little bit different." He bends down on the bar to be eye level with her. "Your fate has to be determined first."

"I don't understand. What's fate?"

"Come here. I'll show you." Gary helps the little girl off the stool and gently takes her hand to guide her behind the bar, positioning her before the grandest slot machine hell ever made. "You see all the streams that surround the area?"

Camilla nods.

"This is one dimension or one angle of a greater plane." Noticing the confusion on Camilla's face, he asks, "Does your Mommy or Daddy ever get lost while driving?"

"Mama does, drives Daddy crazy. He says that she couldn't find her way out of a paper bag to save her life. She turns left when she is supposed to turn right."

"So, what does she do?"

"She calls Daddy, and sometimes he can tell where she is and give her the directions on how to get back. One time, she was so lost that he had to come and find her. Should I call my daddy? I'm lost, aren't I? I should call my daddy. He's real good at finding things. He'll come to find me. I know he will."

"Let me explain again. These rivers have many stops that reach different ports. Most people who arrive at one of the realms are met by Charon, the employee of the month, so to speak, and he takes them to their final destination."

"Am I going to meet Charon?"

"Well, if you do, it will not be today. Charon doesn't handle this realm. Those coins you have …"

Camilla glances down at the two shiny coins still resting in her palm.

"Look at this." Gary points to a gold lever with enameled leaves carved into the side. "You, my dear friend, get to pull this great lever to decide what will happen to you."

"Like a game. Mama says slot machines are grown-up games. I'm not grown-up."

"No, but you sat at a bar, and did you drink a grown-up drink?"

A wide grin spreads on her face as she points to Gary. "No. You drank a kid drink." "Well, I suppose I did, so I guess you get to pull the big handle on the slot."

"Why?"

"Because right now you are sleeping."

"So, is this a dream?"

"In a way. Do you believe that your dreams are true?"

"I suppose, but I don't always remember my dreams, even if I do talk in them. If I'm talking now, Mama's going to be so confused. Especially if I can't remember this."

"Just because you don't remember doesn't mean that dreams are not real."

"So then, how do you know if your dreams come true."

"Faith."

"Faith?"

"Yes. Some see it as an idea to guide them through the rough times, but I see it as more of a muscle. Someone as young as you has a stronger muscle."

"How could I? I am sick. Mama says so with the acute—"

Gary interrupts her, "This muscle does not reside in your body. It inhabits your soul. And there is nothing sick about your soul. And right now, your soul is visiting two different realms." Gary takes a breath and begins again patiently, "The realm where your parents sit by your bedside and pray." He points to the glass where again Camilla's peers in. This time she sees both her parents at her bedside in a dimly lit hospital room with the blinds closed and the privacy curtains pulled partially around.

"Look! Daddy is at the hospital, and he is praying! I didn't think Daddy ever prayed." She begins to choke up again. "I didn't think he ever cried. Why is he crying? Will they be okay?"

"In time."

"How do I wake up?"

"Your coins … place them in the machine and wait."

Camilla looks at him suspiciously. "Wait for what?"

Kitty Kat jumps down and begins intertwining herself between their legs, wrapping her long, black tail around Gary's calf.

"For your fate to be determined." He points to the slits on the side. "You put your coins there, and these blue squares up here will start to spin really fast until they get tired, and then they will stop."

"What happens when they stop?"

"You wait for the message. If it says *mors* [1], then you will go through that door over there." Gary points to a big, heavy, mahogany door behind a golden gate with seven-pointed crowns at the top and a clear flowing brook at the base, carved with cherubs and bright lights coming from underneath.

"If it says *vita*[2], then you will go back through that entrance over there." Gary points to a silver river path leading to the elevator that just opened to disburse out an explosion of bells as a tall man with long, stringy hair steps out, smiling as he notices the gambling events happening around the Cocytus River.

"Roger, my boy!" a loud, boisterous voice says. "'Bout time you got here."

"Guess I've been missing the party," he replies as he hurries to find himself a place at the Blackjack tables.

Gary watches him for a moment and then turns back to the little girl. As if reading her thoughts, he says, "Don't worry, you have nothing to be afraid of here." Then, looking back at the slot machine, he adds, "Oh yes, sometimes *arbitrium*[3]."

"What do those words mean?"

"I'll tell you what … you pull the lever, and whatever word comes up, I will share the meaning with you."

---

1   Mors: Latin for death
2   Vita: Latin for Life
3   Arbitrium: Latin for Choose

"Wait, what about that over there?" Camilla points to a huge mountain to the right of the gold elevators. Colorful flowers have sprung along the sides of the mountains with bright green shrubbery embedded between the flowers. "It is so beautiful. I want to go there."

"Yes, it is." Gary smiles. "That is the Mare Lacrimarum[4]." He looks back at her. "Those are the waters that feed into all of these rivers. As you can see, the waters get a little messy in places along the way, but that waterfall over there … well, I can assure you, those waters come from a place of love." He gently turns her around to face the slot. "Now come on, you have a game to play."

Smiling, Camilla carefully places her coins into the machine's money slots and listens to the loud click and then clang as it registers the commerce. After looking hesitantly at Gary, she places her small hand on the lever, layering it with her other, and uses all her weight to pull it down. Once it hits the bottom, the wheels inside begin to spin. Flashing lights halo on top of it—blue, then red, and then an iridescent color. The sound of what could only be described as the high-pitched but beautiful sound of angels roar overhead. Camilla looks up at the sight that clouds over the beveled ceiling that peeks into the outside world. She spins around in an effort to not miss a sight or sound. Right when the lights slow down, the soft tinkle of bells cascade through the air while the wheels drift to a stop. The words remaining blur until the whooshing and buzzing cease, and then in a sea of blue, the delicate curved marking of 'mors' appear.

"Mors." Camilla looks at it thoughtfully for a moment before turning to Gary. "What does that mean?"

Gary gets down on one knee, looks her straight in the eye, and gently replies, "Death."

Camilla gasps. "That's awful, who died? Not me. I'm dreaming, remember? You saw, in the hospital, I was sleeping

---

4   Mare Lacrimarum: Latin for River of Tears

while Mama and Daddy prayed. They're praying for me. God answers all prayers. Remember, I dedicate myself to Jesus Christ. Besides, I have to get baptized." Quiet tears well up in Camilla's eyes.

The lady barfly gulps as she watches Gary's eyes soften and listens to his voice go gentle and kind. "I have a special feeling that there are some people looking forward to seeing you."

As he speaks, the smell of roses, freshly baked chocolate chips cookies, and hot chocolate fills the air. White doves fly up in the air in balls of protected light as golden steps form over the gentle waters of the Lethe River. A soft, warm light shines onto Camilla's face as the heavenly golden gates clank open followed by the heavy, mahogany double doors. Gary picks her up out of the stool and places her gently on the ground.

She turns in the direction of the right, and a white marble bridge forms with pink pastel with flecks of gold in each step. She bends down and touches one of the steps before grabbing Gary's hand. "Look, the steps are like cotton candy. Can you imagine? Cotton candy steps."

Gary smiles again and holds her hand as they walk over the bridge.

She stops for a moment and points to a blue jay overhead. "Look, Mr. Gary, sir. The blue jays. Aren't they pretty, Mr. Gary, sir? Smart too. They know to stay on this side of the river. Grandpa was right. Animals are real smart." She bounces while they walk, and as she looks up again, she gasps, her jaw dropping as her eyes light up when the doors open and she sees a vision of an inviting, marvelous castle with ivy growing on the walls covered with honeysuckle. The sweet aromas grow stronger as they get off the bridge and a gold path becomes vibrant, punctuated with a line of brightly colored zinnias.

"Look at the flowers. Me and grandpa planted flowers just like those, but they haven't bloomed yet. They are going to look just like those though. I know it because I saw the pictures. Grandpa loves to make the yard pretty. He would love these."

As she speaks, gentle music expels into the air from the door's threshold. In front of the castle, a table is set holding a dainty, porcelain tea set and flowered plates with a platter of assorted, delicious crumpets. Her eyes widen. "It's so beautiful."

A pretty lady, wearing a pantsuit and pearls in her ears, walks into view. Her hair is short and brown.

"Well, come on, darling. I've been waiting."

"Grandma Arlene!" Camilla gasps. Looking back at Gary, she whispers, "But Mama said she died."

Gary lifts his head and nods toward the woman. "You heard the lady, she's been waiting."

"But my Shirley Temple—"

"You finished it, and I have a feeling there will be plenty more waiting for you where you are going. Come on, let's go."

Camilla squeezes his hand right before she lets go. The golden steps over the Lethe stream glisten as Gary walks with Camilla closer to her destination. A spray of mist floats up from the water, and Camilla inhales it.

"It tastes so good."

"There is more where that came from." As he speaks, he nods to the open gates that expose a luscious, green meadow behind the castle where a two Irish Setters come bounding through.

Camilla lets out a squeal. "Dan and Ann!" Turning back to Gary, she explains, "Those are my dogs. They died when I was small. That was before Daddy got Hades." She's breathless with excitement as she says, "Dan got hit by a car, and Daddy had to put down Ann because he said she was ate up with tumors. There they are, my dogs. My dogs. I can't believe they are here. I missed them so much."

"Come on, girl," Grandma Arlene hollers, smiling and holding out her hand.

Gary kneels down, looking her straight in the eye. "Listen to me, little one. You will never feel pain or fear again. You are safe."

Smiling, Camilla hugs Gary's neck and kisses his cheek. She looks back at Grandma Arlene, and then hesitantly at Gary.

"Go on, sweet girl. Sleep with the angels."

Camilla throws her arms around Gary's neck once again and gives his cheek another kiss, and then turns around, darting toward Grandma Arlene with the two dogs in tow, leaping on her and licking her palms.

Gary watches as the doors close completely, only leaving a strand of soft sunlight from underneath and the gentle smell of roses.

The barfly sits quietly for a long moment, watching Gary crossing the bridge over the Lethe, the cotton candy steps disappearing behind him as he strides over. He opens the small swing doors of the bar, gets behind, and carefully cleans Camilla's glass and cherry stems scattered on the bar. During this ritual, he speaks slowly without looking up from his task, "Children get me every time. Never seems quite fair."

"That was so sad. How were you sure she would go through that door and not the one over there?" The barfly points to a metal door behind the river Phlegethon serving as a barrier on the left.

"Watch for a moment."

The barfly watches carefully. "What am I supposed to see?"

"Clear your mind."

The barfly looks at him, then back at the river that slowly began to bubble. "It looks like it is starting to boil."

"Keep watching,"

Suddenly, the water laps into the air, sending out waves of fire licking up to the sky while laughing at the door covered with black smudge marks and knots pounded on the side. A form of three connecting bodies is carved into one side of the door, and on the other, a beast-like man with a long, pointed serpent tail curled around him on the other. Red beams stream from underneath with a faint sound of scratching behind the door teased with the stank odor of sulfur permeating through.

The barfly looks back at Gary, horrified. "Do children ever go there?"

"Ah, the un-baptized babies going to hell is just an obnoxious tale made up by Dante to scare the bejeezus out of young parents to get their children blessed. No loving father would send a small one like that to travel down the dark forest by the side of Charon. Heaven embraces the children. There is no need for an adjustment period when they are surrounded by so much love. In Camilla's innocent mind, it never occurred to her to stop by the casino. Herman sent her straight here."

"That does seem to be a horrid fate." Looking at him thoughtfully, she states, "It must be difficult."

"What?"

"To guide a child like that. I mean, it is awful that they would be forced to come here to begin with."

"She wasn't gone yet, and this is the waiting room for those that are in a coma."

"What do you think she would have chosen if she could?"

"Hard to say. She was in a lot of pain with her cancer, and her grandfather did tell her that her grandmother is here, and that small child has more faith than half the bastards out there." Gary nods toward the casino. "Yes, she had faith. Faith to know that her loved ones that passed would be here waiting for her, although she didn't truly know that at the time of choice, but …" Gary pauses. "Most of the times, the young ones pick life because they are afraid of being without their parents. That's who I feel sorry for the most."

"Kids or parents?"

"No. The ones that have to choose." Then, in a thunderous voice, he bellows out loud enough for the roaring crowd at the casino to hear, "Last call."

Francesca

Gary turns to the barfly. "Sometimes, they are a little timid in coming up. Why, I've been here for days before somebody decides to come and pull the ole slot."

"I didn't think time existed up here."

"They don't feel it, but I do. Part of my penance I suppose."

Smiling affectionately, she asks, "What penance, watching a group of misfits having too much fun with the drink and playing the games?"

"Nah, they are scared is what it is."

"You mentioned that before, but what do you think they are actually scared of?"

"Depends. Sometimes it's judgement, sometimes it's regrets, and sometimes they are scared because they know others are scared so they figure they should be scared, too. You know, when placed in a time of desperation, a person's little fuck ups …oh, excuse me, little mess ups get analyzed so even the slightest little sin gets blown out of proportion." Propping himself on his arms, he looks her in the eyes. "It's the unknown that is the scariest of all."

The barfly's eyes twinkle while her retinas move to the right, causing Gary to take notice of a woman, thirty-something with straight, black hair, big lips, and dark eyes crossing the bridge to the bar, fiercely trying to steady herself, fighting violent winds as they howl in her ears. Sheets of water spray up at her. She holds up her right arm, a useless shield for the river's spit. It takes all her strength to pull herself forward. The barfly watches in mesmerization as the steps behind the woman disappear into the Cocytus stream. She stops at a break.

"You're okay," Gary speaks up, "the Acheron is much calmer. You will make it fine, just one step at a time." He then positions himself in front of the drink selections, hands resting on the bar, anticipating her approach.

She smiles flirtatiously, smoothing her hair behind her ears, chuckling nervously. "Well, that was an experience. Thought I was going to get blown away to oblivion." Hesitating, she flutters her eyes, water still stuck to her left false eyelash. "I'm not sure how this works."

"First, take a seat, and then talk to me." When she gives Gary an inquiring look, he sighs and says, "Tell me whatever is on your mind. The process will work itself out." He twitches his shoulder. "I have no authority on your fate. I'm just the ferryman."

"Ferryman?"

"Uber driver."

The woman, still confused, pulls out a stool and sits. "I'm Francesca."

"Hello, Francesca, what'll you have?"

"Your name for starters."

"Sorry, I am Gary, and I will be your bartender, guide, therapist, monster of your fate, which by the way I'm not really, and whatever other stupid concoction of a story as to who I am that is floating around in sin city over there."

Straightening her posture, she lets out an annoyed sigh. "I'd like an Aperitivo please."

Gary knits his eyebrows. "Nice choice … that is if you are planning on eating a big meal."

"That's what'd I like," Francesca says without wavering. "Do you have a problem with that?"

"Lady, I'm not the one with problems. If you want an Aperitivo then Aperitivo it is."

While Gary pours the drink, Francesca inhales, enjoying the sound of the pour, the sloshing sending music to her ears.

Ignoring the dramatics, Gary slides the drink to her and in a softer tone he asks, "So, Francesca, what ails ya?"

"What makes you think that something ails me?"

"You're at hell's waiting room bar with blood stripes on your wrist. Ya ain't pickin' men up at the Holiday Inn, so spit it out."

"Well, aren't you direct?" Francesca pulls her hands away and rubs her wrists, looking at him, determined. "I don't know how these stripes got here. I did not cut my wrists. They just kept bleeding during my vacation at the demonic arcade over there." When Gary doesn't respond, she straightens herself up in her seat and continues, "It wasn't fair." Placing her glass on her lips, she mutters, "It just wasn't fair."

Gary sits on a stool before her in the back bar. Kitty Kat leaps onto the counter, catching her legs on the drip rail. Gary quickly rescues her so she can nuzzle her head under his chin before she curls up in his lap. Sipping his Aperitivo, he grimaces, and then sips again.

"So, what ails ya?"

"I had it all you know." She rubs the rim of her glass with her right index finger, breathes deeply, and begins again, "I had my own cosmetics store. Beauty was what I specialized in. I had three stores across the Los Angeles area, and I was planning on opening another in New York during the spring. It's pretty that time of year."

"What the skyscrapers turn bright green and the windows spring flowers?"

"You are a smart ass, you know that, right?"

"Huh. I'm usually referred to as an asshole, but I'll take smartass. Anyway, I apologize. Go on."

Looking at Gary, she waits for an impressive response regarding her success, but he stays stone silent, building on her nerves.

"I had a staff of forty ..." Tossing her head, she frowns, "They all hated me though." She looks back at the casino room. "Are any of them going to come forward?"

"Nope, one at a time."

"And her?" She points to the lady barfly listening intently.

Gary looks back at the pretty patron, gives her a wink, and then turns to Francesca. "She's just watching, like an investigator making sure I'm on my game."

"Like a reporter?"

"Well, it seems you know a thing or two about the society pages."

"Maybe I should just go back and play a few more rounds." As she starts to step down, she sees a swarm of slimy maggots at her feet, squirming through putrid blood. "Oh my God!"

"I wouldn't recommend putting your feet down. Not unless you want to walk around in the repugnance of your sins."

"I beg your pardon. Who are you to judge me?"

"Not my job, ma'am. I just speak what I see." Nodding down, he says, "You don't want those maggots sticking to your flesh, do you? Besides, your bridge has done disappeared, and since there are not going to be any outbound buses at this station, you are stuck here for now. So again, I ask, what ails ya?"

She straightens herself on the seat and runs her hand through her hair. "Well, I can agree with you that I know a thing or two about the society pages. In fact, I am known throughout the city. My father, he was a well-off investment broker in real estate. Sold to some of the biggest celebrities in Beverly Hills. Made a fortune. He was the one who fronted me my start up for my first store, right on Rodeo Drive." Looking at Gary again for a glimpse of approval, and again disappointed, she takes a gulp of her drink and continues on, "It was a hit. Before long I had rich housewives praising my products, celebrities shopping from my online stores and making TikToks about my products. Tourists peering through my window dreaming of the ability to be able to afford the products in my shop. I was even featured as the young entrepreneur of the year in 2018." Looking around, she inquires, "Am I really in hell?"

"Not exactly, but this ain't heaven either. You don't qualify to wander through the kingdom of the dead as you are not exactly dead."

"But I'm not living either?"

"Tell me, how are you feeling now?"

Francesca holds her head up, her chin firm as her teeth gritted. "If you must know, I'm sad. Consumed with sadness like none I have ever known before. It is as if an invisible hand has reached into my chest and grabbed my heart, squeezing it with all their might until the blood has turned into tears and let it rain all over my guts.

"Aww, sounds like a storm of melancholy."

"Are you always so sarcastic? Laughing at my pain. My God, I'm pouring my heart out here. I can do without your mockery."

"Entrepreneur of the year you say. That must have made your dad right proud."

"Hmm, he didn't have much to say about it. Too busy screwing his new wife. That bitch is three years younger than me. Disgusting, old man."

"He still helped you get started in your business."

"As well as he should. The old grump owed it to me. You know he never attended anything when it came to me. Not my high school graduation or college or even one of my weddings. But he sure as hell can attend everything to do with that party ho of a wife he has."

"Doesn't explain how he owes you anything."

"The hell it does! I'm his daughter."

"And that obligates him to attend all sacred events pertaining to you? Seems like you are being a bit of a drama queen."

"Don't judge me. Fathers are obligated to their daughters or their children. It isn't like I asked to be born. Hell, I wouldn't be as screwed up as I am if he would have shown just a little bit of love and compassion towards me."

"Doesn't seem to hurt you much. In fact, it seems to me that you relish in the thought of your success as a rich businesswoman."

"Well, I am that." She pauses. "Rodeo Drive." Francesca closes her eyes dreamingly. "I had a nanny who would take me there, window shopping she called it. That's what the poor people do. Window shop and dream knowing that when they wake up their shopping destinations will be Walmart and the bogo sales at Payless. My nanny yearned for so much more." Letting out a chuckle, she says, "She used to make fun of all the ladies that would go into the fancy stores like Gucci with their little dogs dressed in costumes. She'd always bend down and whisper in my ear that it would serve them right if the rugged mop thing took a shit right there on the red carpet embroidered with a G."

"Sounds romantic."

"Oh, it was, and not in the foul way you are thinking of it. I longed to own one of those shops. When it finally happened, I had an opening day party, serving the finest of champagne and caviar. I even brought in a special gourmet dog food that was fit for the finest of French bulldogs." Cocking her head to the side, her hair skims her shoulders. "I found that nanny. Gretchen was her name. I found her and invited her." She wrinkles her nose. "That did not go over well with daddy's second wife. Hmph, she had fired her for sleeping with Daddy, but I didn't care, she was still my favorite out of all my nannies."

After taking a sip of her Aperitivo, she continues, "She was a fake Mary Poppins who always let me have chocolate after dinner. She'd say it was her obligation to give me a spoonful of sugar before she left for the day." Letting out an affectionate laugh, she settles back, thinking, "I wish Daddy married her. She was always so nice to me. You know, I would have been simply fine if I hadn't gotten lonely."

She taps her glass, not noticing that it filled back up on its own. "Oh well, moving on."

"Lonely?"

"Yes, you know, needing the company of a man."

"Seems to me that someone on your class level would have men crawling after you."

"Well, yes, I did, but many of them were such a bore with their meager attempts to impress me." Glaring at Gary, she explains, "I need more than a gentleman that showers me with sparkling presents. After all, I am a woman who can buy her own diamonds. You may not know it to look at me, but amidst this elegant lady that sits before you, I have acquired a unique taste for sex. My appetites go beyond the average woman of my age and stature." Putting down her drink, she rolls her eyes up at Gary. "Did you know that girls from the Trobriander Tribe in New Guinea begin having sex at the age of six?"

"Sounds pretty sick if you ask me. Hope you did not engage in such acts."

"Well, no, unfortunately. But …" she laughs, "I did have an obsession with Dracula, hoping that he would come to my window where I would anxiously let him in so he could have his way with me."

"At six?"

Francesca peers into her wine. "Well look at that, the words … do you see the words?"

"No, read them to me."

"*Love, which in gentlest hearts will soonest bloom, seized my lover with passion for that sweet body from which I was torn unshriven to my doom.*"

"That is Dante, right?" Francesca asks rhetorically, knowing she was right but wanted Gary to be impressed by her master intelligence

"I believe so, but whoever or whatever it is, it doesn't sound pleasant at all."

"Doesn't it? Looking up quickly, "would you follow your love into hell so that you could be with her forever?"

"Well, I don't think—"

"Oh, excuse me, I apologize, the times are changing. Is your lover a her or a him? I can never tell these days." Her voice sniffling into a snooty tone.

Gary stands up straight, dismissing his frustration. "This conversation is not about where I would follow my love to as my love has not led to death." Gary's eyes narrow. "I'm not sure if you can say the same."

Francesca looks behind her, acknowledging the wails of souls leaking from the left. "I wish they would hush their misery. It makes it hard to think."

"Think about what? The sex tribe?"

"Don't be so surprised. Some women start early with their appetites. There is no need to make it sound so scandalous."

Gary remains silent, petting Kitty Kat, his face empty of emotion.

"Anyway, I am a woman that needs company, and despite my prestige I had a difficult time getting it. Besides, I only wanted my appetites satisfied. I never wanted a relationship. That is too much work. Come on, look at me." Straightening herself up, "I am a woman that needs company, and despite my prestige I had a difficult time getting it. Kids, Tupperware parties, little league, PTA." She shudders. "The idea of being a soccer mom puts the taste of vomit in my mouth. Not for me. I want my career with something spicy on the side … so I got clever about it." She narrows her eyes at Gary, anxiously waiting to be questioned, but he stays quiet. "Well, if you are not going to bother to ask, I signed up to a discreet escort service."

"So, you hired male prostitutes."

"God no, there is no excitement in that. I became the escort." Looking smugly back at the lady barfly, who still listens intently but unimpressed, she takes another sip. "You see, I could be the object of desire, making young men's wet dreams come true. That's what I found exhilarating."

"So, you are a whore?"

"No!" Francesca says, aghast. "My, you are an ass! I was the escort. I provided intellectual, conversational stimulation during dinner, allowing the man I was with to feel special. Feel wanted. Asking about his job, pretending to be impressed they were some mediocre regional general managers running a company or promoting a product consumed by the lower-class man."

Pausing for a moment in thought, she drums her fingernails on the glass. "But for the purpose of avoiding an argument with the ferryman, yes, I did have sex with my clients. I mean, if it wasn't going to lead to sex, then I simply didn't want to see them anymore. After all, why bother? I have natural urges, as well as my client, I might add." Her eyes glistened by the bright lights, her lip curls up, "I feasted on them. I don't see how that is bad. Two consenting adults …" lost in thought for a moment, a dirty smile crosses her face, "sometimes three." She sighs. "Do you really think that should lead me to everlasting torment? After all, what woman doesn't occasionally fantasize about being a human succubus?"

"Depends on what else you did."

Francesca rolls her eyes and flips her hair as she speaks again. "Truth is, I was living two different lives. During the day I was a remarkable businesswoman in charge of sculpting beauty on Rodeo Drive. I interacted with some of the most successful businesspeople and philanthropists in all of Los Angeles. And at night …" Francesca pauses, taking a sip, "at night I would put on my five-inch stilettos or knee-high, leather boots—whichever was—preferred and fuck the husbands of the very ladies I negotiated perfume costs with."

"But why?"

"Does there need to be a reason? I mean, can't a person just act without thinking of the reaction? But why is a stupid question."

Gary remains quiet. Francesca's temper flares.

"Because that was what I wanted to do." She softens her tone to a pout. "I would get wet just thinking about it. I had a house high in the hills surrounded by some notable celebrities, and after a while I would let them come there. I even had a special room set up. Help create a fantasy, a few toys and me." Laughing, she shakes her head. "I even had a few of Daddy's friends. You would think that would make them uncomfortable, but it didn't. Nasty, old men." Francesca gets quiet, rubbing the rim of her class, and then looks at the casino crowd again.

She mumbles more to herself than to Gary, "I got rapacious, though. … especially when it came to Lorenzo."

"Lorenzo?"

"Aw, yes. He is different. Not like the disgusting, old men that peruse escort catalogues like yellow pages, or a dating app.

Lorenzo is a fine man of great prestige that wanted to satisfy his own appetites like how I enjoyed satisfying mine. We were a great match from the moment we met each other. We were magnetic together." She takes a sip of her drink. "Oh, how the feeling between my legs throbbed when I knew he was coming over. I eventually gave up all my clients in hopes that he would see that I was willing to dedicate myself to him."

Inhaling and then exhaling deeply, she closes her eyes. "His eyes were deep brown, his hair ebony black with glistening olive skin, and his voice, thick and gentle embedded in an Italian accent. Oh, there are no words as to how hard I fell for him. He became a regular, and instead of initiating my fantasies like I would do with my other clients, I worked to find out his. Anything that man wanted, I would give to him."

The memory triggers a thick waft of Giorgio Armani cologne, which she takes in, leaning her body back. Bending her back farther, her still-damp white blouse sticks to her as she sways back and forth, embracing her lustful memories.

"Lorenzo is magnificent at everything he does. I was sure I could get him to love me." Pulling herself back toward the bar, she snaps at Gary, "Don't look at me like that!" although his expression had not changed. "I am good for Lorenzo. He traveled over here from Italy, a suit designer who liked my company. I even decided to begin a men's line that would complement his product. He could open a shop up in LA, me in Italy. What a match we would make. He told me that he was considering relocating to California, seeing that he had to travel here and to New York so often. He needed an American home, he eventually found one too. He was building an American life, where I could magically fit in."

Francesca stares down at her glass as it magically refills itself again. "Don't see the point of you being here if the bar knows what I want."

Bowing out his chest, he replies, "I'm good for aesthetics. Go on, your story is interesting. Tell me more about Lorenzo."

With a satisfied tone, she continues, "Well, it wasn't long after I made myself exclusive to just him that he realized who I was. He saw me through the store window one day while eating lunch at a bistro across the way." She slaps a hand down on the bar. "Of course I was horrified when I saw him. I mean," taking a deep breath, she rushes to say, "I have come across husbands before that I had screwed when they came in shopping with their wives but toying with them was fun. They never wanted to get caught. Divorce would ruin those guys. Flings were a secret toast to masculinity for them." This time she let out a laugh that shook her curvaceous frame. "It was fun to watch them sweat. I'd blink my eyes, cross my legs. I had a high, metal stool that I sat on. Higher than this one. I would sit as the ladies talked, I'd barely listen while all the while crossing and uncrossing my legs."

"Like Sharon Stone in that movie? Sounds more like you are just some slut-nut caught up in a fantasy land."

Letting out a huff, she knit her brows in a frown, "Oh, you act like I was some kind of Lifetime miscreant. I am not though. I was better than that. You see, they knew my taste, and I made sure they yearned for it. All the while their wives an arm's length away. Serves those bastards right. They'd whine about the money their wives spent, mainly in my little establishment or some other over-priced, marbled floor with a red-carpet runner where the clothes came out of cardboard boxes but hung on cloth hangers as if they are special. The ridiculous amounts put on credit cards for half-jackets and leather boots, and then those hypocrites would turn around and give me even more money at night. I lost count of the times men would call urgently wanting to make sure that I would stay quiet. I must admit, that became somewhat of a turn on in itself. Oftentimes I would see their number come through and I would laugh and decline the call knowing the panic that would be stirring up inside of them." Looking directly at Gary, she states, "Extortion can be sexy you know. I could blackmail all of LA if I really wanted."

"Even Lorenzo?"

"Oh, I didn't want to hurt Lorenzo. Not really, I just wanted him to listen to me. He didn't talk about her when he was with me."

Gary remains quiet as he pets Kitty Kat.

"Is that all you do all day … serve drinks, listen, and pet that stupid cat?"

The cat looks in her direction and lets out a hiss before changing positions and burying her head in Gary's lap.

"She's not stupid. Besides, Kitty Kat likes to listen, too."

Her purr begins to sound loudly.

"You couldn't think of a better name than that?"

"If you must know, her name is Phlegyas[5]. That is what the wife named her, but I didn't care for that, so I just call her Kitty Kat."

"What the hell kind of name is Phlegyas?"

"Phlegyas is the demigod of Ares. You know, God of War?" He nods toward her drink.

She gazes in it to see the image of a handsome man forming. She sighs.

"Lorenzo?"

"Yes, Lorenzo. He was a hell of a lover. I still think he loves me. He just doesn't know it. Anyway, when I saw him at the bistro, I was surprised and a little shocked."

"But you said he liked your project and that you were even putting together a men's line."

"Well … well, I hadn't really had the chance to tell him about it, but I was planning on it. I just wanted to wait until the time was right. I knew that with our heads for business that we would be a perfect pair. A power couple in the beauty and fashion industry."

Gary nods his head while grimacing at another sip of his drink.

"Anyway, it happened so fast. I went to the front of the store

---

5   Phlegyas: Son of Ares

to check out a display when I noticed a car commercial being filmed. I was curious to see if they were using any celebrities that I knew when suddenly I saw him." She lets out a breath. "Well, I quickly dodged back into the store, but it was too late. He saw me. A few hours passed, so I figured he was gone, or perhaps he did not register that it was me diving behind a perfume display. I mean, after all, the lover whom he saw in the leather and lace for so long found in an upscale beauty story wearing a pencil skirt, blazer, and pearls doesn't really seem like a likely scenario. I should have known though."

Smiling, she shakes her head. "He is way too sharp for that. Turns out he just had a long meeting. He came into my store right about three. I held my head up high and greeted him as if he were a stranger stepping in to check out the upscale goods."

She lifts her voice in a way to act out the scene. "Can I help you, sir? Perhaps you would like to buy some nice perfume for your flame."

She shakes her head at Gary. "He said, 'I guess I could get some. I have not surprised the wife in a while.' Can you believe that? Right there as if I were nothing but a tart salesgirl. Well, I thought he had to be kidding but I played along. I pointed out my most expensive bottle. He had the nerve to have it gift wrapped, and I would never see it again. He actually gave it to his wife. What a prick move."

"Guess he didn't see you as his main flame."

"Not even a flamelet. I called him out on it, too. I had not heard from him in a couple of days, and with all my other clients gone, my body began to ache for attention. Besides, I figured by now he would surely understand my affection for him and want more of me. After all, now he knew I was much more than an evening of entertainment. I could be good for him. Me being the success I am and all." She takes a gulp of her drink. "That backfired though. I called him to invite him over. After our pleasuring time together, he got up to leave. He did not say a word about the perfume and that annoyed me. So, I asked him if he was planning a real special present for me. 'I already gave it to you,'" she says, imitating a deep voice while shrugging her shoulders. "Can you believe he had the nerve to say that to me?"

Frowning, she takes another gulp. "He then told me that he did a little research on me and found out about my endeavors and the store. The nosy SOB pulled up my last five years profits. I of course teased and asked if he wanted to be an investor."

Francesca pauses and turns to stare down at the casino. The noise is rolling in, laughter and faint arguing is heard but nothing that seems to cause concern. She watches a waitress walking around passing out Lotus drinks. Without turning back to Gary, she asks, "How long do I have to do this?"

"Do what?"

"I don't know, what we are doing? I am getting tired of talking. Those maggots are disgusting. How are they even alive? They are all black, and God, they smell."

"Until you are done. And please, stay away from the dramatics. I could tell within three minutes of meeting you that you love to talk about yourself."

She turns around and lets out a sniffle before forcing herself in a momentarily silence, sulking, sipping on her drink, diving in and out of her thoughts, relishing on her moments of ravishment and self-pity combined. Silent tears roll down her face.

The lady barfly's gaze passes back and forth between Gary and Francesca, aware of the awkward silence but not willing to break it.

Finally, Francesca sighs. "I really did think I could make him love me you know. And, well, I'm still not convinced that he doesn't."

Gary shifts as Kitty Kat repositions herself.

"I mean, I saw his wife … mousey thing. I can't believe that he would attach himself with something like that." Lowering her voice, she takes her right hand to her mouth as if to shield a secret from an invisible crowd. "She comes from money you know. Probably the only reason why he stuck it out with her." Putting her hand down, she continues, "Anyway, I told him my feelings and he laughed."

She was silent for a minute before slowly raising her drink to her lips and taking a hearty gulp. "Just laughed." Using a bar napkin, Francesca dabs underneath her eye. "Like I am nothing but a joke. Here I am, probably just as successful if not more than he is, and he is laughing at me. He said that I was nothing more than a two-dollar whore. Me, the daughter of the king of real estate of Beverly Hills and entrepreneur of the year, nothing but a two-dollar whore. I guess the Italians are not well educated on what class is." More tears stream down her face. "That cut me deep. I thought him seeing my success would impress him. He would want to be with me instead of that mouse. But no … he just laughed."

"Sounds like you spent a lot of your life trying to impress people."

"I don't need to impress anyone."

Gary holds his hands up. "My bad, just an observation."

The sound of a siren goes off in the back as celebratory hoorays are sounded at somebody's jackpot.

She looks at the crowd. "Stupid fools. Don't they know that they didn't win dooly?" Then sullenly, she redirects herself back to the conversation at hand. "I thought Lorenzo was the real deal and that I had finally found somebody who would love me. I told him that I could give him the world and then he said that he had already got what he wanted from me and that he would not be acquiring my services any longer. I found out that he went back to another escort agency. I don't know how he didn't think I wouldn't find out. That information is easy to come by."

Stretching out her shoulders, she glares down at her drink. "I got so pissed that the next day I waited for him to come to a suit shop that was just two doors down from my store. He sold to all the Fairfax merchants so all it took was a few free complementary products to the sales creeps and I got the whole month schedule of visiting salespersons. Information is so easy to come by. Especially when you have money. Anything can be bought. Anyway, when I knew the moment that he was going to be there, I marched down there and planted myself. Of course, I made sure that I was drop dead gorgeous wearing five-inch stilettos and a droop crawl line blouse that flashed a glimpse of the girls. Had to make him want me. Let him see what he was giving up." Tossing back her head, she stares at the ceiling. "Oh, I didn't make a scene if that is what you are thinking. I waited for him to finish his business. I have enough sense to know that there is nothing more unattractive than a woman scorned. He kept looking at me out of the corner of his eye as he spoke. My god, I made that man nervous. He cut it short, too. He wanted out of there."

She puts her glass down on the bar, stretches her arms again, places them back in her lap, and drops her head. "Lorenzo wanted out of there for sure. He also wanted away from me. As soon as he was done in the store, he grabbed me by my arm and walked me out. Kind of hurt, too. He then proceeded to tell me that he didn't feel the same about me and to leave him alone." Clenching her fists, she shakes her head. "I was so angry. It was everything I could do to stop myself from slapping him right there on Rodeo Drive. I told him that I was going to tell his wife about his evening escapades. He told me that if I did such a thing that he would destroy me. He would tell the press and everyone he could think of my dirty, little secret. He said that he would make me the pariah of Beverly Hills." Francesca waves her arms about, raising her voice. "My business would be gone, my reputation soiled, and for what? A man who made my pussy tingle a time or two."

Picking up her drink, and with a lower voice, she says, "Not worth it, I know, but …" she takes a sip, "I couldn't let it go, I couldn't let him go. The humility, he had to pay." She looks harshly at the barfly, and then back at Gary, and then to her drink. "Nobody was going to make a fool out of me. Nobody."

Gary remains unemotional as he sits, looking at her, stroking Kitty Kat's fur. Glancing over to the lady barfly, he gives her an occasional mischievous smile, causing her to look down at her folded hands resting in her lap.

Francesca ignores the exchange and continues, "That's about right. Nobody wants to hang with the Beverly Hills whore. I get that, but I was more than that. I was more than that to him and he knew that, too. He just had to see it my way. Admit his love for me." She looks down at her drink, noticing the liquid beginning to swirl, creating a water tornado. In the eye she sees a tall, white mansion with a black iron gate coming out of tall bushes guarding the modern house.

She takes a breath and recites the scene as seen in her drink.

"I drove over to his new, fancy house with high bushes as a privacy fence and a winding driveway with a security speaker where only the most desired gained entrance. I confidently announced myself to the box as Francesca Charybid, and I was here with a special delivery." Laughing, she mutters, "Stupid snots fell for it. They opened that gate right up and I drove on through in my sparkling, silver BMW, gliding up the drive."

She winks at Gary. "I looked hot that day, too. My black leather pants, knee-high boots," she wrinkles her nose, "it was really too hot for them, but I had to look good. Wanted that bitch to see what her husband was diddling. My bustier was peeking out through my white jacket." She pauses for a moment, gliding her finger over the rim of her drink, sipping in the scene, welcoming the replay of the memory.

"That twat didn't seem to notice. Can you believe that she answered the door herself? I figured I would have to go through an entourage of maids and other household nuisances. But no, there she was … white T-shirt, Calvin Klein jeans. Calvin Klein of all things! Barefoot like some snippy teen, looking me and smiling like she was expecting me to give her a lollipop or something. She eyed the bag I held for a moment. I brought a nice one from my store, for people who spend over a thousand dollars. We wrap up things in a stiff, linen bag with a firm satchel and pink lace matching the bedazzled high heels and sunglasses on the bag."

Francesca gets quiet as she examines the scene taking place in her glass.

"Teddy," she lets out aggravatedly, "the mouse's name is Teddy."

The image of Teddy becomes clearer—no make-up but still pretty, hair up in a messy bun yet blonde strands fall around her brown eyes.

Reaching for the bag, smiling and giddy, she asked, "What did Lorenzo surprise me with this time?"

Taking a breath, Francesca says, "The house was beautiful. Marble floor, that is what I remember the most. Swirled rose and grays on a marble floor, two winding staircases that framed a high crystal chandelier. So elegant, that chandelier, those staircases, that floor." Francesca's dreamy voice becomes angry. "And there she was tramping on it with her bare feet, with unpolished toes, and no makeup and those stupid, damn Calvin Klein jeans. God! I didn't even know they still sold those."

Looking up at Gary, she asks, "How could Lorenzo possibly love this? This mouse of a person who has no taste, no class, no style." She picks up her drink. "And yet, here she was." Lowering her voice, she mutters, "Tiny little thing really. More of a gnat."

Then firming back up her tone, she goes back to the story, mocking Teddy's voice,

"'Well, what is it?' she gasped, excited like she never got a gift before." She turns to the lady barfly. "Not that she deserves anything as upscale as what would come out of my store." Stretching her arms, she continues, "I said to her, 'Here let me show you.' God you should have seen the look on her face when I pulled out a .380 semi-automatic pistol. 'Sorry, honey, Calvin Klein don't make these in pink!'" Letting out a chuckle, she looks at Gary. "Well, I couldn't help myself. It seemed a little tormenting was in need at that moment." Bending her head to nurse her drink, she stops again, enjoying the replay.

"She didn't have time to respond before I pulled the trigger. *BANG!*, Like an explosion released from my hand. I didn't think twice about it either. I mean, I really thought I would lose my nerve when I got there but it was so easy." Shrugging her shoulders, "answering the door in those damn Calvin Klein jeans eased my mission. Sealing her fate. I don't know how long I watched the blood drain from her head onto that marble floor." She lifts her head. "Such a shame, too … it really was a beautiful shade of rose and gray. Anyway, I thought Lorenzo was out, but apparently not. And oh, what a fit he had when he saw his beloved mouse, Teddy, laying lifeless on the floor."

Her voice raises in a surprised high pitch that echoes off the glass. "He threw such a fit that he attacked me. I started to raise the gun at him, but he was fast. He wrestled me to the floor. Would have been kind of hot if his dead wife's corpse wasn't there leaking blood on the rose-gray floor. What an awful stain." Francesca huffs. "I squirmed under him, curled my right leg around his left, and then suddenly, I pulled myself out. I kicked him but not hard enough. He got up and started toward me again. I only meant to make him stop I turned the gun on me and told him that if he came one step closer that I was going to kill myself."

She watches the scene in her glass.

Lorenzo, breathing hard, snarled, "Go ahead, do it. Kill yourself."

Francesca speaks again, rushing her voice, "I thought he would call my bluff, I thought he would frantically proclaim his love for me. I turned the gun, waiting for him to run to me, beg me to stop, tell me it was going to be okay. We could fix this. We could make it look like Teddy left him, disappeared, something, but …" She looks down at the image again.

Lorenzo growled, "Do it, you bitch!"

"I pulled the trigger and *bang*. I swear that room had

surround sound. It cracked, I took a breath, closed my eyes, and the next thing I know," she glances at the elevators that just let in an old man in a black suit, "I was getting off those."

Then she looks at Gary. "Oh, don't get me wrong, I love to gamble, but this place is beginning to make my skin crawl. It is my understanding I have to see you before I can get out of this hideous establishment with all its doors and smelly rivers. Now don't get me wrong, I am not looking forward to dancing in the city of fire, and considering what I done, I'm pretty much sure that is where I'm heading, but this place has worn on me, and I think it is time to make my exit now."

"This is true." Gary drops Kitty Kat to a maggot free floor, and she threads herself through his legs. "It is true you have to come through me, but I am only the transportation to where you are going. I have no authority as to where your destination leads you."

"Well, I see. Am I supposed to give you these?" Francesca pulls out two large, gold coins.

"Yep, that would be your gambling money."

"I heard something about that. I would just like to forego the whole thing and take my chances in hell. Leave my legacy in Beverly Hills as a jilted romance story. Who knows, maybe I will be a Lifetime movie. I'll definitely make the society pages for sure. Daddy crying with his empty regrets. His latest wife pretending to care by lying and saying we had an oh so close relationship when really, we couldn't stand one another. There will be talk of me for a while. I wonder who will play me on the silver screen. Angelina Jolie? Ooh maybe they will put a Latino spin and Jennifer Lopez. She is so beautiful. Oh, hell, here I come."

"Perhaps, but it is not your call as to where you go. Your fate lies there." Gary points to the large slot machine. "Go ahead."

"But the maggots!" Francesca looks down and realizes they were gone. She gets off her stool, as Gary steps aside, leaving an opening for her to get in front of the big wheel of the slot machine.

"Ah, the big wheel." Looking back at the barfly, she tells her, "I really was expecting something a little more poetic." Then sliding her coins in, she takes a breath and pulls the large, gold lever. "Oh, I can't watch this." She closes her eyes tight as the wheel picks up speed, a whishing sound and a rattling as it spins and whirls. Opening one eye, she asks, "How long does it take?"

"Really, just a moment, but I'd imagine that in your position it seems like eternity."

Then suddenly bells chime, *ding, twinkle, ding, ding, twinkle, twinkle,* and then it stops.

Gary stands to the side, Francesca opens her eyes, slowly, and steadies them on the word *Vita.*

"Vita?" Looking at Gary, she says, "I don't understand."

Suddenly, a harsh wind blows toward the pair, startling the waves of the Styx. A sturdy bridge appears first over the Acheron—firm wood held together with rope, causing it to swing back and forth.

Gary goes around the bar as she gets up.

"Well, it looks like you are going back, and from the looks of it, it ain't gonna be no steady walk."

Then the pair take their first step.

Francesca eyes Gary hesitantly. "This is ludicrous. I will surely fall. Please, I accept my fate. Just take me to the smoldering gates. They are waiting for me anyway. You can't tell me you didn't see those nasty beasts goading me."

"No can do. My orders come from stronger powers than you and your fear of what will show up in the society pages tomorrow."

Francesca looks up at him, horrified. She sees in the distance the gold elevators opening up just past the Styx River.

"Shall we?" He offers his arm for support.

"Wait, I really have to go back?"

"Yes, my dear. You landed on life. You will be waking up soon."

"No, I can't go back. It must be a mistake. Let me go again. I am sure I am to remain here. I can't return. The humility, the society pages. Why, I will have to go to prison, I'm sure. Come on, give me another crack at it."

"Your coins are gone, and I don't get paid overtime."

"Stop it with the analogies and just give me another chance. I sure you have something up your billowing sleeve that you can do."

"No, ma'am. There are no more spins."

A flush of wind zips around the bar and Francesca feels a tugging sensation pulling at her. "Make it stop."

"Walk with me."

Despite her desperation to stop her footsteps, Francesca obediently follows. Her body feels lighter with each step.

The lady barfly holds herself up to watch the two walk the distance.

Francesca becomes quiet. Somber. A soft orange and red light filters over her as she passes the smooth passage by the Lethe Rivers. She looks up at the heavenly gates as she walks past, hearing the sound of playful angels singing.

"I'm sorry," she whispers before taking another step, passing the raging waterfall that divides the gates of Heaven and the golden elevators doors. Pausing, she looks at Gary. "My daddy, my daddy is crying right now. Gretchen has called him. She is praying for me. Alice, my store manager. I am so mean to Alice. In fact, yesterday I told her she was useless, and yet, I can feel the tears she has shed for me. She is grieving, but why? Why do people grieve over the ones that mistreat them? Why would she have so much compassion for somebody that was so awful to her?"

"Perhaps she has the unique ability to look past the actions and love the soul."

Gary gestures her to move forward.

She looks back at the beautiful waterfall and lets the splash of the sweet waters cool her face. Then her gaze turns toward the elevators and then to Gary.

He salutes her.

"Good-bye, Gary." She enters the elevators and presses the only button there, waves at him, Herman the conductor sitting nearby, and takes a deep breath as the doors close.

Gary begins his travels back. He stops at the waterfall, kneels, and splashes his face with the clean waters. After making the sign of the cross, he walks back. He waves to the angels singing in unison as he crosses the Lethe while the bridge behind him disappears with each step he takes until he finally makes it back to his stationed position.

He pats the lady barfly on the arm before returning to his position behind the bar.

"Well, I guess she's gonna have a lot to answer for."

He then turns around to the loud laughter coming from the casino. Waves of cigar smoke floating above Blackjack tables and 1920's fedoras. In his loud, booming voice, he makes his announcement, "Last call!"

Florence

"Oh God!" Gary groans.

"Be nice," the lady barfly says firmly. "Listen to her story. That is what you do, isn't it? Regardless of how pernicious it is."

"Yeah, yeah, yeah." He turns to the huge mountain of a person hobbling forward, the bridge pivoting as it struggles to hold the beast of a woman crushing a walker while grappling to maintain her balance with oxygen tubes tugging at her nose, her chin swaying back and forth with every attempt to stop drowning in sweat. She lets out a shriek as six black crows fight over her head, swooping down two at a time to peck at her hair. Her fat, bulging arms are unable to reach high enough to smack them away. Only a slight lift of her elbow, which exposes a teal butterfly tattoo stretched to deformity. Her face paralyzes in moments of horror as icy rain accompanies her travels, getting splashed by a monstrous three-headed creature, each one growling as their faces twist. One with a bloody face, another whose complexion is yellow and diseased, and another pasty white with gaunt highlights spitting out black maggots. Each one tormenting the obese woman in anger while flaying her with claws, mocking her with howls, weakening her ability for a safe passage.

"See, even the hell hounds are disgusted by her." Gary grimaces as he speaks. "My God, is that a Cheeto stuck in a fat flap," he mumbles.

"Stop that!" the lady barfly snaps at him, her blue-green eyes flickering at him, her lips firming. "You have a job to do, and a bit of kindness would be necessary here."

"Well excuse me but we can't all be as magnanimous as you."

This brings a light chuckle to the patron. "Guess you have touched up on your vocabulary during your time on the job."

"I am a connoisseur of many lives which brings about a variety of vocabulary words. You'd be surprised at the knowledge acquired here, in the Coma's Last Chance Casino Waiting Room." Gary stretched out his right arm making a sweep across the vision field, passing by the heaving woman, strands of thin dirty blonde hair sticking to the sides of her face her glasses cracked by the freezing ice stuck to the rims. She nudges her walker forward, her plump hands tightening around the rails, her legs trembling underneath.

Gary winks at the lady barfly, "why hello Charybdis, what can I get you to drink, and please don't eat my cat, she's my service animal."

He ignores his favored guest's harsh look to fixate on the approaching blob.

"I'm sorry," she huffed out. Taking in a deep breath, "I'm Florence, but you can call me Flo."

"I'd suppose that is amongst the nicer things you have been called."

Finally, within reach of the bar, she fumbles for a stool, initiating the lady barfly to walk around and pull up a wider one with a back.

"Here, this should make you more comfortable." Flo wallowed out a smile, as the lady barfly held the chair sturdy for her.

"Thank you miss, these knees can't take much more standing. Where I came from, I couldn't even walk."

"Fit through the door is more like it," Gary whispers.

The lady barfly lips tighten as she helped Flo get more comfortable.

Gary watched disgruntled, and disgusted. Flo swallowed hard, hurt by his attitude.

"I appreciate your kindness ma'am. It is nice that someone welcomes a person around here." Looking up at Gary who had found his seat on his stool across from her. "That is what I am you know, a person. Not a beast." Kitty Kat took her place on Gary's lap, curled up and purred but her eyes remained open and gazing at the pleading woman yearning respect.

After an awkward silence, Gary sighs and begins with, "I take it you would rather have food than drink."

"Is that an option? Oh, my god yes. If I knew that I would have come up here a long time ago." Her voice was raspy but pleasant and genuinely grateful over the cuisine option. "Those darn flower drinks don't fill up hunger."

"Well, you shouldn't be hun…"

The lady barfly holds up her hand to stop Gary before he could continue. His eyes narrow and then he forces himself to gaze at his newest visitor. He sees a swarm of thick wormy green slush that surrounded her aura. She trembled. "I would imagine that if the smell that has submerged into your skin didn't get you up here, the intense cold would have." Flo gave him a disgusted look.

"I'm hungry."

"Of course, you are."

Gary stretches out his arm, inducing a magical sweep that produced a gluttonous number of pizzas, Shipley's donuts, Little Debbie Snack cakes, litters of sodas, cakes with piles of icing and bowls of M&Ms, jellybeans and Reese's Peanut Buttercups, fried chicken and other items creating a monstrous playground for the diabetic impaired.

Flo giggled with excitement using her stubby sticky arms that seemed to be covered with an aroma filled vomit Vaseline to pull a pizza slathered with cheese and slices of pepperoni towards her. Her pudgy nails fingering one of the slices before picking up the whole box and resting it on her deformed breasts that drooped to her stomach.

"Want a slice?"

Gary released a nauseated gulp and pulled out a water bottle and with a grimace, "no I'm good." Flo's rotten teeth emerged in a sweet smile that she steered towards the lady barfly who nodded her head no but offered her an encouraging smile back.

"I see you looking at me in disgust." Gary remained silent. "Don't even try to pretend. I have seen it all countless of times before. Before I was housebound, I'd go to the grocery store, and I'd see the stares and hear the whispers. I'd curse them out under my breath but never loud enough for them to hear. A blubbering fool like me has no way to defend themselves. Besides, my only concern was to get in and out as quickly as I could, so I loaded more food in my basket. Or I'd get Alex to do it. Alexander. He's, my brother. He's a fat ass too…" with some hesitation, "or he was." She looked at Gary and smiled food in her mouth and all. Sticking in her teeth were remnants of fried cheese crust, mozzarella sauce dripping from her bulging chin dripping on to her curtain of a dress that barely came to her elephant knees.

"Hand me that coke will ya?"

Gary leans to the side and places a two-litter-bottle of coke between her greasy hands.

"Can I get you a glass?"

"Na, I just drink if from the bottle." Then eyeing a pink and blue frosted layer cake, "ooo, I could use a fork though and push that thing closer." Gary pulls a fork out of his apron and stabs it into the cake before pushing it forward. "My god this is good." As she let out a laugh, a piece of escaped crumbs fell out of her mouth, going unnoticed by her. Gary watched quietly as she shoveled the calories into her.

She eyes him through her gorge, "guess I'm supposed to tell you some sad stuff about my childhood. Help you get an understanding as to who I am and why I'm like this huh. Get you to feel sorry for me."

"I am here to listen to your story, but nothing you say can make me feel sorry for you."

"Don't be so sure."

"Oh, I'm sure. You chose to be this way with every repugnant bite you take. Even in a Coma, on life support, you choose to consume a steady stream of food. Hell, even in this realm, you could barely make it over the waters."

"Well, if your disgusting monsters weren't spitting and laughing at me, maybe it wouldn't have taken so long. You know, you aren't so great yourself. You wouldn't be here if you were. What sins are you paying for asshole?"

Gary places Kitty Kat on the counter near the barfly and away from the food, then he straightens his bowtie and speaks firmly. "This isn't about me. It is about you and you reflecting on your own life and how you could have made it better."

"You don't fucking know anything about me. And as for my so-called Coma. I'm diabetic and I have a weak heart."

"By your own doing, I see."

"What do you know. You ain't nothing but a lousy barkeep!"

"Oh, and I suppose you are going to enlighten me with some grand story about how you were a contribution to life. Missionary in a foreign country. Keeper of the light for sailors out to sea?"

"I have you know obesity is in my genes. My whole family is fat, and we know no different. That is how we were brought up. On food. Every holiday was celebrated with food. When kin got married, we ate, when they died, we ate, when kids were born and when they graduated…we ate. Every significant event in my life involved food."

"I get that. I originated from the South in the United States. I know food is part of the culture. And not healthy food. Fried Chicken served with piles of mashed potatoes. Corn on the cob, sweet-iced tea, mama's homemade pecan pie with chocolate chips and a scoop of vanilla bean ice-cream."

Gary eyed Flo as he spoke, noticing her excitement at the sound of the menu urgently replying. "My mama made potato salad with lots of mustard and egg. Every Sunday!" She dropped her head, "until daddy died that is. Then she had to get a job and Alex had to look after me." She waited for Gary to soften, loosen his stance, ask the question, *how did your daddy die*? In a quivering voice, but he just stayed on his stool, rubbing Kitty Kat's back down to her tail which she stood straight up when he got towards the bottom. *Does that cat actually wag her tail for him?*

Escaping from her thoughts, she began again, "my daddy was a good man. He was fat too but that wasn't his vice. It was the booze. He liked to drink." Licking her fork and reaching for the bowls of M&Ms. "I never touched the stuff myself, neither did Alex. We were not going to be like him. Well… not drink like him. He was fat too. Not like Alex or me, but he was fat."

"Seems like you really need to home in on the fact that your daddy was fat too."

Flo sneered but then smiled, giving Gary eye contact through her pie face. "Daddy always said mama made the best fried chicken in all of Kentucky. Said the Colonel may come looking for her to work for him, but he'd keep her all to herself." Thoughtfully, "he did love her, I know that."

"Was there ever a doubt?"

"Nah, not to us. To her maybe because he would work late a lot, but Alex and I knew he loved her." Noticing Gary looking at her. "Don't look at me like that. My daddy was no cheater. He loved my mama!"

His silence enticed an explosive outburst.

"He'd drink though, and it would cause him to lose jobs. Too many DWIs. Best job he had was as a truck driver. It made him be gone for weeks at a time but the money it brought him was the most he had ever made. It was even better than when he worked as a mechanics assembler. Of course, he got fired from that too. They said he was too much of a liability. Assholes. He was just a man trying to support his family." In an excited voice, "is that banana pudding? I love banana pudding!" Flo pushed away the plate that once held a layer cake and reached for a crystal bowl filled with creamy banana pudding topped with whip cream and vanilla wafers. Moving her fat head around, beady blue eyes almost swallowed up by an oversized forehead and pudgy nose.

"Spoon, spoon! I know I saw one somewhere." Her chunky arm could barely reached pass the two empty pizza boxes she had devoured within the first few minutes of conversation, but it managed to siphon through the trash and produce the desired object she searches for. A long silver spoon with LCC engraved on the tip of the handle. She eyed it for a moment before asking, "What does LCC stand for?"

"Last Chance Casino."

"Is that where I am. I don't even gamble."

"Really? Seems to me that you took a gamble with your life."

"Shut the hell up. You know nothing. What are you anyway, an angel, demon, what?"

Gary straitens his bowtie and responds, "somewhere in between, I guess. Like the pudding?"

"This place is disgusting. It feels like moving mud that bites at your ankles. Rather be bedridden than deal with this."

"It wants to slow you down from your indulgences. Let you think. Let you reflect."

"Ain't much to reflect on. Sometimes I did good and sometimes I did bad. Not more or less than any other person that makes it down to this dungeon."

She then shoveled the yellow delight into her mouth staring at Gary. His eyes remained tentative on her with spite channeled to his inner disgust. For a moment he stepped down off his stool to reach for Kitty Kat who had jumped onto her side of the counter managing to steal a piece of pepperoni she had lifted off another pizza to be victimized by Flo.

"What, you don't have any cat food for that thing?" Kitty Kat let out a hiss before Gary could calm her.

"Kitty Kat can have a treat or two. It won't hurt her."

"Yeah right! Maybe you should weigh that fat furball of yours."

"She prefers to be called goddess size."

"I know that." Snorting, and wiping her mouth with the back of her hand with a raspy snicker. "I know about goddess size and husky, thick boned, healthy proportioned. I know all the anecdotes invented to soften the blow of the distinguished triple XL sizes. Retailers are always coming up with creative ways to refer to the obese in attempts to be politically correct. There are even stores that make the sizes smaller than what they are." She spits out pudding as she talks. "I knew this one chic that wore a size eight but in this one establishment, it was a size two. Imagine that shit. Stupid, so stupid. People just need to acknowledge who they are. Even if they are fat asses like me. But no, it's all about the right thing to say to be polite and the wrong thing to say to be cruel. Political correctness is a hoax put out by idiots to make them feel better about themselves. Stupid, so stupid." Licking her index finger, she continues, "school was a nightmare for me. Political correctness doesn't exist in schools. You would think the bullying would motivate me to diet, but I just ate more. High school was even worse. Daddy had just died, and I was dealing with the confusion as to why mama did not bother to have a funeral for him or nothing. She just woke me and Alex one day and said that daddy was in a car crash, and he was in heaven now. We were stunned. I stayed quiet but Alex would not believe it and asked lots of questions. He just wouldn't let it go. He even asked the resource officer at school if he could look into any car accidents that had happened, but the guy just gave him some sad eyed look and told him to go talk to his mama." Reaching for a bottle of orange soda, "Alex was a bigger target than me. You know kids are always meaner to gingers. He grew up okay though. Always stood by me even though I never deserved it." Tiny beads of water dropped out of Flo's eyes. "I was treated real bad. My daddy he died three days before my ninth-grade year in school. I was already over two-hundred pounds and mama said no man would ever want me if I don't stop stuffing my face with twinkies. She even hid the snack cakes and chocolate bars from me at times. I would find them though and eat them all up just out of spite. She'd complained that we didn't have money to waste on candy and then the hypocrite would buy it for herself and hide it from us kids. Hell, when it was Halloween, she'd say we couldn't go trick or treating because that was like begging yet, she sure was the first in the church family's food line every Wednesday morning. Hypocrite she was. Damn hypocrite."

She let out a loud smelly burp. Gary backs up on his stool and grimaces. "That bitch would hide these big Hershey

Chocolate bars on the top shelf of the pantry. Always found them though. Stupid wretch of a woman. Daddy was too good for her. Spending money on chocolate and then taking food from the food pantry. When I was older, she'd send me too. They thought I was older than I was on account I was so big and then we'd get a second helping. You know, churches should check for frauds."

She exhales, Gary steps back with Flo noticing, "oh please, you can't tell me that my breath is any worse that the sulfur that reeks from the left side of the room. Is that the gateway to hell? Is that where I am going?"

"Do you think you need to go to hell?"

Flo lets out a breath, "are you, my judge?"

Gary lets out a disgruntled sigh, "I get asked that a lot. No, I am not your judge. But I do possess the ears that will let you wallow out all of your life's troubles."

"Well, you don't seem much like a therapist."

"I didn't say I was a therapist. If you want a therapist, wait for Dr. Phil. And no, I haven't seen him down here, so you are stuck with the likes of me."

"Yeah, well clearly you are more of a condescending asshole that has prejudices against the obese, if anyone asks me." The lady barfly remained quiet but nodded in agreement.

"I guess we all have our vices."

Flo looks down and notices an image forming at the bottom of the pudding bowl. Spiraling swirls of pink, red, purple, and blue colors and then green circled the bowl in turbid waves. She watched it as if she were looking into a unique kaleidoscope of color glossed with sediments of fresh banana in processed cream. The hypnotic substance slowly emerged into an LED image. Peering into a looking glass that reflected a younger and lighter but still chubby pimpled covered image of Flo in her high school uniform. Her back fat bulging through the strands of her bra that was transparent under her red collared shirt. Her hair pulled up too thin to make an attractive ponytail. Her short crimson polished nails highlighting her portly hands that were held up over her face as Trent, an acne infested football player that spent more time on the bench than in the field tortured her with two of his loser friends Cappy, an ox-size stupid sixteen-year-old still stuck in the ninth grade due to his existence of apathy and video games and Antoine whom pretended to be from a rough mobster family in New York but everyone knows that his dad is a factory worker and his mom runs a daycare out of their house for low-income families. Just another loser with great hair unlike their leader Trent.

Flo's bowl image released a stank of weed woven into her own putrid smell which tickled her nose while sweat beaded around her forehead and her hairy armpits that poked from the edges of her short-sleeved moo-gown.

"I cried out, but nobody heard. I was cornered in the boy's locker room after school. I was told by Saundra, a girl that pretended to be my friend that Alex was in the locker room, and he needed help because he was hurt. They said that he had done something to his ankle and that the nurse had already left for the day and the coaches were out on the field attending to practice. I believed her. It never even dawn on me at the time that Alex would never have been in the locker room. He avoided it at all costs. He caught shit because of his size as much as I did. He had as many wide load signs posted onto his back as I had. Thunder thighs, Lard Ass, Tub Mongrel, we had heard it all. On the bus, in the hallways even in class while unsympathetic teachers turned a blind eye. Those teachers they saw it, they heard it. All the names and spitballs thrown our way. And yet they pretended the torment wasn't happening right in front of them." Flo started to cry. "Those horrible teachers were just as much as a bully as the kids." She cried harder. "School was a never-ending nightmare. From the moment that we stepped on the bus in the morning to the second we walked into our house. Heading for the Oreos and hoping mama would bring home McDonald's. Nobody cared about us. We had no friends. Not really. That bitch Saundra. The last place Alex would go willingly go would be the boy's locker room. Only the fields were sacred to the coaches. Not the locker rooms. A place that remained unguarded, vulnerable for easy targets to be the fledged by the bullies that wondered the ominous hallways at Jefferson's finest high school."

Rubbing her eyes with the back of her wrists she leans over and grabs a brownie. "Yet, I went in. I never thought Saundra would lie to me. I mean, what would she gain from it? She invited me to eat lunch, French braid my hair. She even said she would go shopping with me. Help me pick out things that would make me look nice. Make me look thin, but instead, she lured me into a boy's locker room to be the prey of Trent and his loser friends."

Flo paused for a long time, glancing up and down at the bar where food of all types appeared as she willed it. She reached for a bag of Doritos, tugged on the sides of the bag until it opened and pulled on a large burnt orange triangle, licking a tip before putting the whole thing into her mouth. "I like to suck the flavor out before I chew and swallow. Kind of like how people suck the salt off sunflower seeds before eating them. I don't eat those though." Opening her eyes wide, "surprised, there is actually something that I won't eat?"

Gary remained quiet.

"I'm glad you are not a therapist. Cause, eating is my therapy. That's how I cope. I don't need you." Looking down at the bowl. "Can you see them? Those filthy mongrels that destroyed my life. They poked at me and laughed at me." Taunting voices echoed from the bowl.

"What's wrong Flo? Are you on your Flow?"

"They are so stupid! Can't even come up with a good insult."

Another dark voice floats up, "Awe she can't even find her pussy over her layers of lard." Flo's chin stiffened.

"Assholes, all of them assholes! Make it stop." Stabbing her spoon into the mirage but it kept going and maintaining her attention. She watched her younger self try to run past them, but

Trent pushed her as Cappy gave another shove causing her to fall backward on the floor, hitting her head on a bench. Her skirt pushing up revealing her days-of-the-week panties. Thursday.

They were too small causing redlines around her waist her and her fat chunks of a leg where the connection between her thigh and calf met as the knee was a buried into knots of fat lost among the elephant trunks.

"Oh, is that it." Trent got to the ground and pressed himself on her, unbuttoning his Levi jeans. "Let's see if we can find it. You are a girl aren't you."

"More like a sea-monster." Antonio retorts.

Where the hell is Alex? Where is Saundra. She sent me in here, did she know? She had too." Tears flowing down her rosacea filled cheeks, while she pleads, "make this stop," but her pleas go unheard as the dark voices raise from the bowl.

"Got her down Cappy. Hold her legs."

Helplessly, Flo watched as Trent pushing himself into her as he pretended to know what he was doing. He wouldn't last though. Virgin rapist couldn't get his turn to last long before the other two took a wak at it. Cappy and Antoine had the same amount of luck as Trent. Her body so big that she couldn't turn over between shifts. Thursday panties gone. How was she going to explain this to Mama? Doesn't she know how much new panties are. Even at the thrift store where most of her clothing came. They were in luck if they could find anything large enough to fit. *My panties! How am I going to explain this? Fuck you, Saundra! Fuck you, Alex!*

Looking up at Gary exasperated, "Why are you making me watch this? What kind of twisted fuck are you?"

"I'm so sorry this happened to you."

As Gary spoke tumult sounds echoed from the casino room. Flo looks back and scrunches her mouth. "I still don't get why I would be here. I don't gamble."

"Are you sure about that. Perhaps you don't play the tables or the slots, but were there times when you took a risk?"

Flo shrugged, "I told principal Stevens about what happened, and he did nothing. He didn't call them in or nothing. He said no boy would do that to me. I went to the resource officer too and he didn't do anything…well…he told me to go talk to my mama. That was a line he really liked."

"Did you?"

"She didn't believe me. Nobody believed me. Even when I had a baby."

"Baby?"

Looking down and picking on the fudge of a brownie. "Yeah Dolorous." She sighs. "I can't remember when I ate so much."

"That's because you want to eat. You will not get full. You will eat on desire and not hunger."

"Damn, wish I would have gotten here sooner." Talking with her mouth full as she shoves another brownie in before swallowing the other one, she had already sucked in.

"Dolorous?"

"Couldn't stand the slimy little thing. Didn't know I was pregnant on the account I was never really regular anyway and I was so fat that nobody noticed that part of it was a baby bump. One night, I woke up screaming bloody murder, mama was working late so Alex called the ambulance and a few hours later, that little slimy clam came out. Mama was pretty shaken."

"You?"

"Wouldn't have been if I could have given her away but mama said no. She said if I was going to sin like a woman of the night than I had to pay the consequences and that was Dolorous."

"Did you love her at all?"

"Tried too but could never bring myself to it. Would have aborted her if I knew she was there." She looks up at Gary, "I'm sorry, I know that is wrong. A baby shouldn't pay for the father's crime." Then sighing, "maybe if she would have stuck around long enough, I could have loved her."

"Stuck around?"

Flo discovered a can of icing under one of the empty pizza boxes and began using it to dip her Doritos. Her crunching sounded out the distant rumble in the casino. One compunctious chew after another. At times she studied her food while at others she looked up, but not directly at Gary. She took interest in the lights from the casino bouncing off the liquor bottles on the bar shelves. Her gaze lands on the shimmering wrapper of a Little Debbie Snack cake. Again, the color circles embedded the wrapper beckoning her to look deeper.

"Awe, not this again."

This time falling more quickly into the trance of a fatter teen-aged Florence than what was seen before sitting up on a bed with a frayed blue and white nightgown and a tiny red infant with black hair screaming in her arms. Her mama's voice sounded through the door. "Shut that brat up!" Flo crying at her failed attempts to feed, then burp and feed again threatening looks of frustration at the baby, then the ceiling and then the baby again. An oscillator fan circling back and forth making a clicking sound in rhythm to the clock sitting on the milkcrate nightstand littered with chip bags and gum wrappers.

"She wouldn't stop crying. That's all she did was cry."

Gary remains quiet as Flo watches the scene unfold in front of her. Her mother yelling through the door, her feeble attempt to comfort the crying infant shrieking and squirming in her arms.

"I hated her!" Flo repeated. "I had no business with a baby, but mama said, you made your bed you lie in it. Even though I never wanted those nasty boys on me. And here I was stuck with their abomination."

Anger flooded her face as she watched her younger self take the infant and lay down in bed. Carefully she laid the innocent being beside her, crying out, arms flaying. Teen Flo watched for a moment as her mom's voice shouted again through a shut door, "do something, you'll wake up the whole trailer park."

Teen Flo's emotions flipping between sadness and frustration. Her youth outlined through her plump body, chipped nails, and rosacea cheeks slowly impulsively making a decision amongst the torment of her mother's yells and the shrieks of her hungry baby. She slowly and meticulously rolled over on top of the young life squishing the seven-pound bundle of innocence as the fan covered the sounds of the muffling cries, until there were no more.

Staring at the image, "I don't know how long I laid there." A long pause of silence before she looked up at Gary and yelled, "why won't you say something?"

"This is your story, not mine."

Flo looks back at the image embedded in the wrapper to see Alex walking in, grungy in a McDonald's uniform, carrying a bag of food. "Look, Flo, brought you back a quarter pounder meal just like you asked." Looking down at the empty bassinet. "Where's my niece. I can feed her if you want." His voice kind and innocent.

Slowly Flo rolled back over. Her face sticky with sweat and burning with malice, tugging at the top of her nightgown that slightly stuck to the baby's corpse.

"Oh my god! Oh my god! Flo get up!" Running to the door. "Mom! Mom! Get in here quick!"

Flo laid there, refusing to look at Dolores.

Her mother stumbled in, igniting a smell of stale cigarettes to stink up Flo's aura. Her greasy matted hair, smudged mascara twisted mouth hollering to Alex, "what you bring us to eat?"

Alex stretching out a shaky hand to towards the bed. The hand that still held the McDonald's bag, grease stains forming at the bottom of it. His index finger pointing out towards the bed where Flo remained on her side, motionless next to the silenced child now stiff in broken pieces held together by a thin veil of skin.

"You stupid whore! What have you done?" Her mother wailed while walking over to her, slapping Flo with the back of her hand gashing her lip with a costume ruby ring. Alex slipping out and grabbing the phone. "You stupid girl." Suddenly her screaming mother hears Alex in the hallway.

"Yes, operator, we need an ambulance at 801 Hazelhurst…."

Mama ran out and grabbed the phone from him. Speaking quickly to the operator. "Yes ma'am, there seems to have been an accident. My granddaughter…"

Alex ran back into the room. "What happened?" He approaches Delores, rubbing the bottom of her chin with one stubby finger. Crying, "the paramedics are on their way, they can revive her."

Flo looked up from the memory. "He would have been a good uncle. I know that because he is a good father." Dipping another Dorito into a glob of icing. "He is a good brother."

Gary glanced down into the memory; Flo's gaze follows.

Paramedics in the room, a police car pulling up outside. "My daughter, she fell asleep while feeding her. She must have rolled over on her. Flo, get out of that bed at once."

Flo looked around, the baby was to the right of her, and the bed was up against the wall. No way to get out without going over the child. A female paramedic looks at Flo.

"You stay right here. We have to wait on the ME to come and the police are going to want to ask you a few questions."

"The ME?"

"Medical examiner," the paramedic said hastily.

"I have to go to the bathroom."

The female paramedic looked up at her partner who nodded. He went to the end of the bed and helped pull her up while the other medic kept it steady. Outside a short stout man came in asking an officer as to the whereabouts of the remains. Flo wobbled beside him and slipped into the bathroom that was so small that she could barely fit in. Steadying herself on the toilet, she changed out her pad. She had clotted during the night. She had been doing that since the birth. She never went back for a follow up visit. Mother said they didn't have insurance and her trashiness wasn't worth the money.

She washed her hands, looked at her reflection in the mirror and smiled, then giggled and held her hands over her face to avoid letting out a squeal of laughter. Alex knocked on the door.

"Are you okay?"

"Yes, I'm coming out now."

The memory skips to where she is sitting on a brown torn pleather couch talking to two policemen while gobbling down her cold fries. She did not look up when the baby was taken out. So tiny. The body bag looked like a trash bag. On a stretcher like a grown adult when she was small enough to fit inside a cooler.

Flo feels a pulling sensation, the memory transforms into an ariel view and then became blurry until the last voice drifted off, "it was an accident. A horrible accident."

Flo continued to look into the wrapper even as Alex's voice was long gone.

"He always stood up for me. Even to mother. He protected me at all costs." Wiping sweat off her chin, "If you care, it was ruled an accident. An unfortunate mishap of a teen having a child way to young. She was buried in a plot in Potter's field since we couldn't afford a real funeral and that was that. No more Dolorous. Her name was never mentioned in our house again." She twists her neck, shrugs her shoulders, and added, "anyway, that was many years ago."

"So, nobody questioned you about Delores's murder?"

"I said, it was classified an accident."

"Yes, but we both know it wasn't."

Flo looked angrily at Gary. "I suppose you think that after that I went on to live some sort of nefarious life without guilt but that is not true." Looking down at a chocolate milkshake. "I just moved on. Finished school, took care of mother when she got sick and then Alex took care of me when I got sick. Besides, my body became my jail cell."

"Sick? Disease?"

Rolling her eyes. "You know damn good and well that my

weight made me house bound. Hell, I've been on oxygen for the last three years."

Looking around. "I'm lucky to have Alex you know. He moved back in so he could tend to me. I know it breaks his heart to see me this way."

Inhaling and then exhaling, Flo shrugs. "I don't want any more food."

"Had your fill?"

"By the looks of me, I never had my fill. But I'm tired of the pain."

"Pain? You shouldn't be feeling any pain here."

"Memoires are painful. You didn't bother to show memories of my birthdays and when Alex would bring me special treats. My mother when she wasn't drinking. My daddy. No, you showed me at the most disgusting moments of my life. What for? Why is that?"

"I have no control over your reflections. Your mind does and it brings out your inner demons. You eat to soothe that pain. But as you can see, no matter how much you eat, the pain is still there."

"Where do you think Delores went. I know they wouldn't send her to a place like this."

"Delores was too young to experience a life. You made sure of that."

Flo looked down at her pudgy hands remorsefully.

"Amethyst."

"I'm sorry."

"Amethyst. That was her middle name and her birthstone. I was always planning on getting an Amethyst ring, but I couldn't find a real one that fit on my finger. I wanted it to remember her by. Think of. Just because her name was never brought up again in our house, it doesn't mean that I didn't think of her sometimes."

"Doesn't seem like you ever forgot her."

"Or what I did to her."

"Are you remorseful?"

A choked cry gurgled from Flo's throat as tears swelled again in her eyes. She tried to speak but all she could do was nod her head.

Gary gets up. "I'm not sure if you can get up from there, so let me push this a little closer to you."

A glittery dust forms over the bar, lowers onto the food swallowing it up returning the bar into its original shiny brown and gold surface. The backdrop of glasses shine, and behind Gary lights sparkle and dance across his spectacles. On the bar lay two sparkling gold pieces.

"Here you go."

Gary pushes up the slot machine, the lever at arm's length. Long and dazzling.

Flo picks up the coins and slides them into the slot one at a time, her eyes focused on Gary. Placing her hand firmly on the globe of the lever she struggles to pull it down. The lady barfly gets up, "here let me…" before she could finish her sentence, Gary holds up his hand.

"No, this is the one thing she has to do on her own."

"Maybe I won't be housebound anymore."

"Maybe. I am not privy to the miracles that happen after here."

Flo releases a nervous smile and using the handle to pull herself up, she yanks down as hard as she can, pulling herself back to her specialized chair.

Instantly a breeze picks up as the symbols in the display spin, flashing comments here and, a mangled bit of music sounds, a crunching noise comes from behind and then the ambience subsides as the wheels slowly come to a stop, one by one, resting on the word *Mors*.

Flo looked up. "The last doctor I went to said I wouldn't make it to forty. Guess he was right."

"Guess he was."

Gary walked around the bar and slid Flo's walker to the side. "You won't need this anymore. You will be fine without it."

"Do you think I'm forgiven?"

"That depends on the path we go." As he spoke, green vines grew from the shores of the Lethe River and stretched out towards the Acheron River. A low murmur of music begins to sound and as the bridge vines stretched, the notes became louder. Flo recognized the rich voice or Aretha Franklin, R-E-S-P-E-C-T.

"Oh, I love this song. Turn it up." The song plays louder as Gary comes closer and takes her by her arm, she gets up, legs not trembling to walk beside her escort.

The lady barfly heard a slight chuckle from Flo as she watched the two as they walk down a path filled with tables and casinos.

"This is the closest that I will ever get to walking the aisle."

A green bridge opened to the right; the waters of the Lethe River turn gentle. As the two walked the bridge, the ice of the Acheron began to melt, a warmth shined over Flo as a golden light opens from the heavy mahogany doors.

"There's my baby girl." A tall, chunky, happy man calls out. Flo turned to Gary. "But why? I am not worthy of heaven. I am not worthy of anything. I have sinned. I have killed." Gasping, "I killed my own child."

Light spread across her face, "Come on baby girl," sounds from inside the door. Gary studies her before speaking. "I am only here to guide. I am not the one to accept your request of forgiveness, but I know you have been heard and through your pleas, you have been granted mercy from the greatest parent of all. The Father. Accept his mercy and forgiveness, as you will heal and as you learn to forgive yourself, the pain will melt away."

The lady barfly sat and witnessed the tremendous golden light that silhouetted Gary as he spoke to Flo. She looks at him and then at another man calling to her from the opening of Heaven's door.

"I have so much to tell you, darling," the man yells out to her. Gary gently lets go of her hands and watches her without struggle pass the golden gates and enter the threshold of the mahogany doors.

Gary stands there a moment as the doors close and then turns to go down the green vined bridge that withers away after each one of his footsteps. He smiles at the lady barfly when he reaches the bar, uses the mirrors behind the spirits to straighten up his bowtie, and then turns to face the direction of the roaring casino.

He takes a breath, and then with a loud, southern drawl he hollers out, "Last call."

Bruno

"Jackpot!"

Screams and whoops sound in the distance as people illusioned by intoxication from the Lotus drink, too simple-minded to realize they were engulfed in a euphoric state of glory, indulging in the belief that they struck it rich.

"You can't take it with you!" Gary hollers. He turns to the lady barfly. "Idiots. Every one of them. Idiots. They all come here sucking down a sweet molasses, playing endlessly in a time-forbidden mirage filled with exultation yet fearing me as if I am the one to take it all away from them. Can't say it enough. Idiots. Or is imbecile a better word? What do you think I should go with? Idiot or imbecile? I mean, you are the storyteller, so you must be a superb wordsmith."

Ignoring Gary's sarcasm, the lady barfly responds, "Then where does it all go?" Quick pause while she rethinks her question. "The rewards I mean. The jackpots."

"It recycles, similar to the way people's souls do if they don't learn a lesson the first, second, third … hell, hundredth time around in some cases."

Looking out in the distance, Gary takes notice of the bridge from the Cocytus River opening as a tall, muscular built man struggles through. His movements are slow, hindered by heavy weights tied to his arms, hips, thighs, and ankles. With each step of his journey, the man stops and examines his surroundings. His brows are knitted, his eyes squinting as if he is searching, but as quick as he takes a pause, fiery waters leap out at him, encouraging him to trudge on, grasping at the gold cross dangling on a thick, gold chain around his neck. Each step is accompanied by a prayer as the perversion of desperate demons lunge at him from different directions. Gary studies him as he slowly makes it across, admiring his determination through the tumultuous path.

"Take a look at that." He gestures toward the inbound man.

"Looks like he is having a tough time."

"He is crossing the bridge to get here. The bridge that is

full of hate. See the six-winged beast flapping overhead. It is spitting on him. You can see the droplets of saliva land on his head. Watch. And yet, look at that, clinging to his faith."

The lady barfly watches as a bat-like creature with red eyes and snarling teeth flaps from the top of the rotunda directly above the high-class man. Large drops of mucus and spit drip down, some landing on the bridge, the sizzling acid drops melting the steps away in a way so the traveler must step over them while balancing the heavy weights. A few of the droplet's splash onto him, some bits landing on his arm. Smoke sizzles up from the skin, and yet, he doesn't fall, he doesn't quiver, he only looks straight ahead, the gold glint of the cross-sneaking peeks through the cracks of his fingers. Noticing Gary in the distance, he salutes him and offers him a jolly smile as he maneuvers his way passed the smoking gates of the Phlegethon with an 'I got this' determination.

"Now that is true integrity and machoism at its best. He keeps going. How in the hell does someone keep their cool like that?"

"Do I hear admiration coming from the Great Ferryman of the Last Chance Casino?"

"Hey, it's impressive to me. I sit here many a day watching big ass bullies crying like little girls when they make their path. But not him." He nods toward her. "You probably want to listen to this one. He's got a story to tell."

The two watch together as the elegant man comes forward. Upon his final step between the Phlegethon and the Acheron, he pulls out a handkerchief from his pocket. A thick one, not like a real handkerchief but a cloth napkin found in the finest of restaurants. He shakes it open and wipes the mix of bloody froth and pus that had splashed onto his face. He hears the laughter from above, but he doesn't bother to look up. Instead, he takes his right hand and rubs it through his dark hair, flashing a middle finger.

He then makes eye contact with Gary and says in a loud,

North American accent, "I shall not be anyone's snack today." After throwing the linen cloth over his shoulder, he makes his way onto the now sturdier bridge, not noticing that his handkerchief dissolved the moment it hit the waters.

Keeping his head up, his eyes straight ahead, maintaining eye contact with Gary, he crosses the bridge. He smiles again, pleasant, and despite the journey he just made, he remains classy in his well-tailored suit.

"Excuse me, sir." Upon a closer distance to him, Gary immediately recognizes his dialect from that of the New York region. He tips his head toward the lady barfly.

She herself is impressed by his magnificent muscles rippling through his tailored jaket and finds herself taking an immediate liking to him.

"Greetings, my good man. Please pop a squat," Gary says, quickly positioning himself between the newcomer and the regular.

He looks at him inquisitively while Gary wipes down a section of the bar that was already clean. "Have a seat." He points to a stool. "Guess we ain't from the same neck of the woods."

"Yeah, well, you don't want to be from my parts. It's filled with thorns."

"That is excessively poetic. You a writer or something?"

"Nah, I'm more of an investor I guess you can say."

"Well, nothing to invest in here, but it is your lucky day. Drinks are on the house. What can I get ya to wet your whistle?"

"R&H beer if you have it."

"Can do. The best brand I've got if the gods are interested in my opinion."

Gary turns to a small fridge under the glasses and opens it to reveal shelves of enticing beige and purple cans of R&H Pilsner beer. The man licks his lips and closes his bright green eyes, taking in the glorious sound of the popping of the top of the can, imagining the sloshing sound of its contents as Gary slides it over with an ice-cold mug.

With intense sophistication, the man shifts his position, and being the beer drinking pro he is, he tilts his glass and pours the delicious nectar in it while his eyes glaze over as the suds rise to the top, making a bubbling sound. He looks at Gary, who nods at him while he pours his own. He tastes it. "Damn that's some good ale. Better than I remembered it."

"Well, it probably is. You from the fifties, right?"

"Last I remembered it was December of 1953."

"Yeah." After taking a sip of his own beer, Gary continues, "Time is different here. What you got is the new and improved R&H. Not sure if I even have the older stuff. Which would be a first for this place. You know, we like to carry everything here, but, well ..." Gary takes in another sip and thinks for a moment. "Sometimes, it is just best that you take in the new and let the old stuff remain in the past. That fabric that will one day become known as history."

The sophisticated man lets out a laugh. "Ha. Now look who needs to be the writer." Then he glances at the can. "Thought the label looked different." Rubbing his hand through his hair, he notices Kitty Kat, who jumped onto the bar, placing a white paw on one of the cans. "Won't hurt her, will it?"

Gary reaches out and strokes the cat's back up to the tail. "Nah, nothing hurts her here. It is all about truth. What's your name?"

"Bruno. Named after a patron saint, but I'm not a saint."

"Okay, Bruno," Gary tips his glass toward him, "what's your truth?"

"So that is how this goes. You entice me with my favorite beverage and then you listen to my wallowing about how soulless my life was?"

"Something like that."

Bruno takes a sip of his beer and rubs the scruff on his chin, thinking slowly. "My mother raised me to be a good man. Made me study, do chores, and look after my younger brother and sister. I never minded though. I saw how hard she worked. She cleaned houses, did laundry and other domestic odd jobs. I am not quite sure how she kept the rent paid with what little money she earned. Even took us to church every Sunday and always had spare change for tithes. She was a good woman." Bruno nods his head in thought. "I was so blessed to have her. Didn't know it at the time though. Gave her nothing but trouble, and yet, she never gave up on me." He smiles sadly. "No other like her."

"I take it family is important to you?"

"Yep, and not just the blood kind. Anyone you take into your heart. It's all about loyalty you see. Mom knew that." He takes another sip. "You sound as if you are from the South."

Gary lets out a chuckle. "Well, I guess down here, we are all from the South."

Bruno looks around. "I would have expected to see more fire and brimstone down here."

"What, you don't think that walk across the bridge wasn't hot enough. Say it louder and you may just get sprayed with demon piss."

Bruno lets out a chuckle as he glances at the bubbles in his beer. "Living my sins over and over again like some ominous merry-go-round operated by the devil's zookeepers. Not that I wouldn't deserve it, especially with the way I led my life. I didn't always follow Mom's advice. Drove her nuts, too, but when I do something to deserve a consequence, I sucked it up and took it like a man." Looking down, he pulls up his sleeve and reveals a gold watch with the face encircled in diamonds and the Roman numerals crusted with a sparkling silver.

"Nice piece you got there."

Bruno holds it up with pride. "Yeah, Harry gave me this right after I first started working for him. Said we were going places and when you go places you have to look like that you belong there."

"You don't look like you belong here."

"Yeah, well, my mother always said that the pretty sinners

were the most dangerous 'cause nobody wants to ever punish them so their crimes grow along with a false sense of pride and immortality."

Gary sets another beer in front of Bruno before leaning down on his elbows and sipping on his own. "Look out there," he says, pointing with a nod of his head, red and blue lights bouncing off his wire-framed glasses. Bruno follows the gaze while Gary speaks. "What do you see?"

"Looks like a crowd of folks enjoying eternity gambling and drinking."

"Yeah, they are participating in the same activity, but look at them. Study them, what do they all have in common?"

Gary patiently remains quiet while Bruno observes the crowd for a long time. He enjoys the spectacle of seeing people win the jackpots, the arguments at the tables, and the waitresses passing out the drinks, but when he finally speaks, it is out of confusion. "Sir, with all due respect, I do not understand what you expect me to see. These people don't seem to have anything in common except they are doomed to gamble until they come to meet you. Nothing poetic."

"So, what do you see? Not just the overall image. The details."

"People. So many people. They are dressed different, they look different, they are different ages, different colors … hell, even when I was amongst them, they sounded different. Not sure if they were even speaking my language."

"And yet, somehow you manage to understand them."

"I just figured that was the magic of hell."

"Oh, contrary to your belief, you are not in hell … yet."

"Don't think I care for the 'yet' part."

"Don't imagine you do. After all, who would? Yet, the path a person takes is what leads them there."

"Yes, well, if you are into philosophical conversations, here is something to ponder. What if the person's intent were to follow the right path; the path that represents good and yet somehow …" Bruno takes another sip of his endless beer, "what if the person took a wrong turn? The metaphoric map got the traveler loss if you will. Perhaps swallowed up in their desires. Must they still carry the burden of their sins?" He rubs his wrists that had recently carried heavy weights but became unchained the moment he reached the bar's shore.

"Burdens are a perspective of regretted choices, and … well, I could go on to sing you a chord or two of 'Amazing Grace', but my voice could scare the mold away in outdoor shower stalls." Chuckling, Gary shakes his head. "What I can say is that there is always choice. Even when somebody does not realize it, they have one. The choices may not always seem logical though. Especially when fear enters the perspective."

"Fear of the outcome?"

"Well from my experience of wiping down this bar for a few decades, what I see more of is the fear of the unknown." He places a round coaster under the man's beer. "I know that is what determines the choices that are made up here."

"Yet, it is the choices in life that counts, not the ones here."

"So, you do know where you are."

"Well, I sure as hell am not in heaven," he says, looking around, "but you are right, this doesn't exactly feel like hell either." Picking up his can, Bruno studies the new label. "I like the design." Turning the can around, his eyes fall on a yellow circle outlined with a dark burgundy line and a burgundy drawing of Staten Island. "That's where I hail from," he boasts proudly to Gary. "It is a great place to grow up. When I was a kid—" Bruno suddenly drops the can in mid-sentence.

"You, okay?"

"Yeah, fine, I just got caught off guard." Bruno picks up the can, and embarrassed by his spill, he reaches for Gary's towel to clean up his mess but stops himself.

"What on earth …" His eyes follow the purple lines spinning as the words begin to melt and pull apart. Again, he throws out a "What the hell?"

"It's okay. Part of the process."

Kitty Kat jumps down off Gary's lap to lick up the remains of the spilt brew.

"Good girl, never let a good drink go to waste." Leaning against the back shelves, Gary consoles Bruno, "You're not hallucinating. I promise."

Bruno holds up the empty container in a shaky grasp as the logo continues to spiral until a one-way mirror appears, offering a reflection to a ten-year-old Bruno shooting through the house.

"You're it!" he hollered at Andrea, his younger sister.

She laughed as she grasped her stomach, her pigtails loose with black strands falling in her face. "No fair, you peeked."

"Did not!"

"Yeah, you did," his brother, Bentley, commented without taking his eyes out of his book.

"Didn't see you there hiding on the couch."

"You never do."

Bruno looks up for a moment. "Bentley always wanted attention but never knew how to get it. He just watched life go by while Andrea and I lived it."

"Did that work out for him?" Gary asks as he bends down to pick up Kitty Kat who is currently using his pant leg as a scratching post.

"I guess. He grew up, married Lydia, his high school sweetheart, and had three kids of his own. Even named one after me. He worked as a school librarian." He smiles. "I used to tease him about having a woman's job." Looking down at the image of a young Bentley reading a book, he says, "Guess I should have seen that coming. He loved books. He'd go through thick novels in a week. Swallowing up every bit of knowledge from them and losing himself in their wild tales. He'd say reading was a place to go when you had nowhere to go. Wasn't much of a reader myself so I didn't really know that meant." Smiling, he speaks fondly, "He became a good man. I never told him how proud I am of him. I regret that. While he was living out the American dream doing everything right, I was running with Harry's crowd."

"Harry?"

"Harry, the boss as everyone in the neighborhoods knew him as." Bruno pauses for a moment to look at his watch. "You know, I don't know how long I've been here, but the time stays at three o'clock. You wouldn't happen to have a watch battery around here, would you?"

"You don't need one. Tell me more about Harry."

"I thought he was my ticket to becoming a self-made millionaire. That was my goal, or at least it was until I wizened up to what my real dream was. While Bentley kept his ideals small, I grew to become more avaricious with each passing year. Mother met him in the summer of 1923. We were all still young and did not have any memory of our father, so he was a welcomed existence in the house. Most importantly, he made Mother happy and that was all what us kids cared about. Of course, we did not mind the gifts he showered on us. He gave me my first bike, bought me my first steak at a fancy restaurant, and he gave me my first job. Guess you could say he was grooming me. He operated out of Brooklyn." Chuckling, he shakes his head. "He was the King of Brooklyn, and in my eyes that made me the prince. He told me that I was going to be his apprentice and he'd make me a big success like him. When I walked into a room, everybody would look up and show respect."

"I thought you said you were from Staten Island."

"Yep, loved it there, too. Had good friends, but Harry said that you shouldn't play where you lay. It could get messy if you do. So, he did his business in Brooklyn." As he speaks, he places his hand on his glass. It instantly fills back up with ice-cold beer. "It's funny you know. How you grow up believing someone is your hero, but their vices become your vices and they follow you until the end."

"How so?"

"He was a vicious criminal always chasing the dollar, and well … I guess … so am I."

Kitty Kat meows, and Gary leans down. She licks his nose. He smiles, stroking her back as she repositions herself. Bruno's eyebrows knit at him, waiting on a reaction, but is met with none.

"You're a benevolent sort of gent, aren't ya?"

"Don't want to interrupt a man when he is about to tell me about his 'wrong turn'. Besides, I could use a good gangster story."

"Oh, is that what I am now?"

"Oh, I mean it with great respect. The so-called gangsters from the 90s forward ain't got now style, no class. You, my friend, are the image of the perfect gangster."

The lady barfly lets out a light chuckle.

Bruno nods to her, and Gary winks. "I wasn't always the man you see before you. In fact, there was a time I was one vociferating mother—" He looks over to the lady barfly. "Please excuse my vulgarity, but I was quite the vociferating mother fucker. Fortunately … let us just say that my time here has taught me patience and the ability to not judge."

The lady barfly lets out a, "Ha!"

Bruno smiles. "It is good to see that people can change. I wish I could say I was one of them. There was a time that I thought I was." He takes a swig. "Hanging out with Harry made my head swell. Thought I was untouchable. He had everyone on the payroll. The mayor, the district attorney … hell, the entire police force. He had operations all over Brooklyn. There wasn't a storefront or street corner that didn't know his name. Bets were taking place in plain daylight."

Rolling his mug between his hands, he shrugs. "Think I'm embellishing, don't ya? But I swear on my mother's grave that a man could work a nine to five gambling job and go home to his wife and kids just as easy as he was working the line. Hell, easier since the cops never bothered ya. Even when ya were openly stinking drunk. They would just nod at you, tell you to take it on down the road. Yeah, I was walking on easy street."

Squinting his eyes, he looks sideways at the left door before turning to Gary. "Do ya know what it is like to be able to do whatever ya feel like it and to have it overlooked?"

"Can't say that I do. Lived my life on the up and up."

"Then how the hell did you end up here?"

"Good point." Taking his mug, he gives an air cheers. "Maybe I wasn't always living on the up and up, but hey, this isn't about me, it's about you. This is your show, Bruno. Tell me about your co-star, Harry."

"Good Ole Harry. Head of the Brooklyn gambling syndicate. Nobody else had a chance in profiting on that. Clever bastard he was. Never thought he'd get caught." Winking at the lady barfly, he says, "Ya know, he escaped the cops once."

"Really?" Gary leans in a little closer, surprised at his own interest.

Kitty Kat jumps to the counter and lays down next to the lady barfly's drink.

"Yep, and when he was finally caught and brought up before the judge," he shakes his head, "he still wouldn't narc on the officers who were a part of the ring, staying true to his word to them. What a guy!" He lifts his beer and holds it up as to toast. "They had family, ya know."

Taking a large swig of the beer, he eyes the other that Gary had gotten up and put in front of him. Thoughtfully, he says, "It was a time, ya know. Like in the movies. Thugs in pin-striped suits in fedoras holding two fist-sized bankrolls with a new harlot on their arm each night. And we all worked for Harry, the kingpin of gambling, each and every one of us biding for his approval. I know he kept my pockets filled even though we were recovering from a depression and the people were skittish of war." Taking a deep breath, he smiles. "God, I love New York."

"Looks like New York is not all that you love," Gary says while nodding to the beer that that Bruno just opened. "You know, your glass can fill on its own and still stay cold."

Looking down, his brow furrows. "Well, isn't this something. I have a full beer in a can, and my glass never gets empty. Don't care, I like the sound when the lid pops. Like an explosion." He touches the side of the glass. "Damn, it is cold. Ice cold. Harry wouldn't believe this. Gary, you may have a hard time getting rid of me."

Gary smiles while redirecting Bruno to stay on topic. "Harry seems to mean a lot to you."

"Is that a statement or a question." Rubbing his chin, he asks, "Hey, you got any cigars here?"

With a release of his hand, Gary produces two Cuban cigars and pulls a lighter out of his apron pocket.

Bruno takes a sniff. "Wow, you are feeding all my vices today, aren't ya?" He lights his cigar. "Well, not all of them I guess."

Gary tilts his head, releases a puff of his cigar. "You don't say."

Bruno stops for a thoughtful pause before speaking again slowly. "God knows I love an ice-cold beer and a smoke, but what I really have a fancy for is the loot, and of course, the ladies." After pulling the cigar out of his mouth, he looks at the tip and begins again as if he was telling a story to entertain tired travelers in a drawing room.

"I was surprised when the heat got too hot for Harry. He never came across to me as a quitter, but one day he packs up and takes off to California, leaving all these little stores in limbo and an unsettled atmosphere. He was trying to dodge the government, which by then was coming down hard on what they referred to as illegal gambling rings. Bit silly when ya think about it seeing how nobody got hurt … well, unless they stuck their nose into business that they didn't belong in."

"So, why didn't you just take over when Harry left? You said that you were his apprentice."

"Oh, I tried, but I didn't have the connections like he did. I mean, he would compare his life as to those that ran speakeasies during prohibition. His comings and goings were against the law, but nobody really cared. He acted like he was doing a service for New York. But me? Well, I don't really have that kind of charm." He smiles. "At least not with the politicians that is. They still saw me as some scrawny shit trying to play a big boy's game."

"So, what did you end up doing after he left?"

"Bounced around, attempted the occasional con but I wasn't very good at it. At least not to get the bucks I wanted." Taking another sip, he shrugs. "I even took a stab at opening my own bookie business. Seeing how everyone else was doing it. Boxing was starting to be a thing, ya know, and I figured I could take bets on that. I thought maybe my relationship with Harry would help me out. A lot of people just assumed I was his kid and he never corrected them, even after mother got tired of his running around and booted his ass out." Bruno pauses reflectively. "Another reason to stay loyal to him I guess."

A loud crash sounds, a faint, "Excuse me," came from behind Bruno.

Gary waves at an elderly woman waiting for a bridge to open up.

"Not your turn, ma'am. Wait until I call it," Gary bellows out and then turns back to Bruno. "So, is that how you ended up here? Something went wrong as a bookmaker."

"No, not exactly. As I said, I was not good at the business, or at least not like I thought I was when I was a kid hanging onto Harry's coat tails. You see, I set up shop at a family-owned restaurant, right there in Brooklyn. I had been going there ever since I was a kid when Harry would take me along to help him with his errands. The business is now being run by the owner's son seeing how his old man got caught up with the dementia. Anyway, I loved to watch this young chef they had cook. This kid was fantastic I tell you. Threw the pizza crusts high up into the air, never missed catching them. Not once. His food was to die for. Never had Rizzoli like what he made. The smells made you feel like you were walking the streets of Italy. I tell ya, you cannot even find food that tastes like his in the streets of Manhattan's own Little Italy. If I was the architect of Heaven, that boy would be the chef. Franko, they called him. A true culinary artist. The Van Gogh of chefs if you ask me. Anyways, one day he saw me watching him and he got all miffed." He imitates a thick, rough voice, "'What the fuck ya looking at?' he says to me."

Letting out a chuckle, he shakes his head. "Wouldn't thought that such a young skinny thing would have such a deep voice. Anyway, I says to him that I admired his skills. He got all snarky, thinking that I was making fun of him or something on the account that he was a cook, told me that he wasn't no queer, that he had a pretty wife at home and a baby." He takes a drink. "I let him know real quick that I wasn't foolin' him no how, that I really liked his food and wished I could throw some dough like that. You know what he done?"

"What?" Gary asks as he gets up to the side of the bar and picks up Kitty Kat who had drifted off to sleep next to the lady barfly.

"He threw me an apron and told me to wash my hands. For the next three weeks, I spent more time learning how to make pizza crusts and cut noodles just right. He even took me to the fresh market and showed me how to pick out the best produce. Before I knew it, I realized that I found my niche."

Bruno pauses and stares back down at the label, taking in a glimpse of him and a scrawny man with long, dark hair and aprons, Bruno looking monstrous compared to the little guy but both happy and content to be rolling the dough, throwing it way up. As he looks, the smell of olive-garlic herbs float up, teasing Bruno.

While he watches the scene, he continues to talk, "I gave up the bookie business and started working in the kitchen right beside Franco. Bet you never had egg parm the way I make it. I got real good at cooking. Sure, I would place the occasional bet. Won more than I lost, too, but the magic was in the kitchen. That was where I was meant to be. That was the dream that I didn't know I had until I had it. Didn't pay as much but for the first time that I could remember, I was genuinely happy. Bruno and Franco, we were one cookin' pair. Well … until I messed up that is. Fucked up real bad."

"How did you do that?"

The image melts away from in between the purple lines and Bruno becomes quiet, drinking his beer. Looking down on the label of his beer, he twists the can around, studying it before slowly speaking. "This isn't the original you say?"

"No, some guy after your time bought the company, took the product, and made it his own." Kitty Kat jumps down, allowing Gary to get up and stretch his back. "You like it?"

"I do. When did he buy the company? I thought they were doing well seein how's they survived the Depression and all. Not that I keep up with the legit businesses. I mean, I know the economy got people down and all, but … well, let's face it, everyone gotta have a drink now and then. Besides, the war brought businesses back again."

"Down there, time marches on regardless of who chooses to be aware of what is going on around them. It is not like here, where the clock stops. Remember, the time works different here?"

Bruno knits his brows, looking at Gary. "You're an odd duck, ya know."

"Being down here will do that to you. How'd you mess up?"

"Huh?"

"You said you fucked up. What did you do?"

Bruno turns to the barfly. "Pardon us, ma'am. I may not have lived my life right, but my mother did teach me that is no way to talk around a dame. Especially one as nice as you."

"Save the rhetoric. I want to know what went down with you and Franco," the lady barfly responds with a curious voice.

After taking another sip of his beer, Bruno licks his lips and continues, "Franco wasn't lying about his wife being pretty. She was a sexy little thing. Hell, I bet I am not the first she went running around with. But …" Bruno gets quiet again.

As he drinks his beer, the crowd noise lulls in harmony to twenties jazz band sounds behind the Cocytus in the back of the casino.

In a somber voice, he says, "She first came on to me. Swagging her little skirts. Oh, Dejanira, Dee was what Franco called her. She'd come into the restaurant; I could feel those strumpet eyes fixated on me the moment I walked out to the front. She would leave the baby with her mother and say she was up there to see Franco on the account that she couldn't spend time with him because he worked so late. I knew that weren't true because we always split the shifts so that I could have my evenings out perusing the streets and he could have his with the family. You know, he loved her. Not sure if he even knew she was always up to no good. Even if that little voice in his gut told him, he wouldn't believe it." Taking a breath, he mutters, "Stupid loaf loved her."

Bruno puffs his cigar, pulls it out of his mouth, and looks at the tip thoughtfully before speaking again. "Oh I wanted her just like I want money."

"Sounds like you want a lot of things."

Chuckling, he nods. "You are right there, my friend. You are right there. I can never get enough money, possessions, women. Everything's a conquest you know."

"Sounds like pure greed if you ask me."

"Well what else can I have? Got no wife, got to build up the assets to make myself more attractive."

"Sounds like you weren't on the hunt of a woman of your own."

"Right on the mark again." Bruno makes a gun motion with his right index and thumb, imitating making a shot along with a right squint of his eye. "I never knew how to keep myself clean. Not like Bentley. He always stayed out of trouble. I've never told him this, but I have always been kind of envious of him."

"So, what happened with Dejanira?"

"Yes, well, it wasn't long before we started running around together. You know, behind Franco's back."

"Pretty shitty don't you think? I mean, the kid was trying to earn a living to support his wife and child and you were out banging his girl."

"Hey, man, you don't think that I feel bad enough. Besides, I thought you weren't supposed to judge."

"My bad, go on."

"You're right though." Bruno's eyes glaze over. "Damn, I am a jerk. That boy taught me everything I knew about running a kitchen. Made me a changed man. When I was cooking, I never really thought about breaking the law. The smell of mozzarella didn't remind me that I could make a fortune at the races. Franco made me a better man, and what did I do? I fucked up his life, mine, and … well, Dejanira lost hers because of me. Now that baby is going to be placed in the system and who knows what will happen to him. Be placed in an orphanage, raised by nuns, probably become resentful to religion and all of humanity and it's all my damn fault."

"What do you mean Dejanira lost her life? Did you kill her?"

"Hell no. I've done some bad things, but I never killed anyone. No matter what tight spot I was in." Taking a deep breath, he runs a hand over his face. "One night when I got off early and Franco was to be working late, I went over to their house. It was late enough for her to put her boy to sleep but not late enough for Franco to come home."

He glances over at the lady barfly listening intently. "Ya know, maybe this is not for a woman's ears."

"Go ahead, I'm interested, and at this point and I prefer to determine myself what these ears listen to," she scoffs coyly.

"Fine." He turns back to Gary. "Franco walked in on us, and let's just say we weren't exactly drinking beer." Looking sidewards at the lady barfly, he mutters, "We were right in the middle of … well, you know."

"Yeah, I got it."

"Anyway, when we heard the door swing open, Dejanira pushed me off. Just as she was getting up, I caught glimpse of the little Derringer he pulled out his coat pocket. Looked like a baby gun. Didn't think he'd ever have one but there it was, and he was pointing it straight at Dee. I couldn't believe it; he shot her right square in the forehead between the eyes. Before she even fell backwards onto the bed, I got up and pummeled toward him."

Pausing for a moment, he shakes his head. "I heard the shot, I felt it barrel into my chest, I looked down and saw the blood before my knees buckled and collapsed to the floor. I heard the baby cry, and then stop. I guess Franco got scared when his boy cried and he went to him, leaving me there. I looked up at the ceiling, tasting metal in my mouth, and then … well, then I closed my eyes and felt myself drifting. Nice and slow like. There were no sounds after that for … well, I don't know for how long. Everything went cloudy and all I could see were shapes until I couldn't see shapes anymore. Then I woke up and found myself in the elevators. Right over there." He points to the direction of the elevators shielded by the waves of the Styx River.

"There I was, pretty ladies with long hair and short skirts offering me drinks, coins in my pockets to play the slots, in my finest suit paid for by Harry's nest egg that he had tucked away for us kids, and strange people walking around telling me to have 'peace with myself' as if that would every happen after what I had done. After the life I led. God, why didn't I listen to Mom?" Shaking his head, he mutters, "She always knew what was best."

Bruno stops talking for what seems like a long time. Deep in thought, Franco's hurt eyes embedded in his mind, the label reopening up, playing out the scene in a loop. Finally, Bruno manages to pull himself away, tears creeping into the corner of his eyes. He looks up at Gary, then glances at the barfly and then back at Gary. "It's not losing my life that I am crying over. I can deal with that. I fucked up, and I can pay for that. It's just," He hesitates for a moment before speaking again, "I just can't get over the pain in Franco's eyes. Him knowing, his best friend and his girl were going at it. He is the best man I have ever known. Better than Harry even on account he worked to live a straight life. The one person that I can truly classify as his best friend." He drops his head, "I banged my best friend's girl. God, I'm such a selfish bastard."

Bruno turns quickly around to look out in the casino, not caring what is happening out there but too embarrassed for Gary to see the tears, the shame veiled in his eyes. Without turning, he says loudly, "I really hurt a lot of people. Like I said, I really fucked up."

Gary remains quiet, looking down at his cat who is currently threading herself between his legs. He does not look up when he hears Bruno say, "Guess there isn't much I can do about that now."

"The past is the past, and the present is the gift of reflection, to see our wrongdoings, what we would change if the opportunity arose," Gary says somberly. "The tapestry of your history has been made."

"Ha! That's very poetic of you to say, but there's not much I can do here." Fishing in his pockets, Bruno pulls out his two shiny, gold dollar coins. "Guess these are for that slot," Bruno says while nodding toward the large, shiny machine behind Gary.

"Ready to give it a whirl?"

"Guess so, I got nothing else to do. Well, unless you consider going to hell that is."

Bruno gets up and stretches his legs, brushes off his sleeves, stopping to take note of his watch with the glittering diamonds, shining three o'clock.

Gary stands, waiting patiently.

Bruno hesitates and then takes off his watch and hands it to Gary. "Life is about time. The good and the bad. There were periods in my life where I thought I had plenty of it, but I didn't. I thought I had plenty of time to take care of Mama when she had a stroke. It was Andrea who took care of her in her final days, not me. My excuse was I didn't have the time. I claimed I had to work, but I was out banging some dames whose names I don't even remember. Not sure I would even recognize any of them if I passed them on the street."

Taking a deep breath, he continues, "I never bothered to attend my niece and nephew's birthday parties, because of time. I didn't have time for a wife, or to track down my father. I didn't have time for Harry when he was on his last limb. And now, I don't have time because I wasted it."

Gary reaches for the watch.

"Take this, give it to someone who deserves more time."

Without argument, Gary takes the precious watch, turns, and pulls out a mahogany chest underneath the bar. Opening it, he reveals a treasure of precious mementos of heavy sentimental value from wedding rings, rosaries, and children's drawings as well as homemade arts and crafts to a variety of other once cherished items magically tucked away in a bin of recycled memories. A tinkle of bells sound as he carefully lifts a tan teddy bear, smaller than his palm, places the watch in a compartment carpeted with silk, and then tenderly puts the little bear back on top. He waits a moment before closing the chest, praying silently, before using the bar to pull himself up and turning to face Bruno again.

Solemnly, Gary opens a half swing door and beckons Bruno to come through.

"I do like to gamble," Bruno says with a half-hearted laugh. Then he carefully places the coins into the slot and rests his hand on the lever. Looking over at the lady barfly nervously, he says, "Wish me luck, little lady."

She smiles and says, "I don't think tonight is about luck. I would prefer to pray if you don't mind."

Bruno nods. "I would be mighty obliged." And then he takes a deep breath, turns to the enormous magical machine, and pulls the lever. "Here we go! Luck be a lady tonight."

The dials begin to spin, laughter sounds from the casino

behind him, and rays of colors dance before him. Red, blue, beige, purple, all a flurry. With a can of beer still in his hand, Bruno lets out a whistle. "Come on, darling, don't let me down."

Bells began to ring loudly as Gary lets out a jocund laugh, chanting out words of encouragement. "Whatever happens, you got this."

Bruno turns his head to him as the sounds and wheels begin to slow down. The spinners stop with an unexpected thrust. And then the word *Arbitrium* appears.

Bruno looks at Gary. "I'm confused. What does that mean?"

Looking at the slot machine, his brow furrows. "Uh, an interesting turn of events. Always makes the play interesting." He then focuses on Bruno. "You, my friend, have the unique option to choose."

"I don't follow."

"You can stay and allow me to walk you to your final destination …" Gary pauses for dramatic effect, "which I don't know by the way until it is revealed to me so don't bother asking, or you can take another spin."

"A spin on the slot machine?"

"Oh no, dear friend. A spin at life. You can choose to go back and live out the remainder of your years. The gift of time, so to speak."

"Why would I want to go back? I told you how bad I screwed up. I don't think there is going to be a welcoming party for me."

"Perhaps not. The choice is yours. Take what is in plan for you now or go back and see what you can do with the rest of your life."

"Well, what is the plan for me if I stay? 'Cause if it means drinking more beer and gambling, I would be game for that."

"No, my friend, that journey is complete for you. It is time to face the unknown, whatever that may be."

Bruno glances around and then down on his hands. "I could be a great chef. I was good at that." He looks to Gary for approval. "If I stay?"

Gary sits back. "Again, I can't answer that. As I said, I am not made aware of outcomes. I'm not an angel. I am not a demon. I am just a man who is put in this station as a guide, and not a spirit one at that, to lead you to your fate, whatever that may be. Which river that we cross will not be revealed until it is time to walk the metaphoric plank. Make your choice wisely, friend. You are one of the few fortunate who get such a chance to do so."

Bruno takes a deep breath. "Well, ferryman, guess you won't be taking me across tonight. I'm going back."

Gary reaches into the small fridge, where one last R&H stands. Chilled condensation smiling at Bruno. Gary takes it, walks around from behind the bar as a sturdy bridge form over the Acheron River, this time leading to the Lethe River.

"Come with me."

The two gentlemen cross the bridge and stop for a moment to honor the glory of the heavenly gates.

"Is that big band music I hear in there?" Bruno asks Gary jovially.

"Oh yeah, those angles really know how to keep a party going." Then looking at him, he says, "Don't worry, you will have the chance another time to get an invitation." They then quietly walk over the bridge and stop for a moment at the great waterfall, [6]Mare Lacrimarum.

"These waters feed our distributaries here. Listen carefully."

The two men stop and listen. Sounds of laughter, cries, and music with what sound like dancing is heard. A cool breeze releases from it, giving both men a feeling of peace.

"I never believed in magic until now," Bruno says, feeling overwhelmed.

"Well, if magic is a combination of grief and love, tragedy and happiness, then here it is. I like to think of this place of more of an area to rejoice in my faith."

"More so than the heavenly gates?"

"Yes, these waters are the reminders of the ones who we

6   Mare Lacrimarum: Sea of Tears in Latin

have left behind that will join us one day. Go ahead and touch it if you want, it feels great."

As Bruno leans down and takes in a handful of the delicious water, the bridge over the Styx River opens up.

"I suspect that some of this is made by the sheer joy that you will spread in your life."

Bruno breathes in, embracing the crispness of the wind that accompanies the waters. He then rises, and feeling refreshed he edges over to step on to the bridge of Styx.

"Well come on, ferryman. It's your job to see me off, isn't it?"

Gary steps on and puts his hand on his shoulder as they take the final steps that places them in front of the gold elevators, the clock above still reading three o'clock. A single emerald jewel with no direction or floor level awaits. Gary presses it and it lights up a glaring green. As the doors open, a bell sounds in the distance, and Gary stretches his arm toward the stall, inviting Bruno in where Herman, the elevator operator, stands inside.

Bruno nods and then enters the transportation cell. He turns around and accepts a final offering. The last beer.

"One for the road," Bruno says as he reaches for it.

"One as a reminder."

Bruno looks at him inquisitively. "What do you mean?"

"You like the beer so much, maybe you can learn from the lesson behind it. Follow its lead."

"I'm sorry. What do you mean?"

"You know, take something that you have. Examine it carefully and then with every ounce of creative talent that you have been gifted with and the faith embedded in your heart, you take that something and make it better."

Bruno pops the lid, holds the beer up, and with a smile he says, "Cheers!" as the door closes.

Gary stands at the closed doors for a moment. "Cheers" he whispers, and then makes his way back, past the bubbling spring of the waterfall, the singing angels on the other side of the Lethe River, and the smooth waters gently lapping waters of the Acheron River.

Upon arrival, he takes notices he has a sip left of his R&H and gulps down the last swig.

"Wow, Bruno was right."

"About what?" the lady barfly asks.

"That is damn good beer."

Turning toward the direction of the casino, he yells, "Last call."

Julio

Red, wide eyes and shaking with terror, Julio stumbles on the bridge. It is not until it begins to wobble, and he pulls himself up, that he realizes the bridge is alive. Walking on a horrid beast's belly, it chuckles each time he falls. Grappling on fur, side walls of paws, and vomiting when he reaches the goat's genitalia.

Gary watches in the distance, shaking his head. "This ain't right," he mutters to himself.

"Look at that," he points while speaking to the lady barfly.

The shear atrocity of what she sees causes her to turn her head away in an uncomfortable stance.

"My God, he doesn't even know what direction to go in. And you can't tell me he is on his way to hell. Well, you know," he says with a shrug of his shoulders, "the real hell that is. He's just a kid. He ain't even got a real mustache. Dust. That's all he's got. Dust on the lip."

Julio walks slowly, crawling at times, looking side to side between each tiny movement. He is just a kid in age. Not in mind. In mind he does not know what he is but the secrets he holds within are vile. Just as vile as the repugnant smell rising from the goat's breath that he is forced to trudge on. He is nothing more than a product of unfortunate circumstances which veiled his ability to love and laugh like a child. Yet, never make decisions like an adult. His ability to reason stolen by a life full of choices made for him and not model ones at that. But it didn't matter. The devil doesn't discriminate, and he doesn't stop to consider poor upbringing and vulgar circumstances. It was far more entertaining to humiliate and instill fear in the child. Just a child … in age.

The casino scene was as foreign to him as old age. The beast evaporates as he makes it to the shore of the Acheron. With the sturdiness of the new passage, he runs 'til he reaches approximately three feet from the bar. At that point, his jaw drops, and he stares wide-eyed, frightened to approach and knowing that turning back is not an option. He waits, eyes bulging, his mouth gaped opened, sweat dancing on his brow.

Finally, Gary calls out, "Well, come on up, boy. I ain't gonna bite ya." Then, he mumbles under his breath, "Looks like you have been bit enough."

Julio groans in relief, loosens up his shoulders, and comes forward, sitting carefully on the stool.

"What can I get ya?"

"Well, sir, I'm not old enough to drink. I don't think there is much you can get me."

"Boy, you are at my bar, you can have what you want, but just one. I gotta feeling that you have put plenty down your gullet in your short sprint on Earth."

"Well, I guess that I like me some Mad Dog."

Gary lets out a roaring laugh. "See you like the cheap stuff." He pounds the bar twice with the palm of his hand. "Mad Dog it is, my man." He pulls out a bottle of Mad Dog from the end of the counter, brings down a short glass, and begins to pour. "Here you are." He slides the glass over. "So, what's your story?"

"Story?"

Gary shrugs his shoulders and looks over at the lady, who appears more attractive with each and every glance. "Sometimes it's hard to get 'em started." Then he turns to the boy, "Tell me about yourself, Julio."

"How do you know my name?"

"It's on your halo, now start talking."

"Well, yeah, my name is Julio. I live with my mother and brother, Peter. Ain't got no daddy." He looks at Gary, who is sitting adjacent to him on a stool, Kitty Kat in his lap, shaking her head when she stole a sip of Gary's glass of Mad Dog.

"What, don't you like it, Kitty Kat?" He grins at the boy. "Sometimes she has a bit more of a classy taste for her alcohol." He then picks her up and carries her to the lady barfly who immediately starts stroking the cat and nuzzling her face in the feline's fur.

Julio looks down at his glass again. "I'm not exactly sure what I should be talking to you about."

"Just start yapping. Eventually, what you need to say will fall out. How old are you anyway?"

"Sixteen, sir." He takes a sip of the bitter liquid, grimaces, but continues pushing his shoulders back in a feeble attempt to prove that he is a man.

"Even without a daddy, I have a nice home. My mom, she worked hard to get us where we are now. When I was little and we were living in the shelter, she worked two jobs and she went to a place that me and my brother could play while she learned English."

"Really? Take it you are from Mexico originally."

"Yes … well, me and my mom. My brother was born in Texas. Mom was pregnant with him when we came over. I was little, though, so I don't remember much. Just a whole lot of walking in shoes that were too big. I tripped a lot, so Mom stuffed the toes with grass, but then I ended up with a horrible rash. Nits bit my toes."

The boy looks anxiously at him, rolling the glass between his palms. "I remember that I was four. I know that cuz I had gotten those shoes for my birthday. They were my favorite. I knew they were just hand-me-downs, but I loved them. When we stopped to rest, I pulled the grass out. I could not stand the feeling of it scratching on my feet. That was a stupid thing to do. I done a lot of stupid things." He stops talking for a moment and stars into his drink. When he begins speaking again, his voice loses its effect and becomes trance-like while the liquid in his glass begins to bubble.

"One night when we were sleeping in an abandoned schoolhouse, we heard gunshots and pounding from outside. Mom pushed me through a small window that had shards of glass on the sides. When I fell, I landed in a puddle of glass and cement. I cut my hands. Not bad, but the blood scared me, and I began to cry. Then Mama forced herself through the window. She could barely fit. She picked me up and told me to stop crying. She was whispering but she was angry with me. I could tell. I thought that if I didn't do what she said that she would hurt me, which made me want to cry harder. But I didn't." Julio looks up. "I was always wanting to prove that I was good and brave. When she told me to run, I ran. No questions. No argument. I ran faster than I ever moved in my life. Faster than my mom. I'd look back and saw her running, too, cradling her belly as she did. I stopped for her, and when she caught up, she pushed me forward and told me to keep going, but my shoes were too big. One fell off. I wanted to go back for it, but Mama yelled at me to come on. I was so angry. I hated her for that."

Julio smells his drink, grimaces, and makes a face.

"Maybe you should get something else. I can get you a Coke if you want."

"No, sir, this is fine. It takes away from the smell."

"Smell?"

"You don't smell it? The stinking waters from the river over there. It smells like old, rotten trash that has been sitting for a while in the heat. It is gross and slimy looking. I reached down to touch it but that guy over there," Julio points to a group of men on the other side of the where the Cocytus flowed, "he told me not to touch it. He said the waters might suck me in and I would drown or boil or something. Don't know if it was true or if he was just trying to scare me."

"Ah, yes, there are a lot of theories about the water. Just the same, there is nothing good about the black waters. Me, myself, I don't even smell the sulfur coming from the Phlegethon. It's good you listened though." Gary looks around. "When I was first assigned here, I thought the place was just all smoke and mirrors. You know, trying to fool ya, but," he pauses, "well, let's just say that I have seen some things that makes me believe that magic is real. Especially black magic." Gary takes another drink. "Go on, boy. Your story has me interested."

Julio looks at Kitty Kat, his broken English becoming more articulate, when he asks, "Sir, do you think I can pet the cat?"

The lady barfly reluctantly gives up the companion so that Gary can bring her over. "I don't see any harm in that. She's real sweet. Well, except when she's bitin' ya."

Julio carefully reaches out and begins petting her. Relaxing with each stroke, he continues, "I hated my mother. I'm so ashamed. She risked our lives to bring us to America, to get away from the violence, and I hated her over a shoe."

He drops his head shamefully down. "That was a long trip you know. I lost count of how many trains we jumped. Mama called it the iron beast because we had to board while it was moving and if we lost our step then we could get eaten up by the rails." Suddenly, the bubbles in his drink manifest into a scene. Julio's eyes widen. He's still petting the cat but staring into his drink. He takes a deep breath and gulps.

Gary leans forward. "What do you see?"

"Mama. When we first got to the US three men at the boarder stopped us. One grabbed me by the shoulders and then they handcuffed Mama. I didn't know English then, so I didn't know what they were saying but I knew whatever was happening was bad. They put me in a small, cold room without a window and a small television on a station that I didn't know the language. Guess it didn't matter, though; there wasn't a lot of talking going on in the show. Just a coyote chasing some stupid looking bird. All day, that stupid cartoon played. They only checked on me to bring me a Coke and let me go to the bathroom. Later, I don't know how long, they brought me McDonald's. It was the first time I ever had it. I like the fries, but the chicken nuggets were cold. My uncle used to say that they don't use real chicken, but when they are hot, I like them anyhow. Anyway, finally, I don't know how long after that, a white lady came to see me. Her Spanish was broken, and what she thought she was saying, she didn't say right." Julio looks up and takes a bigger swig of his drink.

Gary never breaks his attention away from him, despite the yelling in the casino and the roaring of beasts to the left.

"I'm sorry, sir. I guess I said some of that before. I'm nervous, you know. I tend to ramble when I'm nervous."

"Don't you worry, boy. Sometimes I have a hard time following along, so I appreciate a little repetition every now and then. You said you were four when this happened. Tell me, what happened with your mother?"

"Well, sir, I didn't see her for months after that." Julio looks at Gary, anticipating the question that never come, so he answers it himself.

"I was kept at a detention center in South Texas. I had family in the States, but I couldn't tell them where or even what their names were, so they kept me there. The people were nice I guess, and I did have some friends, but I still felt lonely. Lonely and scared."

Julio's voice becomes stern as he looks up, choking back tears. "You see, sir, when you are in one of those places you are alone. It doesn't matter how many bright pictures are painted on the wall or how many American officials come to visit to make sure that you are well cared for, you are alone. A kid without a mama is alone. It doesn't matter that you are four. There are no bedtime stories or snuggles of kindness. You are a child, being clothed and fed by people that speak a different language than you and look at you with eyes of pity. What little that a child can pick up is that they are not supposed to be here which is confusing because all through the journey, the god awful journey where you are walking for miles on end, in shoes that are too big that they bounce off your feet and you have to wear all your clothes so that you don't lose them even though it is ninety degrees out, you are told, that you are going to a better place where life will be easier and then you get there and you find out that it was all lies. Nothing but lies. There is not a plan when you get there because you are not supposed to be there. It's like crashing a party. You think it will be fun but then when you get in, you know that you were not really invited and no matter how hard you work, you are unwanted."

Tears fall out of Julio's eyes. "I was unwanted in that center. I was another mouth to feed, with no family to go to, learning in a school that I did not know the language. It would be six months before I found out that Mama gave birth somewhere in Laredo and then was immediately deported to Guatemala. It would be almost a year before we could see each other again. And I never really understood why. Because I was four, and then I turned five and I didn't have a birthday because nobody knew. Not even myself because I never knew the date. I never saw a calendar, just the moon go up at night, marking another day being alone. Eventually, Mama was able to call me, but I hated it when she did because all she would do was cry. I hated to hear her cry. I couldn't cry because you see, I was her big, strong boy, but I was scared. I was so scared. I didn't know nobody. I hated her for that, too." Julio forces down another sip. "I was just a kid! A kid who had a birthday and nobody knew."

Feeling touched by the young man's story, the lady barfly scoots over toward him, despite Gary lifting his hand in defiance but she spoke up anyway. "Were you eventually reunited with your mother?"

"Yes, ma'am. Mama got an advocate from Catholic Charities to take our case. They were able to get me out of the center and place me with family. Then Mom applied for asylum. She was lucky, you know; it usually takes longer for people to get to be with their families again." Looking around, he asks, "Is my uncle here?"

"Are you close to your uncle?"

"Not really. Actually, I hate him, too, on the account of some of the shit he would make me do. But he's family, and he should be here. This is hell, isn't it?'

"Did you see him when you got off the elevators or in the casino?"

"No … well, I'm not sure what he would look like. He was murdered by the same gang that threatened Mom. That's why we went to America in the first place. Lots of people die in Mexico."

"Lots of people die everywhere."

"Yeah, but do they get their throats slit while their children are forced to watch, knowing that their murderer will rape their wife before the blood drains out of their corpse?"

"You sound angry."

"Fuck yeah, I'm angry. My mama left to avoid getting raped over and over again, and then they killed my uncle." Julio's voice rises, and he swings his arm around.

Gary sits still, Kitty Kat flicks her tail and jumps back to where the lady barfly had been sitting. She joins her. Veins throb in Julio's neck.

Concerned, Gary speaks up. "Careful now, I can't have you choking on your rage. Why are you so angry?"

"Because everything is fucked up. My mama, my uncle, my life."

"Yet you made it."

"Excuse me?"

"You made it to America. It was hard, and you were separated from your mother, but it sounds like you got away from the violence. You said that your uncle made you do things. Like what?"

"In Mexico he made me his [7]chico de entrega."

"What's that?"

"You know, his delivery boy." He takes a swallow. "He would make his money running ammo and drugs up the village and he would have me do it. Thought nobody would stop a boy. Asshole! I was fucking three. Fucking three-year-old boy walking a block down the way. In America, children that age are barely potty-trained. You can't tell me that's not fucked up."

"But your mother put an end to it when you got here."

"Yeah, but I didn't know the language. Had to go to school and teachers be telling us to read Shakespeare and shit and I barely knew the English ABCs."

"How did you cope?"

---

7   chico de entrega: Delivery boy

"I faked mostly. Pretended to be sleepy or not paying attention when the teacher would call hoping that I could make it just difficult enough so that they would give up and go on to the next kid on her list. Cheated too when I could get away with it." Julio shrugs his shoulders. "I never wanted to go to school anyhow. All those damn teachers care about is the state testing, not if we could understand a Midsummer's Dream. School isn't a big deal in Mexico. Work, that was a big deal. Especially if it was honest."

"Did you work?"

"Yeah, when I could. I started helping my other uncle that was already in America when I was nine. We were living with him at the time, and if we wanted to eat, we would do what he told us to do. He told me I was the most perfect delivery boy because I was cute. People couldn't pass up my adorable dimples. A kid that looked like me could do no harm. I was an asset he said. So, I did what he told me to do. I delivered his product. Just like in Mexico. But I was older and tougher. I used my looks to get away with stuff, but I always had my eyes open just in case someone was going to jump me."

"Did you earn any money doing that?" Gary asks intently, treading softly when noticing the mounting frustration on the boy's face.

"Sometimes, but not until after I knew what I was doing. When I was small, I had no idea. I would just take the delivery to the apartment he pointed to, and I would be given a bundle of cash and sometimes a sweet treat or a popsicle. Everyone was nice to me. It wasn't until one day when I was about eleven and the old man at the drop off told me they would pay me later that I understood what was happening. When I came back empty handed, my uncle beat me in a way that I never thought anyone could be beat. I was more afraid of him than the gunman that chased us out of the schoolhouse." The thought made Julio shudder. "You know, it is one thing to be afraid of strangers with guns, but when the gun is in the hand of the one that feeds you, that's when you really know you are up a river." He gets quiet, uncomfortable by Gary's silence.

The barfly speaks up, "I'm so sorry that happened to you, Julio."

Gary looks at her, dropping his head. "Guess I never realized how rough it was for those that came over." Looking up at him, he says, "Even though it is a felony to cross the border illegally."

"Take it up with my mama. I never asked to come here. Blame a kid will ya? Call ICE if you must."

"Now settle down, I meant no harm. Continue on."

Julio remains silent for a long time before starting back up again. When he does look up, he studies the elegant woman at the end of the bar and appreciates her compassion.

"It's okay. I'm fine now. My mama, she was upset that it happened, but said I had to continue to make drop offs so that we could stay there. I wasn't exactly sure as to why because by this time she had gotten a job working at a hotel cleaning rooms, but she said that the way that she was paid, she wouldn't be able to get us our own place, so we had to listen to Uncle."

Gary nods. "She must have been paid under the table. Employers taking advantage of illegals to avoid paying taxes and cheap labor to boot. The system has always been a little screwed up. They get treated like they were fresh off the skiff but some of them have college degrees." He shrugs his shoulders. "Of course most of the time they weren't worth the paper they were printed on in America but that's not the point. These were smart, educated people being forced to clean toilets."

"Yeah, well, Mama didn't have any fancy degrees no how, but she did finish high school which is a lot more than I can say for the rest of my family." Putting his head down, he mutters, "Me included."

"So, coming to America was important to your mom?"

"That's what she said. I will never forget when we finally made it to the border. There were two tall buildings. Looked like towers, and they had the bright red lights coming from it.

"Mama said we couldn't go through those gates that we had to cross a different way." Julio lets out a chuckle. "In my mind, I was a superhero trudging through a swampy marsh, and it was my mission to get my mother over the wall, away from violence … away from hell." He looks up. "Didn't matter though how we crossed. We still got caught. I know what Americans think of us. Coming over illegally. I understand the law, but I also remember the violence. People weren't treated like humans. Mama really did believe that our survival counted on us getting to America. Besides, I never really considered myself as an illegal but more of a noncitizen."

Gary interjects, "Regardless, when you arrived you engaged in a life of crime."

"I didn't know that at first, I swear. As far as I was concerned, that was never the plan."

"How long was it before you found out the truth about what you were delivering?"

"Shortly after I fought with my uncle for not collecting the money that was owed to him. One night mother took us boys out for ice cream. Peter was just a toddler and didn't understand much as to what we were talking about, so I cornered her into telling me the truth. She said that Uncle remained close with people back in Mexico and that was how he was able to get so much at once. I never had bothered to ask why he would be gone for long periods of time before. I was happy when he was gone. Mother would joke and play with us more. My uncle had a terrible temper, so his being gone was a nice break. Anyway, I was angry about everything. My life, my family, where I lived. Not being able to have my friends from school over. I told her that I didn't want to do errands for Uncle anymore. He was mean, and I knew I could do better for myself. I told her that I wanted to be a good man and get a degree like the teachers in school. I was going to invent things." Julio gets quiet.

"I take it that didn't go over to well with your mom."

"My mama, she's a good woman. She said that there were

other laws in life besides those written by politicians and important government people. She said that people had to follow silent laws. The laws of society, and the laws of family. That family had to stick together. We follow the laws of the land the best we can, but we are to follow the laws of family no matter what the consequences were. She said it was best we do that." Julio takes another swallow of his Mad Dog. "She said it was the best for me."

"What did you think when she told you that?"

"I listened. She was telling me how to survive, I guess. Mama says we got to live for the now. Dreams are a waste if you have no means to accomplish them. And I have no means. Except for what uncle tells us what to do. I'm told to deliver product, I deliver product." He pounds his fist into the bar. "Things just got worse though." He picks up the bottle of Mad Dog that Gary sat beside him.

"You know this stuff is harsh. Maybe you should take a break from this. I can still get you a Coke. You're not even old enough to drink."

"Speak for yourself. I live by no rules. Uncle used to bring this stuff home all the time. Numb me I guess." The MD on the bottle begins to blur Julio's vision. Blending in and out, and then begins to swirl.

"Damn, guess I am toasted ... a little."

"Vision blurring?"

"Yep."

"You are not toasted. Just keep looking. It will clear up."

Julio peers down at the label again. The MD still swirling as the 20/20 opens, engulfing the letters. Suddenly, they form together in a white and gold circle, spinning before turning a milky mirror color and opening up to reveal Julio standing in his living room. Backing up each time Uncle pushes him on his shoulder.

"You do what I say, boy!"

Julio squints at the sight.

"I've got a good mind to kick you and your mom and your brother right out of here. Then where will you be? They'll deport your asses right back to that shithole that you came from."

"Bullshit! Mama got her papers. That lady from Catholic Charities helped her. You just want me to do your dirty business. I know what you do ain't straight and you're sending me out with it. I want out!"

"Do you want to eat? Do you want to wear those damn Nikes or your Supreme shirts?"

Julio stood straight, pooching his chest out. "We'd be fine."

"Julio, no!" Mom yelled from the side vision, Peter at her side. "We've got no place to go. We need the money."

"Mom, what he is doing is no good. You don't have to listen to him. You have papers, you can quit the hotel and get a better job. You can rent an apartment on your own now."

"Shut the fuck up, boy!"

"Jose, please let me handle this." She turned to her son. "Julio, don't you bad mouth your uncle like that. He rescued us when we had nothing."

"I'm not bad-mouthing nobody. I'm speaking truth." He pointed at his uncle. "And that son-of-a-bitch knows it."

"Don't use language like that, Julio."

"What, I can go deliver his dimes, but I can't curse? Please! Even with his help we still don't have nothing, Mom. All he's done is taken us into a life of crime. You think that when the police catch wind that we are related that they are not going to send us back? You promised to abide by the laws in order to get your papers and yet you help this asshole. They can take your papers away for this."

"Boy, you don't know shit."

Desperately, he addressed his mother, "People are coming over by the truck loads, dying in the cargo carriers, and for what? A so-called better life. How is our life better, Mom?"

"Don't you speak like that. My lord. Have you forgotten? The violence in the street. The gangs. Your other uncle was killed by them. You have been witness to spilt blood at such a young age. Do you want that for Peter? Here you are, with your blasphemy, when we should be praising our Lord and thanking him for his mercy and gifts."

Julio raised his voice louder, a cross between a screech and a cry. "Mother, I am not blind to what we have, and I am not blind to how we got it. They call us wetback criminals. Do you know that? And that is one of the nicer things they say."

"They are an ignorant group of people who know nothing about us."

"Do they? Do they not know anything about us? Think about it. Uncle is selling drugs. Where do you think they come from? The nice lady at Catholic Charities, the teachers, the owner of the no-tell motel that pays you under the table. We are not living an honest life. But we can, Mama. We can."

Julio looks up at Gary. "I can't believe I spoke to her like that. She was only trying to keep us safe. Keep food on the table."

"What about your uncle? It seems to me he had his own agenda."

Julio looks back at the Mad Dog label. The scene is still playing out. This time, though, his uncle walks back into the room, joining in the conversation once again.

Julio whispers as he watched the scene, "It was always about money for him. Pretty stupid when you think as to how he spent it as soon as he had it. Never had anything for the good things in life. The things Mama dreamed about."

In the mirage, his uncle is speaking between English and Spanish. "Boy I'm going to knock you alongside your head if you don't shut your mouth. It's bad enough you disrespect me, but now your mother …"

"Mama, the drugs, he's getting them from the very people that you said we had to run from."

"Boy, you don't know shit."

Julio watches his uncle knock him down and punch him in the head. He falls into a stand holding a plant and a picture of white Jesus. Julio attempts to stand back up in the scene.

Julio narrates, adding his thoughts, "White Jesus was supposed to save us. Give us a better life in America. Mama went to church every Sunday, dragging Peter along, and me when I wasn't working for Uncle. She loved the white pastor who was fluent in Spanish. Even exaggerated her own accent thinking it would impress him. Meanwhile, the entire time, her own son was running drugs even in the apartment building she lived in."

"Do you still work for your uncle?"

"I stopped for a while. Not officially, I just managed to not be around when he needed me to do his bidding. I would stay at school for as long as I could and then wander around until I knew my mother was home. He would treat me better when she was home."

"From the looks of what you just saw, it doesn't seem like much better."

"Yeah, well, he had a right to be pissed at me. After a while when I wouldn't show, he would stop getting us stuff. Mama's pay could barely buy food and he would say he couldn't pay the rent. One day I got so pissed off that I stole some of his stuff and sold it. He knocked the shit out of me for that. I tried to deny it, but he knew it was me." Smiling, he says, "Guess I'm not a very good thief."

"What all did you steal?"

"A stereo and speakers. Also, his radio right out of his car. What I got the most money from, though, was these three rings that he kept in his drawer. Two were his father's and the other one was my other uncle's that was killed back in Mexico. That one had a ruby stone. I didn't know that was his at the time. If I did, I would have kept that one." Looking up at Gary, he explains, "For my mama you know. She always said that he was the kinder of the two. They were twins. His name was Julio like me, and my other uncle is Jose. Julio was good and Jose was bad. Not sure exactly what I am. Guess somewhere in the middle. I only broke the law when instructed. I began to follow the rule of family."

"Do you believe in the rule of family?"

"It's not really something that I thought about. It was something that I was supposed to do. Didn't have anyone to talk to about it." He lets out a chuckle. "One time I wrote an essay about my uncle when he started smuggling in people. The teacher put a note on the paper that the story was interesting, but I needed to work on my mechanics. Can you believe that? My real life was seen as not real and only worth a C-minus."

"Sometimes it is easier to perceive something as fiction than acknowledge how screwed up things are in the world. Do you believe your life was better by being in America?" Gary asked.

"I'm not sure. But I do know that many people snuck over thinking that they would get a better life. Some to have their babies, some to work and send money back home, some just because they were raised to believe that was the thing to do."

Julio's becomes quiet for a moment, thinking while refocusing on the on the mirage in the bottle.

Kitty Kat jumps up beside him and he lets her lick his fingers. He pulls her closer and begins to nuzzle her.

"My grandmother once said that my father was a supine. I didn't know what that meant so I looked it up. Probably the only time I ever used a dictionary." Julio pauses as if Gary is going to define it for him, but he remains quiet. "My grandmother thought that my pop, wherever he was, failed to act or protest due to moral weakness. I'm still not clear as to what that means, but I do know that he failed to ever acknowledge me. He failed to support Mama. He failed to be a part of the decent side of humanity. Thinking of it, I guess I did, too."

"What do you mean?"

"Well, I failed to be supportive to my family."

"Did you go back to delivering product for your uncle?"

Julio shrugs his shoulders. "Had too. We needed to survive. But the product ended up being people. That was his plan.

Uncle always had plans. You see, the people crossing over started having problems with the laws. The border patrol got stricter, and even though laws were always in place, there were more agents making sure that they were being followed. Uncle said that these people were needing help crossing over and a place to stay when they got here. Uncle said it would be really easy to take money from them because some of these people were desperate and had nowhere else to go. Nobody wanted to go to the detention centers because they knew that they were really prisons painted in pretty colors to make it not look so bad. Uncle, he got smart. Him and his friends bought one of those big hauling trucks. He figured he could smuggle up to a hundred people at a time. One guy would pick up a load close to the border in a van and take them to a drop house. Then uncle would come with his trailer car and pick the people up from the house and drop them off at different locations." Julio lets out a laugh. "He'd get people to wire the money through Western Union and Apple Pay. Can you believe that? Human smuggling compliments of the easy app Apple Pay. He'd even drive people out to as far as Chicago if they paid him enough."

"Sounds like a lucrative operation. Did he ever get caught?"

"Oh, the feds caught wind of the operation, but there were so many of us it was hard to catch us all. That is where I came in. Again, Uncle used my youth. He thought if he could teach me to drive, that I could help take loads of people to where they wanted to go, and we could get even more cash."

"Were you even old enough to drive?"

"No, but Uncle didn't care, and Mama wasn't going to step in. Besides, driving age doesn't really matter in Mexico so she didn't see the problem here. By this time, she had become infatuated with one of Uncle's friends, and once they officially started seeing each other, it was another person for her to try and make happy." Julio takes another drink. "If I got caught, I was to say that I was here alone. An unaccompanied minor. I'd be treated better if they thought I was here alone."

"But wouldn't you have been sent to a detention center again?"

"I suppose. People weren't exactly hosting illegal immigrants as exchange students. Of course, if they did, who's to say that I would ever go back to the family. Besides, at least now, I kind of know the language." Julio looks down at his twirling mirage where he sees his uncle in handcuffs accompanied by a muscular guard holding him by his upper right arm before a judge.

The judge's voice is somber and theatrical. "In addition to the crimes of human trafficking, we find you guilty of federal entrapment, possession of an unlawful handgun, forty-seven assault rifles to be exact, and possession of stolen vehicles." His voice echoed out, intimidating as he looked down on Julio's uncle. "How do you plead?"

His uncle, seeming smaller and sullen, bowed his head to let out his remorseful plea, "Guilty."

Without looking up or changing his tone, Julio starts up again, "We were screwed. My whole family. There was no way we could live once he pled out. Even before, we had no way to post bond or help him in any kind of way. We weren't even supposed to be in the apartment that we were living at. Not that the landlord cared. They just wanted their rent money at the beginning of the month. Otherwise, they didn't give a shit as to who was being housed or what they were selling. Rent was a problem. We had to figure out something real fast, and mother lost her boyfriend at this time and the endless trail of men that came through the house was never anybody we could count on. Uncle pled guilty on the 30th. We needed rent in two days."

The barfly shifts in her seat quietly. Kitty Kat stretches on the bar, and Gary remains still.

"I had to be the man of the house now. I had to help Mom pay the rent. I had to go get a load. My uncle's colleagues were waiting on me."

"So, you are the man of the family?"

"I always was. Uncle would disagree, but I always was. It

was just time to prove it, so I got in the truck, and I drove all day and night."

"Without a license."

"Don't matter. I had a job to do. I was careful to obey all traffic laws. Got to International Street about midnight. I could see two people, one a lady carrying bundles on her back. Not sure if it was small children or pot but I saw them. I got out and waved. Beckoned them to me. Suddenly, from behind, I heard gunfire."

Sharp, loud sounds beam up from the Mad Dog label. Julio looks back down at it. "I felt bad. I don't know if those bundles were babies or not. They threw them down. Didn't hear crying, though, but I heard more gunshots. The people dropped to the ground and all I saw was bright lights with the shadows of rocks flying in the air. It was like a movie. Someone hollered, 'Get down!' so I started to get down, but then I was hit in the back by something sharp. Dude, I wasn't even carrying. I had no gun. I know that is stupid, but I didn't want to touch Uncle's gun. He would get angry if I touched his guns and he is a mother fucker when he is mad. He'd kill me as sure as I'm standing here." Julio stopped talking. He stuck his tongue out and then rubbed it back and forth between his teeth.

"What's wrong?"

"Metal. My mouth tastes like metal." Julio finally accepts the Coke that Gary gave him. He takes a drink from the straw, sucking down almost half before speaking again. "I couldn't roll over, couldn't move, but I could taste metal in my mouth. It was awful. I could smell the rocks on the road. They cut into my cheek. I could smell the combination of dirt and cement on them. I could hear voices coming toward me until I couldn't hear anything at all." The reflection in the label goes dark. Julio keeps staring at it, watching the darkness mold into a fully developed Mad Dog label again.

"My mother is praying for me right now. I can feel it. She loves Jesus. She don't care what color he is. Says he is all colors, just that people make him white on the saint cards because that makes him pretty, but he's all colors. Brown like me. White like you. All colors."

Julio puts his hand in his jean jacket and pulls out two shiny, gold coins. "Damn, this looks like real gold. Wonder what I could buy with this. Cover the rent at least."

"I'm afraid that we don't collect rent down there. That's what you pay the ferryman with."

"Who is the ferryman?"

"You are looking at him. Care to take a spin?" Gary points to the heavy slot machine.

Julio stands up. "Never used a slot machine before. I'm just a kid, you know. Guess it is as good as a time as any though."

Julio takes the coins and slowly puts them into the slot. He pulls down the lever, and the bells begin to tinkle, the lights sway, the wheels whoosh, and Julio closes his eyes.

"Dios perdoname[8]."

"Don't worry, child. He already has."

The wheels stop but Julio doesn't look at the message. Instead, he turns to Gary who places both of his on Julio's shoulders. "It's now time for you learn to forgive yourself."

A heavy, warm light shines on Julio's face, adding a glow of yellow and orange to his face. He turns and looks at the message. *Mors.*

"Grandmother made us learn some Latin. I know what that means."

"But he is so young!" the barfly spits out, tears in her eyes.

Julio turns to her. "Don't cry for me, lady. I'm saved. Cry for those who are still lost." Choked up by his maturity and unable to speak, the barfly nods. Julio then looks to Gary. "Okay, where are you taking me?"

Gary looks up to the rivers as the bridge over the Acheron opens. He steps forward, and Julio follows in silence. As they make their footprints across the bridge, the hot waters

---

8   God Forgive me

occasionally leap over gently. When they get to a crosswalk, Julio looks to Gary.

"Will Mama and Peter be okay."

"Does your mama have her faith?"

"She does."

"Then she will pass it on, just like she did for you."

"I never really thought I believed in God or white Jesus. Not like Mama. I mean, look at everything we went through."

Another sturdy bridge appears, leading the way over the Lethe River. In the distance, Julio and Gary see the golden gates dividing, the large, mahogany doors slowly opening, releasing a blare of traditional Mariachi music muffled with the sounds of children laughing, spices of Julio's favorite food wafting through the air.

"Can you smell that? The sopapillas. They are delicious. Grandmother use to make them before we left Mexico. I think I see her. My family, I have family in there."

"You do."

"And they have sopapillas and sweet milk in there."

"They do."

Julio and Gary walk side by side over the bridge.

"My last stop is here," Gary says as they reached the last plank before to get off at Heaven's Gate."

"Thank you, sir, for your trouble and listening to my story."

"It was my pleasure, Julio. And for what it is worth, Jesus is made of love, which contains all colors. Now go on. Your family is waiting."

"I don't think I deserve to be there. Mama begged me to go to church, but I wouldn't go. I always made excuses. Even claiming to not believe in God. I don't know if I really believed that, but I know I couldn't always find a reason to. Now I am here. An illegal, an un-citizen."

"Son, there are no visas needed in the land of God. Besides, you may not have always believed in God, but he has always believed in you."

Julio steps forward, he walks through the gates, but turns one last time and waves as the cherub door closes.

Gary waves back and walks back on the bridge. He stops at a crossroads between the Acheron and the Cocytus, and waves toward the direction of the bar. "Last call!"

Henry

"This is not what I would consider to be a confessional."

Gary, who had begun an embarrassing attempt to flirt with the barfly, didn't notice the little man that had walked up to the bar. His hand was burned brown with age spots, his eyes a twinkling blue, and his hair white as snow … or at least as white as the color around his neck.

"Sorry, Father … or is it pastor?"

"Well, young man, I have been called both, but I am a priest. A Catholic priest."

"Well, Father, I'm pleased to have you at my humble bar."

"Please, young man, call me Henry." Looking around, he nods. "Seems to me we are on the same level around here."

"Appreciate that, but my mom made me say plenty enough Hail Mary's to not disrespect the man of the cloth."

"Sounds like your mom taught you right. What've you got behind that bar?"

"Ahh, Father, that's the beauty of it. Here you can have anything you ask for. It will manifest itself within my reach."

"I see." He rubs his chin in thought. "Never been one to believe in magic, but then again, I've never been in a position like this." Pausing, he eyes the bottles. "You know, I am not much of a drinker, but I do enjoy a good red wine."

Gary reaches underneath the counter and brings out a 1960 bottle of Petrus. "How about this?" Gary asks as he takes down a crystal wine flute and pours the priest a glass and then himself one.

"Classy." Father Henry swirls the drink around the wine glass and then tastes it. The two men sit quietly for several minutes: Henry enjoying his wine, Gary enjoying his presence.

Finally, the silence is broken by the elderly man. "I suppose you hear quite a few fancy stories here."

"Mainly stories of pain and grief. The tragedies that people would choose to forget about. Some they caused, some they suffered. I guess you could say the same with your profession." Henry laughs. "Almost made me rethink my career choices.

When I was in monastery, I did time as a religious council for a high security prison where I was privy to hear tales of murder. Oh, my stomach and heart ached when man after man detailed their crimes."

Grimacing, he shakes his head. "I am embarrassed to say that there were times that I wanted to reach right into the convict's chest and pull his heart out and squeeze it so tight that I could feel the last heartbeat pop in my clenched fist." He holds up his wine glass. "Some had the nerve to be boastful about their crimes they even go so far as to romanticize them as if their confessions were walks down a treasured memory lane. You know, I had one guy that committed his first murder at just ten years old. Little girl from his class. Hit her in the back of the head with a cement brick and then stuffed her in a culvert. He committed another murder at fifteen because the girl wouldn't return her affection. Said they found her body down by a pond where he stuffed her mouth with dirt and rocks to keep her quiet just in case she wasn't as dead as he like her to be. Sick. Just sick."

Gary nods in agreement, not daring to use the language that he felt best interpreted the crimes.

"Some were even repeat offenders. They would get fifteen years or so, get released, and then turn around and do it again." Looking up at Gary, he cocks he head to the side. "How would you explain forgiveness to a family who just lost their child to murder? Knowing their last moments were of humiliation and fear. That the bodies were found by strangers, strangled and raped, left to lay by the railroad tracks or some dumpster behind a seedy bar. It gets to you, you know. Having to preach God's love and forgiveness when all that you encounter is violence and hate. It gets to you."

Henry stays quiet for a bit, deep in thought, listening to the waters that he came over. His bridge made of hardened sand that spread over low, deep blue waters. So blue that they had a tint of black. Loud, crashing waves pummeling the shores of the

Phlegethon River. "It tried to trick me you know."

"What did?" Gary asks curiously.

"The wicked waters of hell. Splashing me with cool waters. Trying to manipulate me that it wasn't so bad over there. That is rather nice in fact. But I knew that it was a lie. The waters were a lie. I've made some mistakes but I'm no fool."

"Well, isn't that what Satan does to recruit? Make you think that things aren't so bad, so naïve imbeciles join his band of evildoers?"

"I suppose so, but you know some of the evilest doers in the world were quite intelligent."

"Like politicians?" Gary asks with a chuckle.

"Well, maybe. Hitler for sure, and we can throw Stalin into the mix, but history tattled on them. People of that time, especially their constituents followed them blindly. You see, we think of the evil that they did with the concentration camps. And it was. The horror is unbelievable. But what was also unbelievable is the theft of emotions."

"I don't follow." Gary scoots up closer to the priest.

The lady barfly's ears prickle up as well.

"Those horrible people, and many more like them, get followers. The followers have minds that are already weaken by low confidence or the feeling of needing to belong, or any variety of reason, they get caught in and the wicked minds can convince them that the villainous crime is for the greater good. For society but it is not. It is about eliminating society and people still fall for it today. You see, their gut tells them that the acts that the evildoer wants them to do is wrong, but the manipulation makes them question themselves and everything they know in their world to be right and moral. They see other people they know doing the requested acts and it is people they know and respect. Family even, so they figure that what they know to be true is the actual lie and the lie before them is truth. And the evil beckons them on to victimize others, until it is time for them to be the victim."

"And what happens to them when they become the victim?"

Henry sips his wine and looks over to the waters. "They go there. To the rivers of oblivion. Away from the Lethe, their denied fate. Stolen by evil." Taking another sip, he turns back to them. "The way I figure is that evil is a disease, and without the cure, it will eat you up until the infected dissolves into those very waters."

The two men remain quiet for two more glasses of wine. Gary follows Henry's gaze toward the bellowing cries of the left, wondering how he chooses to not look away. Men and women flailing near the gates, crying.

"Don't ever look away from the evil. Stare at it head-on and win." Henry said as if he was reading Gary's mind. "Let those who are suffering know you see it, and share compassion with them, even when the lending hand you offer gets grazed by the fire." Henry swallows another sip of wine. "You know, I was so sick that I could barely speak. All my organs started to fail all at once."

"I take it that is what brings you here to this little hovel."

"Why yes, of course. I just didn't expect it to be like this." He winks at the barfly. "Tell me, sir, am I to believe that I am in hell?"

"Now why on earth do you think you are in hell?" Attempting to imitate the priest, Gary swishes his glass of wine as he speaks, "After all, you are a servant of God."

"Servants can get fired, my good man. Especially if they don't agree with their boss." Bringing the glass to his lips, he nods. "I've committed heresy more times than anyone can possibly imagine."

"Well, Father, is that a true mortal sin. I mean, it doesn't appear that you have left God." Gary eyes the gold rosary peeking out of the priest's pocket.

"No, son, but I did have full knowledge of what I was doing and the gravity of the sin. However," he says with a bit of hesitation, "I suppose that my love for God never died."

"So how did your teaching contradict with your faith?"

"Gary, is it?"

"Yes, Father."

"Well, my good man, I have been a servant of God for forty-five years. And in that time, I have seen a lot of changes. Some for the good. Some not so much. And some a combination of both." Father Henry stops talking for a moment, noticing a look of confusion on the barkeep's face.

"Let me explain. The world moves faster than the priesthood, much less the Vatican. Many of us are stuck in our ways. We don't always recognize the good of medical advancements, the traps of technology, and the revolving needs of our flocks. Many of us are stuck. Though we may be careful observers of the present, we don't use it to predict the future." He looks up at Gary. "Excuse me, dear sir. I am old and I do tend to talk in unpredictable metaphors." Then, smiling, Father Henry takes a sip of his red wine and places it down carefully on a coaster.

"I wasn't always a priest. I didn't always do what was right. I mean, I did go to seminary at a young age, but … well, I dropped out and it would be nearly fifteen years before I would come back." He looks squarely at Gary. "I lived a life you know. A life before the priesthood. I knew things that a young man going into seminary may not know."

He nods and says to himself, "It was good that I did, too. I was able to offer real life advice. From experience, not some twisted intuition on a subject that I have not a clue about. Unlike those men who go to counseling without ever experiencing hard labor, conflict," he winks at the barfly, "romance." Leaning back, the man stretches out his arms. "I lived through them all." As he speaks, he turns around and looks at the activity behind him. "You know, I was supposed to give mass the morning that my temperature spiked so high. By three-thirty, I had so many priests and nuns bickering over me. I do not remember going to the hospital, but I recognized it. I had given so many last rites there before. Now I guess it was time for mine. I even asked the

Lord to let me go to him." He chuckles. "Guess he is not ready for me yet. Still getting me a room prepared I suppose. Perhaps it will have a nice view."

"Father, you say you sinned, but somehow you don't seem like much of a sinner to me."

"Oh yes." Letting out an even bigger chuckle leads to a boisterous laugh. "Surprise, surprise, boy did I." Taking a breath, Henry notices the red and yellow label on the Petrus bottle spin. "Well look at that."

"I think it is meant for you to look at," Gary says with a smile as he sips his own wine. "Can you believe they get over six thousand for this stuff?"

Father Henry holds his hand up. "Shhh, I want to see this." The label turns into a reflection and then into a visionary portal that shows a much younger Henry baptizing a female infant. "I was in India then. You know girls born in India are hardly ever celebrated. Especially in poor families. Can you imagine your life never being celebrated?"

Gary nods sadly, thinking of Julio.

"Poverty there is an infection that chokes the life out of their women. Treated like household slaves, being neglected, or abused, and oftentimes assaulted. And yet, nobody will do anything about it. There is no protection for them. Regardless of their innocence."

"Why is that?" the barfly asks, genuinely curious.

"Boys bring fortune. Girls require dowries that families cannot afford. I would not be surprised if harijans or others of the lowest caste murder the girls born at home."

"That's awful," the barfly exclaims, horrified.

"It is, but so is the extreme unemployment and disease that plague the poorer regions," Gary adds.

"No, it's not. I tried to help raise money so that the poorest of the families could get medical care. A goat."

"A goat?" Gary hiccups.

"Oh yes, you would be surprised at the many ways you can

profit off a goat. But that isn't why I wanted to be a missionary in India. I wanted to help the women."

"Why women? I'm sure more than women are suffering from poverty."

"Yes, but men had a chance to walk out their door and not get hurt. A chance to get a job and to make something of themself. Women … well, let us just say that it is different for them. Their hope relies on the prospect of marriage, which seems easy, but marriage to a good man that will not beat them? Not so simple. If they complain, well, they get brushed off as if they have a mental disorder. Just like the old ages. It's pathetic." After taking a gulp of wine, he continues, "Lot of suicides there."

Suddenly, his bushy eyebrows raise at the sight of the glass filling itself. "Good thing I'm not driving I guess."

"You feel inebriated?"

"No. Actually, I feel great. At peace even. You know what I did? I told those women what their rights would be if they came to America." Father Henry looks back down at the mirage—him with a circle of women, different religions. He did not care, he told them in English and Arabic about birth control, HIV, and severe depressive disorders.

"You can file for what is called asylum," he was telling the women. "You are persecuted just for being a woman and the government will not help."

"But it is my mother-in-law that beats me," a sullen woman spoke up in almost in a whisper, looking cautiously around. "She says it is her duty to teach me to be a proper wife, but I do everything she asks, and she still whips me and tells my husband it is my fault. He sides with her all the time."

"How do we file for this asylum?" a woman interrupted.

"I know no one in America," another piped in.

"You can seek refuge with the Catholic Church. We have ministries in every big city, and they can help.

Still looking down, Father Henry speaks to Gary, "That was not why I was there, but I saw a much bigger need. A need that perhaps went against the church with the vows and sacraments of marriage, but I do not believe that the powers of the church saw what we saw. Perhaps they would reevaluate if they did." Looking up, Father Henry sighs. "Again, we were stuck. Blind to what was real and before us because we were too focused on what was written."

His attention returns down to the mirage. "Community centers. That's what we were to build. Grand community centers with electricity to boot. Those women, living in mud huts, silently praying that their husbands will not beat them for some little absurdity while their children watched, and our goal was to give their kids a place to study and for us to hold mass, so we would not be burdened by not having power. Construction! That is what I was there for. The ministry of construction!"

Standing up, Father Henry slams his hand down on the bar counter. "Construction of buildings we thought they needed it so that they would have light while they gave birth. God, what arrogance!" Taking a breath, he looks helplessly at the barfly. "Please excuse my temper."

He sits back down. "In their world, where the foul-smelling feces on the streets illuminate the skyline, and women were being beaten, we wanted to provide air conditioning to preach God's love, an emotion they never felt toward them. They did not have to worry about hell. They were already living it."

"Your passion is noble."

Gary's voice startles Father Henry as he's lost in the vision that had captured his attention again upon sitting down.

"I take it that you questioned the position of the church often."

"A time or two, but never in front of my elders. I should have spoken up more. I mean, imagine being plopped down in the middle of the world, seeing humanity so close to each other that it is suffocating while every other young woman you saw was in a motherly way."

"I know India has a huge population." Gary winks at the

barfly. "The wife, she always wanted to go to India. 'Got to see the Taj Mahal before I die!' she would say. I couldn't stomach the thought of it myself. All those people squeezing up next to you. Hell, I couldn't breathe with all those people around." Taking a sip of wine, he shakes his head. "I regret it now though. The wife wanted to see much of the world, but my beliefs held me down … or my prejudices that is. I guess I held her down, too."

"You are exactly right about the population piece. Dare I say, despite the heresy in it, is birth control really such a bad thing? I mean think about it, the poor, the neglectful, the abusive, do they really need to add to the population?"

"The birth of a child is a miracle," the barfly says softly.

"Perhaps, but when the child brought into this world has no chances of a strong future, shall we entertain the prospects. Dear lady, I do see where you are coming from, and I mean no disrespect to your position, but … well, have you ever looked into the eyes of a starved child? Their feet bare, their stomachs protruding outwards, their sense of wonder zapped by the demons of poverty and the unwanted."

He turns back to Gary. "This was not just happening in India. It was in so many places where we were sent to build our Catholic empire." Henry's voice softens. "We shouldn't have been focusing on the construction of buildings. It was the construction of souls that we needed to have our sights on. We claimed that we were out to spread the gospel and support the erection of new churches around the world to provide the faithful and the poor a spiritual home, but we neglected the repair of the heart. Where the real spirit begins. The waters of life are a portal to new beginnings. But we failed at seeing it through. Distributing baptisms as if we were the filter of eternal life, but we abandoned them for our next mission. That certainly cannot be the wants of an ever so loving father." Realizing he is standing again, he suddenly becomes embarrassed by his emotions. He sits back onto his stool, drinking from the glass that magically fills up again. Drinking, he savors the flavor before breaking the silence.

"The love of the Holy Spirt is a mysterious thing. Not like what we know as a romance story." He pins Gary with his gaze. "You know, I can understand why a woman wants to go to India, especially if they are a romantic at heart. The story of the Taj Mahal is a beautiful story. A fairytale really. Built out of love. Places of faith should be treated with the same amount of sacredness. Built on love as well. Not arrogance. How can you tell a woman not to take birth control when they don't have the funds to feed a child? How do you plead with a woman to hold strong to the sacrament of marriage, when the man abuses her so terribly that she has to use colorful scarves to cover the blue and black battle wounds circling her body?" Shaking his head, he frowns. "It wasn't just in the foreign countries. America has hidden pockets all over her country sheltering the same story."

Father Henry looks at the wine bottle again. The label still in mirror form opens and reveals a little bit older Henry. He is sitting in a dull living room with a torn couch and a coffee table with tattered magazines, a bible with a faded cover and an empty sippy cup. A young woman of about twenty with long, stringy hair is hunched over, rocking back and forth, occasionally looking at an infant in a small car seat carrier.

In a sobbing, desperate voice, she said, "I know I've sinned, Father, but I have no place to go. My father said, 'You made your bed, now lie in it!' My mother said nothing, she just hung her head down in shame. So, I drink, and I pop pills, and I …" She gulped, unable to look Father Henry in the eye. "And many other things. Now I am pregnant again, and soon I won't be able to dance."

"The shelter will keep you safe for now," Henry attempted to calm her. "They have programs that can help you get back on your feet."

"My parish priest has told me not to leave my husband. Not to take birth control."

"We are told many things, but until we live in the situation ourselves, we do not know what the right answer is for us."

The girl shook her head. "Father, I want an abortion. I can't have this child. I can't even take care of Agatha."

Father Henry took a deep breath. "You know I cannot condone that. You are five weeks along. The child has limbs, lungs even though they are tiny. A heartbeat."

"But it is my body and you said that until somebody lives in a situation, they don't know what the right answer is."

"The moment you became pregnant, you share your body with an innocent human being. That child is alive. He or she may not be viable without your blood feeding them, but they are a life. You are no longer one, you are two. Respect all life womb to the tomb."

"We are also not to judge our neighbor, Father. Are you judging me?"

The young girl's shoulders shook, and she ignored the cries of Agatha, her baby.

"I'm preaching the word. I'm telling truth. Abortion is murder. It is just as much murder as if you smothered your crying baby."

Agatha screamed harder.

"Do you really think God wants an innocent life to suffer like this? Look at me, I'm an addict in a shelter, my husband is running from the cops, and my parents think I am a disgrace." She was crying harder now. "How can a loving god want this for anybody, much less a child?"

"You just said a blessed word. Child. You recognize that you are carrying life."

"What do you expect of me?"

"To give yourself a chance. To give this life inside of you a chance."

Looking up at Gary, Father Henry says solemnly, "She aborted the child anyway. I thought I was making a difference, but the next day she had another resident from the shelter take her to a Planned Parenthood and aborted the child while her friend and Agatha waited in the car for her."

"You tried."

"And for what? I had one job, and that was to show the faithfulness of the Lord, Jesus Christ." He looks at the image again. "I failed her. I failed him. I let him down more times than I care to mention." Dropping his head, he shakes it. "I failed that child. That unborn, innocent life."

"Many Christians are persecuted in the name of cleansing. As a Catholic you stood up against the persecution, the killings, and you spread the message of the gospel, even when it was not the popular thing to do."

"The world turned evil. Messages of hate embedded in political correctness. Even at my bedside, I could hear the news in the background. Protests, crimes … a loss of consciousness for all of humanity. Before I slipped into coma, I prayed that no aggressive measures be used to save my life. I could not speak for myself, as my words are lost in my disease, but I can still pray. Do you think they still have a candle lit in my room?"

"I'm sure they do." Gary leans down on the bar. "You know, in my experience up here, I have often seen that the best of men and women are the hardest on themselves. Conflict with personal beliefs and what the morality of what their heart is telling them."

"What are you trying to say?"

"Well, I am not your judge by any means, but it seems to me that you are a good man, you know your sins and when you know your sins, you are able to ask forgiveness. The church may have been your life, but your faith resides in your soul."

Taking a deep breath, he nods. "Maybe you should have been a priest."

Gary chuckles. "No, sir, not me. Like the ladies too much."

"One time, in Ecuador, I was serving a small community, teaching. We didn't have electricity …" Father Henry jumps up, startled when Kitty Kat leaps up on the bar and meows at him. "Well, where did you come from?"

"That's my furry helper. She likes to listen, too."

Father Henry reaches out and gently pets her head. She lifts her chin so he can scratch underneath, and when he pulls his hand away, she lays her paw on his wrist.

"She likes you. She always likes a gentle soul." Looking at the cat, Gary instructs, "Go on, you were serving a small community in Ecuador that didn't have electricity."

"Oh yes. It was a tiny place, and the people were always so grateful." Smiling, he continues, "You know, I once told a villager that I would love a Coca Cola and that guy walked nearly twenty miles to the nearest market just to get me one. Then he apologized that it was not cold." He takes a sip of wine "Can you believe that?"

"You were respected. Hell, adored even. Often people don't realize the impact that they are having at the time they are having it. My wife used to tell me stories about her students. She was a teacher. Anyway, she would have students come to her years after just to say thank her for something she said or did. Sometimes she didn't even remember the student or vaguely the interaction. And you know what, mostly, it was the quiet ones. You know the ones that sit in the back that may not always engage but they listened, and somehow her words, her crazy, quirky advice would stick with them." Taking a drink of his own, Gary makes eye contact with Father Henry. "Bet it is the same for you, too. You don't know how much of an impact that your words or your actions had, but they last. You made a footprint on lives, more than you will ever know."

Father Henry buries his head in his hands. "Dear sir, I do not deserve your praise. I preached in the four corners of the world, but I let my own beliefs interfere. My message was not always that of the church. There were times, dare I say, after seeing so much misery, poverty, and transgressions that I transgressed myself. I lost my faith when I was supposed to be instilling it. I cursed God in the darkness of night, when I could hear the bombs in the distance, the crying in the tents marked to be hospitals, during the sick smells of famine passing out communion with my plump hands to the mouths of the gaunt, some consuming for the hopes of nourishment. In the hopes that their brittle bones will not break through the exhaustion of impeding death."

Father Henry begins to cry, Kitty Kat curls up closer to him, Gary waits for the sobs to subside.

"You don't think that God hears your lamentation now?" Gary puts his hand on Father Henry's shoulder. "Father, you have created your own hell while completely missing the obvious."

Father Henry looks at him, tears stinging his eyes.

The barfly silently watches, pressing back her own salty tears. She lets out a breath as if she had held it during the entire exchange.

"I am not quite sure I know what you mean."

"When you first sat down, you referred to evil as a disease. And, I agree, it is." Taking a breath, Gary composes himself. "Yet, you have spent your life working to the be the cure."

The old priest looks down while opening his wrinkled hand and exposes two large, gold coins. "I suppose I'm supposed to pay you with this."

"Nope, take it to the machine."

Father Henry eyes the odd-looking contraption with its high back, flashing lights, and Latin numbers. Slowly, he gets down off his stool and hobbles to it, places the coins in the slot, pulls the handle, and nods his head in prayer as the sounds, the bells and whistles start to ring out. He holds on to the sides as the dizziness of the machine vibrates through him, engulfing him in a tornado of life. He can hear the children's voices from Thailand thanking him and clapping as he sang to them "This Little Light of Mine". He hears the desperate whispers of gratitude from three women in India as he held out papers to help them reach the borders, the nuns embracing them in. Smells surround him as well, chocolate brownies that he would make for the men late at night after seminary classes, the tapping of his mother's heels when she taught him how to tap dance on the hard-wood floors that covered his childhood home. The Nebraska fields, a baby wren chirping that his dad helped him save. *"It's okay, boy. It's okay to set him free. He will still never forget you."*

The sounds stopped. A word appears: *Mors.*

As he looks up at Gary, the light from underneath the mahogany doors warm the room. "Mind if I walk you?" Gary asks as he put an arm around the man's shoulder.

"I would be honored."

The barfly watches as Father Henry and Gary cross the Acheron River. The priest's salt and pepper hair turn an ebony black and he begins to walk straighter as his youthful stride manifests in him. When the pair reaches the crossover to the Lethe River, the sound of angel voices ring out, singing.

I, the Lord of sea and sky
I have heard my people cry

The large, mahogany doors open, expelling soft oranges, reds, and pinks with a collage of shadows hollering at him. "Come on, Henry. It's about time you got here."

The angels continued:

All who dwell in dark and sin,
My hand will save

The lady barfly embraces the heavenly moment, enjoying the beauty of the crowd whose praises sound out the hissing of the door on the left, the laughing and brawling of the casino, the thoughts floating in her own head.

I who made the stars of night
I will make their darkness bright
Who will bear my light to them?
Whom shall I send?

Not wanting to miss the force of the heavenly light, the lady barfly sits straight up. The distance is not far enough for her to see the man place his hand on Gary's shoulder while shaking his other. Squinting, she is able to read his lips:

"Let me go to the Lord."

Gary's face softens. He stands there longer than he did with the others after the door has closed, listening to the choir singing. "Here I am, Lord. Is it I, Lord?"

After the bell-like click of the door shuts, Gary turns back to cross the bridge. The Lethe tickling his feet as he returns, the Acheron harsh but bearable. When he reaches his station, he picks up his cat and nuzzles her head, hiding from the barfly what may have been a tear. Then he turns, eyes the casino crowd, and hollers, "Last call."

Dion

Gary turns to the barfly. "So, have you gathered some stories of interest?"

"I must admit, it has been interesting. So many people grieving over venial sins that they may be flippant about if not trapped in this situation where they beg for simony as if they were at some devilish black market."

"So, you don't believe that all of my patrons are truly repentant for their sins?"

"I'm just saying that is seems awfully convenient. I mean, look around … isn't it odd how a person gets so trapped in the world around them, they forget the cruelty that happens outside of their own walls?" She lets out a breath. "Is the good lord a helicopter parent?"

"I'm sorry, I don't follow."

"Some parents think the entire world surrounds them and their child and only them and their child. They forget that their world is not the same as others around them. They pester teachers, daycare workers, Sunday school teachers, and anyone who has a hand in their child's life to stop what they are doing and focusing on only their kid, forgetting that their kid is not the entirety of their world." Rethinking her words, she says, "God has billions of children. He can't possibly be ready to condemn each person who stole a cookie out of the cookie jar."

"Maybe not, but," he pauses for a moment, "have you ever noticed a hole in a tooth and although you know it is bad and that you need to get it filled, you put it off for days, weeks, and even months?"

The lady barfly nods. "But—"

"Wait, hear me out," Gary interrupts her. "Then suddenly you wake up in gasping pain and realize that you have to do something and right then. No matter the cost because the pain is too much, and your jaw is swelling, and your face is burning, and your hands are trembling all from what seemed like a little hole that all of sudden bubbled into an abscess overnight."

The lady barfly looks at him tentatively. "Are you comparing sin to a cavity?"

Gary straightens up. "I tried not to think about it when I was up there." He points up, motioning to the world of the living. "Cavities that is. I really don't quite know my reasoning for that. I feel now that if a person does, then they must acknowledge evil is happening. Then they must make a conscious choice to do something about it. That entails getting involved. And face it, nobody wants to do that."

Gary picks up a crystal bowl from the back counter and dispenses Meow Mix into it, placing it next to his observer. "I guess I am working overtime being my own personal shrink."

"Surprised you can get that here." She nods toward the bowl as she strokes the cat's back.

"Only stuff she will eat. Well, besides cat treats and the occasional table food left by a gluttonous being."

Suddenly, the bar glasses clatter together, and the floor begins to shake. The bridge over the Acheron forms but the steps manifest as jagged, sharp rocks while the river's water boils, leaping up at a tall, skinny man with long, straggly, black hair wearing stained, white jeans and a white tee shirt. A tattoo of a devil encircled by roses sizzles on his arm left. The scalding water burns his skin with each blistering step he forcefully makes forward. A beastly minotaur had taken position rising from the waters, gashing at the man's flesh, tasting his blood.

Kitty Kat hisses and cries before jumping down and hiding behind Gary's legs. The rivers turn to fire, licking the oncoming intruder with passion while the waves of the Cocytus laughs thundery behind him. He looks up, his beady, dark eyes searching desperately for the shore and the path that leads to the bar. He makes a final leap, mutilating his left leg in the process before dragging himself up to a stool.

The lady barfly starts to get up to give the man a hand but is stopped by Gary who holds up his palm and firmly says, "No, let him do it himself."

Although annoyed by his tone, she obediently sits down, horrified by the streaks of blood dripping from the man's scalp and the burned leg peeking through his shredded jeans where skin is visibly seen peeling off.

He groans as he pulls himself up, and stares intently at Gary.

Finally, he breaks the silence, harshly barking, "What do you want?"

The man licks his burnt chapped lips, and, in a growl, he utters, "Johnny Walker, Black Label, and leave the bottle."

Gary turns, takes down two shot glasses, while hidden from the patron's view, he spits into one before pouring the brown delight into them. Turning around, he hands the one with the saliva treat to the haggard man, then takes his position on the stool directly in front of him, making sure to leave the bottle on the back counter.

"See you got a bit of attitude."

"Seems like my attitude is not what you need to be worried about. Looks like you have greater demons to slay."

The man's white tee shirt still sticking to his flesh looks back and shakes his head. "Oh, that ain't nothing."

"Looks like something to me. You got a name or shall I just call you asshole."

Unshaken by Gary's abruptness, he nods his head. "Dion Ford is my name. Before I got down here, it was a household name."

"Well from the looks of your arrival it doesn't appear that it is something that you should be proud of."

"I don't know what all you know about me, but the grand jury declined to indict me on all of those accusations."

"Accusations? Accusations of what?"

"So here you are on your high horse, and you don't even know. Damn. Back in Louisiana where I come from, you'd get your ass kicked and fed to the swamp gators for talking to a man like that."

"Well, I'd be happy to escort you over there ..." Gary points to a malebolge, where on one side stood a burning, thorny mountain and on the other, a lava formed pool. "Or" Gary drops his hand, "you can tell me, Dion, what brings you to my fine bar this evening?"

"Really?" Dion shakes his head from left to right. "You can tell the difference between night and day here?"

"Well, I don't want to think of the likes of you prowling around in the day hours."

Dion hesitates, the veins on his hand decorated with grungy dirt seamed together with barbed wire tattoos exaggerates his bone white knuckles every time he throws back a shot down his gullet.

"I ran a boarding school. It was a good one, too. Meant to help wayward teens find their way back to the church and to their homes. Unfortunately, during my tenure, let's just say there were some unsavory reports about the establishment. Some people objected to our means of cleansing the souls of the trite and difficult to treat."

"Well maybe, what you were treating didn't need to be treated."

"I'll have you know that our services were widely regarded and well needed." Dion holds his glass up to the light and studies it while he speaks.

"We specialized in converting boys who … well, you know, found themselves possessed by demons that led them in the feminine way."

"Really now. So, you say, possessed. Sure those exorcisms cost pitiful parents a pretty penny, too."

"It had to be done!" Dion's nostrils flare as his beady, black eyes open wide. "Society can't be dirtied up with those perversions. No, we couldn't have that. Homosexuality is a sin. It was my duty to help the incorrigible, the unwanted rejects before they spread their disease to the innocent. There's plenty of them you know. Hiding in the seedy city streets, spreading their disgusting influences. We saved those wretched people from that fate and treated them."

"Hmm, conversion therapy. I've heard of that quackery. So how old were these so-called teens of yours that you subjected this 'conversion therapy'?" Gary makes it a point to hold up his index fingers and middle fingers to create quotation marks around his words. A gesture that Dion chose to ignore.

"Oh, they got sent to us as young as ten." Pausing, he cocks his head to the side to think for a moment. "But I guess the average age was about fourteen. Parents wanted them treated before the high school years. Didn't want them to act on it. Fear they'd bring home the Aids." A crooked smile flashes on the man's face as his shot glass fills on its own. "It was much more enjoyable when they came to us young though. They got frightened much easier. Fear is a magnificent teaching tool." After swallowing down another shot, he asks, "Want to know how we worked with them?"

"I prefer not."

"Why? You homophobic?" Releasing a smirk, he nods at him. "Bet you are." Dion begins to speak in a sing-song voice. "Gary the Ferryman, afraid of a little dick. Don't like to butt fuck, do ya?"

Gary's facial features harden, his voice grows firm. "I have no problem with whatever floats anybody's boat. What I don't like is you."

Dion lets out a boisterous laugh. "Guess you do catch wind of the headlines from the other world." He pulls himself closer to the counter. "I'll have you know, it's not all like those media fleas would lead you to believe." Then a wicked smile spreads across his face, he leans back in his chair, and in a taunting whisper, tells him, "It is so much more."

"So, were all the boys that came forward fleas, too? If I recall right, which I am sure that I do, boys described decades of abuse. And state social workers collaborated all of it." Finishing off a shot, Gary glares at him. "Some even mentioned the disappearance of several of the so-called students."

"Oh, pish posh with those damn do-gooder social workers. They have no clout where I came from. I'll have you know that we followed the guidelines of the Fundamental Baptist Church. Residents were to adhere to strict rules, and if they did not then they were to be subjected to harsh punishment. It was our code. We kept them with us, away from the outside world and all distractions so that we can focus on their recovery." He straightens his shoulders. "Of course, sometimes there were some unforeseen consequences."

"Yeah, I'd imagine some of those consequences involved being fed to those swamp gators you speak so highly of. Do you really believe you were helping those boys or were they just income until you got sick of them?"

"Please, do you think that their families would have sent them away to us if they wanted them around? We didn't just have fags in our midst you know … we dealt with prostitutes, drug addicts, and violent offenders. A house of freaks we had up there. Disgusting, pathetic freaks. They all deserved to die, or at least burn in those fucking waters you see yonder." Dion turns around on his stool, his back leaning on the bar while he faces the rapid torture of a woman stuck on a wobbly bridge.

"This does not sound like a school. It sounds more like your judgments were a shooting gallery. Bullets hitting innocent adolescents that you beckon into your control."

"We took in hundreds of children, and we helped them all."

"Really, then why did so many of them press charges against you?" Gary's voice raises, echoing against a beast resting on the shoreline. "Why were so many of them never heard from again? The school pictures your kids' parents had to look forward to would be on the back of a milk carton!"

"Just give me the fucking bottle."

Gary becomes silent, Kitty Kat still hidden behind him, hissing at Dion every time he comes into her view. Dion's shot glass fills up again.

"Some couldn't handle the treatment." His voice has deepened.

"Some couldn't handle being electrocuted and raped," Gary counters.

"You don't understand."

"So, explain it to me, asshole."

"My name is Dion."

"So, explain it to me, Mr. Asshole Dion."

"Teenagers are demons who will go to extraordinary lengths to escape the claws of their parents and the church. Some will commit unimaginable and unholy crimes to destroy the images of the family. Parents needed the ministry's help to set them straight. That is what I did." Dion taps his glass on his teeth and laughs. "Now give me that fucking bottle."

"What is the point? Your glass fills up on its own." Gary grabs the bottle by the neck and pounds it down hard next to Dion, the brown whiskey swishing inside.

Dion's voice growls a little when he states, "Because I demand equal treatment." Placing a hand on the bottle, he moves it fast, startled by the heat from it. Looking into it, the brown liquid starts to bubble and slosh around with a sizzling sound on its own. Waves become faces, the stink of blood and rotting flesh rise out of it as the label bubbles in and back out again. "What the fuck?"

"Look at it," Gary snarls.

An image forms of a young teen, pale with rosacea on his cheeks, scalp recently shaved bald wearing brown corduroy pants and a thick, striped, mustard yellow and orange, short-sleeved shirt, rocking himself on a hard concrete floor in a small room with a slit of a window letting in a thin stream of sunlight.

"Strip," a shadow of a younger Dion is heard directing toward the boy.

The boy stood and began to shake as he started to take off his shirt. Dion walked closer to him, slamming a hard paddle to the boy's side, leaving an oar-sized red mark on the skin exposed by the slightly released pants.

Dion's eyes stays fixated on the scene as he speaks, "This one was a real moron. He tore his body up one night when he scaled the chain-link fence that enclosed the school. Stupid fucker crawled over the barbed wire and ran through the woods. Died the night he tried to escape. Stupid, stupid, stupid."

"Maybe to him, death was his only escape."

Dion ignores Gary's comment and laughs as more of the scene unfolds.

The boy, now in his underwear, gets snatched by Dion and another man dressed in pastor's clothing, throwing him on what appears to be a rough dentist chair that has shackles attached to the bottom and side where they lock the child in, pinching his skin. All the while, Dion and the pastor holler obscenities and taunts toward the child.

"You want food? You want to go home? You will follow this program," the pastor yelled at the boy."

Dion turned on a film projector.

"Shall we find out if you need an exorcism?" The pastor's voice rung out over the click, click, click of the film as the reel turned and projected reflective images of nude women touching themselves. Then men doing the same.

The boy cried out, as Dion flipped a switch that sent electric shock waves through the adolescent's already frail body.

"You, child, are cursed with a mental illness demon that we must expel from to save your soul." As the pastor spoke, he would give Dion occasional nods, initiating more shockwaves through the boy's body.

With each nod, Dion laughs harder as the scene continues.

"How do you find this funny?" Gary asks disgustedly.

Gulping down another drink, Dion lets out a mocking, "Aww," his breath stinking of the harsh whiskey. "You see this and think that I am inflicting a harrowing torture, but it wasn't me that tortured that child. Todd, that was his name, Todd." Dion, still holding his shot glass, uses his little finger to point at Gary. "Todd's desires for the same sex were the fault of his own psychosocial maladjustment resulting from a much younger age than what you see here." He squints at the image in the bottle. "This one is fifteen. I remember, I thought the kid was thirteen judging by his puny dick. Probably not his fault he was a fag though. He had no daddy, and his mother was a whore coming on to every man in the church. He had no role model to take after. The pastor took pity on the poor bastard. Ordered for him to have conversion therapy three times a day."

"All through electric shock?"

"No, no. No, kid that small couldn't handle that. He'd get hosed down and kept in a caged room where he could have an assortment of magazines to raise his arousal. When that didn't work, I'd go in and show him what his perversions subjected men to."

"So, in efforts to make him straight you'd rape him. Sounds like you're a fag, too!"

"Fuck you!" Dion reaches over the counter, grabbing Gary by his shirt.

"What ya gonna do, punch me? Trust me, you don't want to get me fired up." Enormous hot waves splash onto the shore, hitting Dion in the back as the ground below him shakes. He lets out a scalding scream, releasing Gary and slinking back into his stool. His arms shake as he reaches for another shot of drink.

"You know nothing of rehabilitation and what it takes," Dion whimpers. He glances at the JW Black bottle again, still twirling with scenes. This time he is taken into another where a different child, smaller, around ten, again head shaved, shivers as Dion holds a hose to him with a violent blast. He watches the scene unfold. Him turning off the water, taking out a whip and lashing at him, leaving streaks of blood on his back and thighs.

"We tried hypnosis on this one. Didn't work. Tried it seven times and the boy still got an erection when he saw images of men masturbating. Sick little turd." Glaring at Gary, he says, "Committed suicide three weeks after he was released. So, Mr. All-mighty, who's the sinner now?"

"And you don't think your therapies had anything to do with his self-hatred?"

"Let's see how you would be if you were to be surrounded with a bunch of deviants, sinful queers."

"Did it ever occur to you that was their nature? They were born that way?"

"Hey, we did all sorts of things to help. We even had a medical doctor working for us. When the parents signed their rights away, we tried medical surgeries. Castration, even transplant surgery with their testicles."

A gasp is heard from the end of the bar where the lady barfly sits. Gary and Dion turn to her as she asks, horrified, "Where exactly did the donors come from?"

Laughing, he swallows another shot. "As I said, that wasn't the only type of degenerate we let come to the school." He watches his glass refill. "It was at first, but when we saw how there was so many parents in need of our help, we started taking in different kind of cases. We figured," he shrugs his shoulders, "if we can condition the mind out of homosexuality, we can cure all sorts of things." He glances at her. "I had some very inventive colleagues."

Composing herself, the lady barfly asks, "So were you involved in giving lobotomies?"

"Well of course. We had to. There were extreme cases that easier methods didn't work."

"Such as?"

"Sorry."

Firming her voice, the lady barfly asks, "What other methods?"

Turning his body to face her, he answers, "Sometimes we distributed drugs that would induce vomiting while they looked at pictures of people, they found attractive."

"Why did you do this work?"

"Why does anybody do anything? Money, prestige."

"It seems to me you enjoyed it."

Gary is silent. Kitty Kat has jumped into his lap. He strokes her, calming her shaking. Dion shifts uncomfortably, but the lady barfly—who suddenly seems larger in stature and her eyes sparkling blue green a little bit more—maintains her stance.

"How many of them did you kill?"

Dion lets out an uncomfortable laugh, speaking in Gary's direction. "Seems like your friend has an active imagination."

"There are no secrets down here," she continues. "They know every detail of every grotesque act of sin that you committed in your pathetic little life. So, go ahead and explain yourself. I bet you have many stories to boast about."

"Well, I met the good pastor when he bailed me out of jail."

"The first time?" Gary pipes in.

Dion looks at him, annoyed, but hesitantly says, "Yes."

He takes a breath. "Two freaks in my neighborhood accused me of rape and the police held me in county. They tried to pin the disappearance of a twelve-year-old boy on me, but they couldn't prove it. I'm not stupid. My mother called Pastor Mack and he came and got me. He vouched for me and told them that if they would drop the investigation on me then he would make sure that I had a good job at the school he ran."

Gary nods to the liquor bottle where the liquid inside began to slosh around.

Dion follows his gaze as a scene unfolds of a team of police searching his childhood home, his mother screaming that her baby did nothing, a young Dion slouching outside. "Stupid pigs, do they think I would really be so stupid to leave evidence at my own home?"

Looking up, he grins. "I was messy though. Hell, I was just a kid. But I knew better than to lure that boy to my mother's house. I did all of my business in an abandoned house three streets away. The body wasn't discovered until I was already out of there."

"Wait, what?" Gary interrupts. "Why did you leave him there?"

"I wanted to go back and visit him. I didn't cut him up too bad, and until he began to smell really bad, I enjoyed his company."

"The company of a corpse?"

"I wanted him close, but I couldn't take him home."

"So how many did you kill before you began working at the school?"

Dion is quiet for a minute as he counts on his fingers. "Eight," he finally says. "I killed eight, but they all knew what I wanted from them when I took them to the house on Maple Street."

"They knew you wanted to kill them?"

"No! I wouldn't ever get them to follow me if I told them that." Taking a breath, he says thoughtfully, "They knew I liked to experiment. There were times I felt bad for them. They were just so stupid." He watches his drink refill again. "Things were much easier for me at the school."

"How so?"

"The property was big, and the grounds were awesome! Pastor Mack let me have the run of it. Before I started counseling the students, I was a caretaker. Even had a one-bedroom cabin on the edge of a wooded area. Really loved it there, too. It was so nice and peaceful. Walking outside and seeing nothing but trees. That's special there. Not a whole lot of wooded areas in Louisiana. Mainly swampland. Anyway, the land was rough in areas, and it was hot. Louisiana. It gets hot there a lot. Had to buy a lot of lime."

"You're sick!" the lady barfly huffs.

Gary looks at her sideways before turning to Dion. "She's got a point."

"Yeah, that's what the lawyers argued when I was taken into custody." Letting out another boisterous laugh, he grins maliciously. "You know, I bet they make a movie about me."

Again, the liquid in the bottle sloshes. This time, he is seen explaining to Pastor Mack that he had not seen Marcus and did not know how he could have escaped.

Dion speaks as he watches. "His body was in the bedroom. I had a crawl space that led from my closet to a trench on the property." Never taking his eyes of the scene, he continues, "I had four other boys there, but their parents didn't make a fuss. Didn't think Marcus' mom would either, but I think she had regrets after having him committed. Little bastard must have gotten a letter or a message through to her somehow."

Gary peers at the scene. "How did you explain the blood on you?"

"He didn't notice."

"Probably didn't want to."

"Did he eventually find out what you were doing?"

"Yeah, he got pissed by the way the house smelled. Tried to tell him that rodents were getting in and stinking the place up, but he didn't believe me. He went in there one day and found the trap door in the closet that led to my inventory. Thought I was gonna get fired but instead he offered me a proposition."

"He did, did he?"

"Yeah, he said if I was going to play with the boys that I had to do it in one of the cement cells so that it could be hosed down easier. He also wanted to watch."

"Birds of a feather flock together. I guess sociopaths do, too."

"It's not like that. He was a man of God. He knew that God wouldn't care if these people were dead since they were degenerates and using their bodies for sex and money. Sometimes he would offer them drugs to calm them so the moment wouldn't be destroyed by the boy's cries."

"Yeah, well, wouldn't want the fun be destroyed for you."

"It wasn't like that. We prayed for them. After all, they were lost souls. Those miscreants have nobody to blame but themselves for dying."

"Oh, so this gets better. Now you are victim blaming."

"All the students at the school had been threatened by it long before the parents give up and admit them to our care. We didn't go out and search for them. They came to us. An offering if you will."

Dion quiets down.

"You can be a help here, Dion," Pastor Mack said. "Some of these students that get released go back and tell the authorities things that can get us in trouble. Maybe even shut down."

"Aww, come on. They're kids. Nobody's gonna believe their stories. They all make shit up when they feel disgruntled."

"True, but some are more dangerous than others. The ones that won't shut up and let go."

"So, I take it, you need me to shut them up."

"Well, not right away. You can have your fun with them. It may even straighten them out enough to where we can let them go."

"Were there a lot of people let go?"

"Let's just say that there were a lot of suicides those few years. When we knew that there would be parent questioning, we would take the ones that couldn't be saved by our therapies and slash their wrists right there in the woods. The blood was good to feed the trees. It brought in the rodents. We'd wait a few days, call the police, and by the time that a discovery on the far edges of the property was made there would be too much animal damage and decay to be able to determine trauma on the bodies. It's brilliant if I do say so myself."

"Doesn't seem like you got away with it for long."

"No. That little shit Peter went running his flaps."

"I won't tell anybody. Just please stop," shrieked from the bottle.

The nude boy was pushed up against a cement slab with Dion forcing himself against him. Pastor Mack, on the other side of the slab, appeared to be high on something, laughing. His eyes shone red, his shadow forming on the wall behind him as tall as ten feet.

"We shouldn't have let him go. His brother made me mad and hit me when I was wrestling him into the room, so I stabbed him. Peter seen it and promised not to tell. Said if we let him go, he would say that Jake had run away, and he didn't know where to. Holy sh:t! I don't remember that happening," Dion says, his eyes widen:ng.

In the scene, Pastor Mack warped into a winged, beastly demon. His ears pointed, eyes red, spitting while laughing with yelling gnarling teeth. Peter shrieking louder, Dion laughing in the scene, the demon masturbating at the sight.

Dion starts to gasp, "I had no idea, I swear. I mean, when the police finally came, they found over thirty-three bodies on the property. They didn't know about the ones we burned." He looks back down. "Sitting in jail, I kept wondering how he was not arrested, too. Why it was only me that they suspected. I told them too. I told them that Pastor Mack had helped and even committed most of the murders, but my attorneys claimed that it was an alternate personality that helped me and that I was crazy." Raising his voice in a panic, he cries, "But look, I'm not crazy." He stares back down at the winged beast torturing Peter.

"But that demon didn't commit the murders, did he? You did. Every last one of them. He just watched."

Ignoring the question, he mutters, "My life has been hell since I was arrested."

The beast image turns and then blurs to show him in jail. Numerous inmates corner him in the shower are heard saying vile things to him.

"You like to fuck little boys?" says one.

"You kill little boys. Well, how about we just kill you?" The men start beating on Dion, ripping his shirt, punching him.

One jumps on him as he falls to the ground, picking up his head and smashing it again and again onto the cement.

"Guess that's how I got here, isn't it?"

"Well, it didn't help you much," Gary says while grinding his teeth. "You want to find out if you are staying?"

Dion nods and pulls two coins out of his jean pockets. His arm, still burning from the watery fires, his deformed leg crippling him as he holds himself up, struggling to get to the slot machine. Gary offers no assistance.

"Damn, I drank so much and yet my mouth feels dry." He pokes his tongue in and out of his mouth. "Think I could trouble you for some water?"

"Mr. Dion Asshole Ford, I wouldn't give it to you if you were on fire. Oh, wait, you are!" Gary points to a small flame at the tail of his shirt.

Dion shakes it off and then looks straight ahead at the machine. Making his best attempt to stand straight, he slides his gold coins into the slot and waits as the clunk of the coins sound and the wheels begin to spin. Lights streak up from the machine, sounds of wicked laughter chorus the scene as the waves of the Phlegethon River becomes turbulent. Click, click, sounds as the spinner comes to a stop.

Mors.

Dion stares at it for a moment before timidly asking, "What the fuck does that mean?"

"It means now you will have to answer to God."

Before Dion can respond, Gary grabs him by his collar, dragging him over the jagged rocks that tickle his skin, leaving streaks of blood smearing his path.

Dion screeches, "Help me!"

"Like you helped those little boys?" Gary's eyes flare; his muscles bulge as a bionic strength overtakes him. A hideous beast flaps overhead, shadowing the two as they walk the path over the waters over the Cocytus which boil and lap up, blistering Dion's skin, leaving Gary unscathed.

"You imposed your twisted fantasies on those boys, torturing them. Throwing their mutilated bodies away like they were trash for the compost heap only to be eaten by wild animals."

As the two reached the bridge to the Phlegethon River, six harpies flew upon them with open talons. Dion looks up and lets out a wail as one single claw snatches at his eye, ripping it out of its socket, blood pouring out as a minotaur releases a wicked screech. The three demons on the metal door become three dimensional as smoke creeps out of the slowly opening door. Then coming to life, snatching at Dion as the two men come closer, the ominous shadow still flapping overhead.

Dion clutches onto Gary, who had begun beating him with his left fist. Pounding and pounding. Harder and harder. Each blow leaving a piercing red mark that instantly became bloodied and purple as each thrust left another puncture.

"You wanted to be the devil, well now you can meet your mentor." Gary's voice echoes across the room, calming the rivers as it floats over.

Dion gives him one desperate look, pleading for mercy.

Gary responds, "I'm not the one to ask mercy from."

Then, with one final punch, Dion is forced into the claws of the metal door. Wicked, salacious screams sound from inside as the door slams shut, leaving only a thin veil of curly, black smoke to dissipate in the air.

The three beasts nod at Gary as they fade back into the design of the metal door. The escorting beast swoops down, then up, and dissipate into the top of the rotunda. A smooth path opens up over the Phlegethon River. When he comes to the corner of the Phlegethon and the Acheron Rivers, he hollers at the crowd in the casino.

"Can see why some of you are afraid to come up here?"

He spots the lady barfly looking at him, visibly shaken and holding Kitty Kat close to her. His shirt becomes miraculously white and crisp again. His bowtie straightens and his suspenders smooth out. Smiling at her, he walks calmly to the bar.

"Don't worry, you have nothing to fear. This is just all part of the job." Then he wipes his counter, and in loud, echoing voice, hollers out, "Last call."

Violet/Geraldine

A dull silence sweeps through the casino floor, as it always does when a soul meets the gates of hell. Even the barfly, who thought she knew her beloved bartender, is shocked at the wrath that Gary inflicted on the twisted character. The red that pierced his eyes, his enhanced strength conjured by adrenaline and rage frightened her. Although, it did raise her curiosity more. She watches him for a long time before finally speaking.

"Have you ever been inside of the doors?" she asks cautiously.

Gary doesn't look up from petting Kitty Kat and sipping a Coke. "The gates of hell you mean?"

"Yes. It seems like such an awful walk."

"It is. In fact, before the spin of the slot I get a queasy feeling that travels from my brain to the tips of my toes. It's like when you feel like you are okay and yet you have a fever. You know the infection is there, but you don't know what it is, so you don't know how to fight it. That's how it is with the unremorseful evildoers."

As he speaks, the barfly's eyes grow wide, and she gulps down another Lotus drink in one swallow.

"People like that," Gary nods toward the direction of hell's gate, "people like that are burdened the moment they take a breath. A cancer on society. Like weeds, one is pulled and three more sprouts up. The difference is, your garden laughs and loves and lives through the commandments of accountability and kindness until a weed invades their soil, strangling the life out of them, hiding them from the sun." He turns back to the lady barfly. "But it's all good. I seldom go there. You see, Father, that's how I come to call him, Father is an all-forgiving God, and his end goal is to have everyone join him. He doesn't want demons to feast on the souls of the unholy."

"So why does it happen?"

"It's hard to explain. You heard him. He had no remorse. Hell, he even laughed when he witnessed the replay of his past sins. The sick, twisted soul got off on being the star of his own horrid fright fest." Gary pauses for a moment to let that sink in. "You see, when I was up there, I thought differently." He points up, and the barfly follows his gaze.

She didn't notice before … at first glance, the ceiling is mirrored, but when examined closer, it serves as a looking glass to the living. A portal.

Gary smiles. "If you focus on the image, you can hear what is going on up there. I look at it a lot when things are slow here."

The barfly focuses and slowly recognizes a playground and the sound of children's laughter echoing through. She wants to wave at a child who drops his ball and bends down to pick it up, but even though she can see his long, brown hair blowing in his face, his bright blue eyes, and missing two front teeth, she realizes he can't see her. He just sees the scattered grass mixed in the dirt, and the dandelions that his ball made its way to the center of. His life is quiet, peaceful, and filled with hope. No knowledge of the treacherous things that lay beneath the living universe.

"It's amazing," the lady barfly says. Then she looks over to what Gary is watching.

He is fixated on a busy parking lot. A strip club's neon sign is flickering, *Babes, Babes, Babes*. She listens and hears a man laughing at a young girl in a short skirt and heels trying to squeeze past him to get in her car, but the drunk, burly man is blocking her way.

"Come on, darling. Just one more dance for your buddy Nick."

"I told you; my shift is over. Now please let me go."

The barfly takes a swallow of her Lotus drink. "I don't think I care to look at that anymore."

"Why, do you blame her? Think it is her fault because she works in an industry where she has to show her breasts?"

"Well, she made the choice."

"So, she did. She made the choice so that she can pay for her college tuition. Believe it or not, that young lady has big dreams of becoming a pediatrician. But college is expensive and since her parents chose to kick her out when she became pregnant, and since she chose to let the kid live and not abort it like her father suggested, then she had to make choices in order for her, the baby, and her college career to thrive."

"How do you know so much about her?"

"I'm privy to sneak peeks in people's lives if I concentrate on them. It keeps me from getting bored." Lifting his head, he looks up at the ceiling again. "Life isn't always easy regardless of the choice made. I'm really not that much different than you. There was a time that I would have taken a glance at such a young girl and think she was nothing but trash that needed to go back to the trailer. But … well, I'm just not like that anymore. You see, the cool thing is I can glance into any country that I don't even know the language to and the words automatically translate to English in my ears. I learn their stories. Everyone has them you know. Some are silver-spooned masterpieces. Timeless classics that need to be placed on the pretty shelves with glass doors in magnificent libraries. Some are tragic and they belong in the dusty section of the Goodwill thrift stores. But everyone has a story. Just like us. Pretty cool, huh?"

"I guess. But if you can do all of that, why focus on the hooker from the club?"

"Again, with the judgment. She had to make choices. Like everyone, it's just hers were made out of desperation. Some have the time to consider consequences, some do it out of fright, and some out of pure selfishness. Besides, if she really was a hooker, wouldn't she be blowing old Nick right now for an extra hundred bucks?"

"I suppose." The lady barfly peers down at her hands. The wrinkles she had in them when she sat down had begun to fade. The age spots sprinkled over her thumb area and a childhood scar on her left hand blended into a silk, ivory glove of softness. "Guess I never realized how complicated things were."

"Neither did I when I was up there," he states, pointing again to the scenes that gathered back together as an image.

"It is interesting what our intuitions focus on. Think about the homeless on the streets. We know they are there, and yet consider how many people continue to look straight ahead when they are walking up and down the aisles of traffic or lounging under the freeways wanting drivers to stop and give them a dollar for food."

Again, she nods her head. "Yeah, well, many of them are scam artists."

"Oh, I know. And several of them choose to beg versus going to one of the shelters and getting on their waiting lists for the many programs available to get them back on their feet."

"My point exactly. Give the dollar to a program for those who choose to work them instead of those only wanting a hand-out."

"Give a fish, feed for a day. Teach to fish …"

"Feed for life, I get it. But it is all about choice."

"Yet, what if a person doesn't know about the choices, do we blame them?"

"I don't follow." The lady barfly looks at Gary with some confusion.

"Think about this. You talked about the scam artists. Some of them actually go into those desperately desired programs after waiting what seems like eternity and they manage to manipulate their caseworker that they are working it, but they don't."

"Then the caseworker eventually figures it out, the scammer gets kicked out of the program, and the spot goes to someone more deserving."

"Perhaps, and that is the ideal scenario, but you left out a piece." The lady barfly shifts on her chair as Gary continues, "You see, if they have kids, and the only life they know is shelters and safehouses with intermittent street life, the lessons they learn do not revolve around the programs and how to improve themselves economically or spiritually. They learn to manipulate a massive system. Instead of Algebra, they learn calculation of benefits and the tricks to get more. They learn the right words to get a warm bed and free clothing. Parents are charged with teaching their children the difference between right and wrong. But that is an ambiguous idea as the scammers right is how to get something for free. Instead of right and wrong, its live or live better. Cycles of free Christmas gifts from do-gooders and limited of real education."

The lady barfly slowly processes Gary's words. "Creating the cycle of situational poverty."

"Absolutely. Knowledge and circumstances impact choices. This is where complications come in. It appears we are judging the person, but we are really judging the choices. You know, like the stripper."

She looks down at her drink in embarrassment. "That doesn't answer my question about how it gets determined who goes to hell or not."

"I'm getting there. When I was a cop, up there ..." again, he points up and the barfly catches a glimpse of several feet walking up and down a sidewalk in Manhattan, "I used to say some people just need killing."

"People who are on death row?"

"Well, yeah, but I would also say it about rapists, mothers that kill their children, or people who hurt animals." Laughing, he shakes his head. "People that would cut me off in traffic."

The lady barfly lets out a chuckle, adding, "Anyone who got on your nerves."

"Yeah, I guess, but now I see these people that come in."

"But you don't see all of them though. I mean, there are different waiting rooms and this one is for people who aren't dead yet."

"Got me there. These people are in between life and death. I can't even imagine if I had to do the whole thing alone. At least a million people die a year. But I do get to see some of the sweetest lives that ever existed and some of the living demons."

"Living demons?"

"I don't know what else to call them. I have learned a lot about people up here and how circumstances made them the way they are. You know, like the shelter hopper, the stripper, and even the sweet church lady who talks holier than thou to the priest and then curses at the cars to get out of her way as she leaves the church parking lot. I still say they are hypocrites."

Kitty Kat shifts and then rolls on her back so Gary can scratch her belly.

The lady barfly nods her head to the cat. "Guess she doesn't know that cats aren't supposed to like their bellies being rubbed."

"Why would she? She doesn't have any cat role models to follow. Just like the kid of the shelter hopper. He follows the only thing he knows. The actions of his only present parent." Gary gestures with his arms at the area around him. "You see, I am beginning to have a grasp on mental illness and timid folks as well as follower's behavior. I get now that there are different consequences for different crimes. The idea that some people really don't know better. And although I haven't grasped it yet, I am learning about forgiveness and seeking redemption." He gets closer to his customer. "Dion did not want forgiveness. He wanted to boast about the evil things that he did with his gift. He was proud of it."

"Gift? What gift?"

"Life." Gary takes a deep breath. "We all make mistakes. People don't always make things right when they do, but that doesn't mean that they didn't want to, or in some cases realize they should have. Even when they do, circumstances may prevent it. But the opportunity for prayer never goes away. We can talk to Father whenever we want to. And although those we trespassed against may refuse forgiveness, he never will."

The lady barfly gazes at him in admiration. "Seems like you have come far since you have been here."

"Well, I can't say this has been my favorite job, but it has given me an education on mankind. The humanity that resides in most of us."

A tall, pretty woman with a short, blonde bob, hazel eyes, and polished nails wearing an elegant suit approaches the bar.

"Hello," she says in an intellectual voice.

"Oh, hi, Geraldine. You snuck up on me." She gives him a startled look, so Gary quickly composes himself. "I'm sorry, do you prefer Gerri or Violet instead?"

"Violet. I like Violet."

"Yes, the name you gave yourself."

"It's quite pretty," the lady barfly chirps.

Violet steadies herself on a barstool. Turning back to the Cocytus waters, she eyes a large, distorted shape swimming silently, leaping out of the water on occasion and tasting the filthy air of the abyss.

"What would you like to drink?"

"A Red Manhattan if you would be so kind to make."

"Hmm, a Red Manhattan. Are you sure you don't want a margarita to wet those taste buds of yours? One with extra lime and lots of salt. It could be your last you know."

Violet looks at him steadily, then thoughtfully replies, "That does sound good."

"You don't really like Red Manhattans, do you?"

Violet pauses for a moment to contemplate her answer. "I didn't catch your name."

"Sorry, ma'am. It's Gary." He extends his hand, allowing her to give him a firm handshake, relaxing her a bit.

"Here's the thing, Gary. Violet likes a Red Manhattan in one of those fancy Martina glasses, but Gerri, the person I was born as, loves a huge margarita with lots of salt."

"Margarita it is, and I must admit, that has always been my preference as well."

The lady barfly desperately wants Gary to ask about why the name change, but after the last customer that came through, she felt it best to observe in silence. It's clear that Violet is not as much of a talker as some of the other visitors that have stopped by, so Gary waits for time to take its course.

Violet is on her third tall, icy cold margarita before she finally speaks.

"I changed my name to match my new life. Violet, a beautiful, vibrant color. Geraldine is so common. So boring. Named after my father and looked like him, too." Staring down at her drink, she shakes her head. "He wasn't exactly what some would call handsome. Neither was my mother for that matter." She looks at Gary, wondering when he's going to start asking questions, but he's focused on his drink and petting his cat. Straightening her shoulders, she says, "I settled into a rather boring life. My grades were about as average as my looks, so the best that I could do after graduation was to go to the local junior college and live at home while I waited tables."

"There's nothing wrong with that," Gary says in a matter-of-fact tone.

"It's not what I wanted though. It was what was expected of me. Graduate, go to college, find someone to marry. Have kids and raise them to be just as boring as their parents are." Her words lead into another long pause.

Gary and the barfly keep it company until they hear a soft gasp. Violet's elegant hands loosen on her glass when her small drink straw starts to twirl in the drink on its own. Pulling her hands away, she stares in mesmerism as some of the drink's salt flakes off its rim and dives into the lime green funnel cloud forming inside of the glass.

Gary nods to it with a smile. "Pretty cool looking, huh?"

Violet glances at him and then back down at her drink, catching a glimpse of what is to come in the eye of the tunnel. Bells sound up from it, and as it begins to settle down an image of a twenty-year-old Geraldine, or Gerri, is seen in a long, white wedding gown fitted with a veil and a light blue clasp on her pearl necklace. Her eyes focus on her younger self walking down the aisle with an excited young man waiting for her. She takes a deep breath. "I really did love him." Lifting her head, she meets Gary's gaze. "Wyatt that is. I loved Wyatt."

The lady barfly fidgets in her stool, wishing to see what Violet and Gary could see.

"He seems like a fine young man."

"He was my first. I'd known him since elementary school, but it wasn't until my freshmen year in high school that we really started talking. We were both in the band. I played the flute, and he played the drums." She becomes silent for a moment, but this time Gary interrupts it.

"Was it your freshmen year that you fell in love?"

"I'm not sure really. We talked a lot that year, and in our sophomore year he asked me to the homecoming dance. That is when we became a couple. We never fought like our friends did in their relationships. So many of them would date for a month or two and then be off to the next. Wyatt and I never broke up. We never fought, and we were accepted by each other's parents. He was comfortable. Safe. With him, I didn't have to worry about rejection. He saw past my big nose and chubby waistline, and I saw past his adolescent acne and thick glasses. Then we graduated." She takes a drink. "We grew up really."

"Highschool sweethearts. I like stories like that."

"I guess you can say that. He asked me to marry him. I think that was what he thought he had to do. He lost his acne, got contacts, and became handsome. I talked my parents into giving me a nose job for a graduation present and started eating healthier. The year we got married was when I started dying my hair. The year I got pregnant; he went to work for his dad. He didn't want to be a welder, but his parents talked him into getting his certifications, and then he was offered a job at where his dad worked. And, well … well, he found that he could make a good living from it, so he gave in."

"Is that what you felt like you did. Give in?"

Violet hesitates for a moment before answering. "I did love him. I still do. I just wanted so much more." She looks down at the image. Aunts, uncles, and cousins surround her at a reception hall. Smaller children telling her how pretty her dress is, older ladies telling her she is going to make a marvelous wife and what a delight it will be when wee ones come along. Wyatt sits next to her, collecting cash gifts, smiling ear to ear.

"Look at him. He was so happy. He took me to Wichita for our honeymoon. Wanted to see the old Cowtown Museum. Wyatt wasn't exactly a romantic type, but then again, it wasn't like we had the money to go to Paris. Not that he would ever plan a trip to Paris for me."

"I take it that he didn't make you happy."

"Oh, he did the best he could. Hard worker, provided for his family, but … well, when it came to treating me like a woman, it was like I didn't exist. He would only take me out on a date if I made the arrangements. Even then, I could tell he never really wanted to go. Appeasing me was his duty, not his desire." Chewing on her straw, her brows knit together in thought. "You know, he never planned anything for us. Not an outing, a vacation, much less a weekend getaway. I was too much trouble I guess."

"That does sound boring. Shame. Traveling really opens the mind," Gary says quietly.

"Oh, don't pity me. We did travel a few times. Went to New York and Massachusetts. It was fun, but … well, I had to plan it all. He was never the spontaneous type. And definitely not the planning type."

She stares back down into the funnel's eye again.

"My parents were proud. So were his, I guess. Marriage was the next necessary step in life, so we took it." As she speaks, the funnel calms down. She stares at it until it becomes liquid over salted ice. Then she circles her glass with her hand, before taking a swallow, chewing on the ice, then spitting a cube back into the glass. "That was such a long time ago."

"Losing time has a way of creeping up on you."

Violet lets out a laugh. "How would you know? Seems like everything stands still up here."

"No, here it overlaps. Here you just become more aware of it."

Violet shrugs her shoulders again and looks out into the crowd. "Why so many rivers?"

"They provide barriers to each destination. No one crosses unless the river allows it."

"I thought hell would be hotter than this. You know, fire everywhere," she states, nodding toward a winged monster releasing a baleful cackle at the gamblers, dangling from a vast cliff poking out from a mountainous wall. Some look up occasionally with worried, scared eyes, but most continue to drink their drinks, play at the tables, and ignore all the beasts dancing off the fiery chandeliers occasionally lashing out with sharp talon dripping hideous blobs of acid saliva from their mouths. Some with three heads, a few with conjoined bodies, reptilian appendages flying over. Occasionally, one shielding a normal, sometimes even pleasant looking face plastered on a grotesque body engulfed with tumors.

"The architect of this place must have done some serious acid." She starts to stand on the bar at the bottom of her stool to get a better look at the amphitheater shape but nearly loses her balance, her left foot falling directly on a sharp rock protruding near the stool.

"Careful, you don't want to lose your step. People think that once they are in this realm, they can't get hurt, but this is not the place to try out that theory." Stepping closer to her, he motions to the walls. "You see how it is curved like this."

Violet nods.

"It is said that the demons who come out of the left door can send messages to the angels at the right door by speaking into the walls. They can hear each other's voices as they vibrate through them while all of the patrons coming out of the elevators, the gamblers in the casino, or even myself at the bar cannot hear them." Taking a drink, he shrugs. "Pretty cool, huh?"

"But why would the demons want to talk with the angels?"

"Haven't you ever conversed with someone you don't agree with? Especially at work. People come in all sorts of fabric and different threads that weave their belief systems. Often, they are similar except for one little thing, and that one thing opens the doorway for all the bickering to begin." Gary shakes is glass watching the ice rattle together. "It is not so different here. The demons bickering with the angels."

"I don't understand."

"What is the difference between good and evil?"

"That's a stupid question," Violet snaps in irritation. "Those that don't sin go to heaven, and those that do evil acts go to hell. You make it sound like it is some complex decision when it is not."

"So how do you determine what a sin is?" Gary's voice is sturdy.

Violet's eyes flicker while her mind races in confusing circles.

"I'm not quite sure that I know what you mean. It seems pretty obvious."

"Is it? We have all heard the scenario where a person steals a loaf of bread to feed their family. Stealing is a sin, and yet what do you do if your family is starving? Do you let them go hungry?"

"You are right. I have heard that a hundred times at least, and everyone I know gives the answer to steal the bread."

"But stealing is a sin. Should they go to hell?"

Taking a sip of her margarita, and then licking the salt off her lips, she finally responds, "I am very sure that I am not qualified to answer that dilemma."

"Maybe so, but I bet you have been placed in that position. I am quite positive that you have been placed in a situation, and you have made decisions that you were sure were justified."

"Nope, I can honestly say that I have never been in that position."

"Think abstractly. It doesn't have to involve starving children or bread. It can involve other propositions. Even internal ones that involve your soul. Has your soul ever starved for nourishment?"

"I'm afraid this is way too philosophical for me, and I certainly can't see angels and demons bickering over such nonsense," Violet says, her voice softening as she notices the funnel cloud forming again in her drink. It kidnaps her mind to a scene where this time she is in her old living room with the torn, plaid couch and yellowish stained blinds keeping out a blistering sun. She is flustered, a crying baby in her arms, her blue nightgown torn and baby spit-up stained, and her hair a tangled nightmare mess.

"Please take her," she begs a young Wyatt who just walked in.

"Let me change first. What's for dinner?"

"Wyatt! I'm exhausted. Mother has gone home, and your mom doesn't like me. I am alone all day with no help."

"Mom likes you fine."

"Wyatt, the baby, please!"

"What? She's three months old. She sleeps, eats, shits, and sleeps again. How hard is that?"

"She cries nonstop, and I can't figure out what's wrong."

Wyatt kisses her cheek and takes the infant. Talking in a cooing voice, he says to the baby, "What are you doing, Giselle? Making Mommy a little crazy." As he speaks, the baby begins to calm down.

Gerri, as she was then, watches the two in admiration. "That's the calmest she's been all day."

She glances up from the drink for a moment. "Wyatt was a natural parent. I could never get the hang of it." She then looks down at herself as Gerri, the conversation continuing. "Maybe I'm not cut out for this mommy thing."

"It's a little too late for that."

"I feel like I am moving backwards." She stands and looks at her reflection in the mirror, her body still distorted from birth. "Wyatt, I want to go back to college. You know, get my degree. I've always wanted to be a writer, but I can't get publishers to take me seriously."

"You can't go back now. Giselle's too little. Aren't you, little one?" Wyatt says affectionately to the baby girl who had begun to drift off to sleep, a tiny hand wrapped around his index finger. "Wait until she starts school."

She protests, "But by then we are sure to have another baby and all my dreams will be put on hold for even longer."

"Here's an idea … if you want to write, then write. Nobody is stopping you. What's for dinner?"

"It's not that simple. And if you are hungry then make your own damn dinner."

"Hey, don't use language like that around my little girl. I've been at work all day. What have you done?"

"I've been taking care of your little girl," she says exasperatedly.

"Funny, because from the look of the phone bill you have been spending most of your time talking to your so-called physic. I told you to stop that. They charge by the minute, and they are all nothing but frauds."

"I'll have you know that I have gotten some insightful advice from Angela. She says that I have a future in broadcast journalism and that I am wasting away here in Coldspring. I should be living in Manhattan where my talents will be recognized."

"Yeah, well, I'd say anything you want to hear too for $4.95 a minute, Gerri. But we have a baby to feed, and a house note to pay. Angela does not need to be on our payroll."

Still engaged with the scene, she speaks, "I was Gerri then, or Geraldine. My birth name. I believe it was at that instant I had made the decision to change it. I had begun to plot my move to New York City that very moment, and for the move, I would need a name that would be more marketable."

"Was it?"

She doesn't respond. Instead, she continues to watch the scene that's still unfolding.

"I know you have dreams," Wyatt's voice floats up, "but you have a family now. Dreams are just that: dreams. It's time to wake up and smell the baby vomit. Besides, look at her, she's so cute." Wyatt held the child closer to his chest, kissing her head. Gerri plopped down on the couch, exhausted, picking at the oozing stuffing scab purging from a hole partly patched with duct tape.

"Have you even changed out of your nightclothes from last night? Jesus, Gerri, you look awful."

"I loved her so much. Him too." Her voice becomes melancholy. "I don't know why I couldn't be happy. Mom shrugged it off as post-partum depression. But …" She wipes away a tear. "But my depression lasted for years. Right into the time that Virgil was born and then longer."

She glances over to the lady barfly and then to Gary. "I knew that was going to happen, too. I watched Wyatt climb up the career ladder and the social ladder. He landed a job in the office, became his own dad's boss, and made great money in no time. The only thing that I could make was milk, and even that eventually dried up. He was such a good man, too. Never even looked at another woman or ran around with the boys. There were times that he would stop and have a beer with the other managers at work." Her voice starts to get harsher. "I actually resented him for that. Why could he have friends and I was expected to stay at home with the kids instead of going to work?"

Directing her voice to the lady barfly, she asks, "Do you know that when I would ask him to watch the kids on a Saturday so I could get my hair done, or do some shopping, he would refer it as babysitting?" She then looks over to Gary. "When it is your own kid, you are not babysitting. You are doing your job." Staring down at her hands, she shakes her head. "He didn't see it that way though. Here I was married to a great man and had two beautiful children, and yet, I felt so lonely."

The lime green funnel cloud turns and twists again, this time revealing a little bit older Gerri with a six-year-old Giselle and a two-year-old Virgil in the eye of the storm. The boy climbed on her back while she tied her daughter's shoes. "I didn't appreciate their playfulness or their growth. I was too absorbed, pining away about the disintegration of every social relationship that I once had and the only outside interaction I got was from an occasional wave in the car drop-offline at Giselle's school." Faking a chuckle, "I use to fantasize that the school crossing guard was my friend and the elderly checkout clerk at the grocery store had a crush on me."

She then got quiet for a while until she felt a scalding spray of water hit her back. Turning her stool, she looks around to see a horned demon pulling himself up from the hot waters, pointing a long, boney finger at her, laughing … taunting her.

"Pity Party for the shit collector," it cackles.

Then two more swoop down from the ceiling, diving into the waters, letting out a howl before beginning a water fire splash fight among themselves. A fizzling sounds each time waves splash against the jagged shores.

"Don't mind them," Gary says. "That's how they get their jollies by messing with my customers." He glances down at his newly refilled margarita. "So, how exactly did you go from Gerri to Violet?"

She turns her head in embarrassment. "It wasn't my intention to abandon them. At first, I convinced myself that I was just going to go away for a few days. Teach Wyatt a lesson. Get him to appreciate my brain, my feelings. Wakeup call so to speak"

"And did you appreciate his?"

"Don't be judgmental! I talked, and he wouldn't listen." She fiddles with the ring on her hand. "Instead of talking back, sharing what he would dream about, he just went into the garage. Watching old black and white television shows. *Hogan's Heros* was more important than me." She's sorrowful when she explains, "That's why I left."

She looks back at the waters, taking note of the large rocks with deadly points poking out, glistening as each wave smashes against it. "I don't deserve this!" Violet shudders as she watches.

"I was lonely. I know I had two kids and a wonderful husband, but I was so lonely inside. I yearned for more. I wanted to travel more but Wyatt didn't want to spend the money. I couldn't go to work because the children were small, and with what little education I had, I wouldn't be able to earn enough to cover the cost of childcare. I couldn't be the person that I wanted to be." Violet looks back down at her freshly filled glass, mountains of salt sticking to the rim, the silent image inside of her hiding a suitcase in the trunk of her car. Her snuggling baby Virgil and gently rubbing Giselle's hair. She pulled away when the doorbell rang. It's Wyatt's mother.

"Nana!" the child happily hollered out.

Stooping down to capture the bouncing girl, the older woman exclaimed, "There's my girl!"

Wyatt's mom was energetic with a young heart despite her sixty-five years of life and arthritic hip.

"She loved the kids. I knew that she would be a good help to Wyatt," she says softly. "I'm sure he relied on her quite a bit for the next few years. A person would never have known she was just a few years away from having a deadly stroke. She never told us she had high blood pressure, and she hid her anxiety well. I guess she had to … after I left."

"Left?"

"Yes."

Looking down again, she watches as Wyatt's friendly mother says, "Go on now, dear. Don't worry about the kids. You deserve a day to yourself. If you are not back by five, I'll go ahead and start dinner."

Without lifting her head, Violet tells them, "I've heard so many stories of women having horrible mothers-in-law that would try and control the house and belittle them, but … well, she was never like that. She adored her grandchildren, and she treated me as if I was her real daughter. I mean, there were times that I didn't think she liked me, but I guess all women feel that way sometimes about their mother-in-law."

The scene shifts to an image of her younger face, then pulls back like a special lens camera, showing her in the car, driving down the driveway, turning left down the street in her neighborhood.

"Good-bye, Debbie Lane," she whispers. Then she takes a left on a major road right outside of the neighborhood, passes the hair salon where she got her hair done yesterday. Wyatt didn't notice but Gladys, Wyatt's mom, would have noticed if she hadn't had a scarf tied around her hair. Gladys noticed every time there was something new. Giselle in a new dress, Gerri's nails when she got them done, when Wyatt had new boots. She even noticed the new kitchen towels at Thanksgiving. She was like that. Tentative and nurturing. Born to be a mother. Gerri envied that. She was not like that, and she knew she never would be. She turns on Highway six, leaving behind Gladys, her high school sweetheart, her two beautiful children, and herself. Geraldine, AKA Gerri. The farther she drove, the less she was Gerri and the more she became Violet.

She explains herself to Gary, "I thought about going back. Even at that moment that I was driving away, I thought about turning the car around, running into the house, grabbing Giselle and Virgil, and holding them close to me to beg for forgiveness. That night, in the hotel, I cried and cried. I wondered what Wyatt said when he got home. I wondered if he thought I was out late or if he called the police or at least checked the hospitals. He probably figured the old, beat-up beater that I drove wouldn't get me far but the mechanic, Jason, who I took it to two weeks before said it was a mechanical brute and as long as I changed the oil every six months and didn't try to jump a canyon, it would last, not like these newer, foreign cars that were getting so popular with their complicated computers that had to be set often."

She looks back down at her drink, seeing herself crying on a musty smelling bed in a small hotel room that is so close to Coney Island that she can hear the sounds of the Ferris wheel's tinkling music and the banter of two young men outside on the streets.

"I don't know how long I stayed up that night, but I knew when I eventually woke up from a restless night, had a stale bagel and gross coffee, that I wasn't going back. The next day I found a nice, clean extended stay near the bridge, and after flirting with a neighbor he got me identification introducing me as Violet Price. I had less than a thousand dollars cash, so I had to do something fast. I waited tables for a few weeks and interviewed for more elaborate vocations. It wasn't long before I landed a job with Simon Barrator, a congressman for the ninth district in New York."

"Wow." Gary interjects, "I wouldn't have figured you for a politician.

Laughing, she shakes her head. "Well, neither would I, but I wanted something with prestige, so while I served pancakes and syrup at an all-night diner, I answered phones and promoted his well doings during the day."

"Did you agree with his politics?"

"Well, I didn't come from a family of liberals if that is what you are asking, but I didn't completely disagree with the party. It's just …" She pauses, searching for the right words.

Gary lets her process for a few minutes before asking, "It's just what?"

She takes a breath, then slowly releases it. "Simon did some things that I didn't always agree with. Things that had nothing to do with his political career. He was a lawyer, but he made investments in real estate." Pausing, she frowns. "He liked me a lot." Her eyebrows rise when she says it. "He offered me a place in one of his *investment condos.*" As she speaks, she holds up her fingers to make quotation marks. "It was a hell of a lot better than the place I was at. I just had to be his friend." Violet's cheeks burn from embarrassment. "I felt bad. I abandoned my husband. I didn't divorce him."

"How much time had gone by before you got involved with Simon?"

"Well, I began working for him two months after I left, but

it was about six before he set me up in the condo. I didn't have to pay rent, so I stopped waiting tables at night." Placing her drink down on the bar, she says, "I should have never let him get his evil claws into me."

"Evil claws? A bit harsh don't you think?"

"Like I said, it wasn't his politics that I disagreed with. He had a huge warehouse near the docks."

Suddenly, the ground begins to tremble and then shake, causing stalactites to become massive missiles as they whizz into the waters.

"What was that?"

"Don't mind that. The boss just likes to shake things up occasionally to remind lost souls where they are." Winking at the lady barfly, he tells her, "Keeps them on their talons. Can't have too much fun down here." He nods at Violet. "Tell me why Simon is so evil."

"Well, he spent a lot of time with me at the condo. He even took me to Florida a few times. Not sure what he told his wife about me, but if she minded, she never confronted me about it." Taking a drink, she shrugs. "Anyway, Coconut Grove was beautiful. I felt like I was always meant to be there. It was where the dreamers and beautiful people lived."

"Really? I thought that was where people go when they have one foot in the coffin."

"Stop it," the lady barfly hisses at him. "You are being rude."

"All right, all right." He looks back at Violet. "And which one was you?"

"Huh?"

"A beautiful person or a dreamer?"

"I suppose both. I didn't always look like this though. Florida was where I had all my surgeries. My breasts, a chin to match my graduation nose. Simon even gave me a new butt. I'm not even sure if Wyatt would recognize me from all that I got done. I went from frumpy housewife to millionaire barbie trophy."

"Was that your goal?"

Violet's face stiffens. "No, but I was better off than I was, and to get further I needed money. Simon had money."

"But you said he was evil." Violet gets quite at his remark, but Gary probes anyway. "Why go to Florida? I'm sure they have great plastic surgeons in New York." He lets Violet stay quiet longer, stroking the back of Kitty Kat who is snuggled up close to the lady barfly, purring in her sleep.

"Like I said, he had business in Florida. He had connections with the Venezuelan government. Except ..." She gets quiet again.

Not doing well in hiding his impatience, Gary blurts out, "You know, I'm not your judge here. I have no control over your destiny. I'm just here for you to reflect on your past choices. Drink more margaritas. The beauty about being here is that no matter how much you drink, you will not become intoxicated. You will not lose control of your facilities. Hell, you won't even have to pee. So, relax and enjoy the memories."

"I'm afraid what I am telling you is not bringing me any joy."

"You made the choices that you made for a reason, it's time to face that."

"I was attracted to Simon because of his wealth. He was a real jet setter. He had properties in both New York and Miami, and he had negotiations for more in Texas and Colorado. He had a privileged life. One that I wanted."

"What part did you play in his life?"

"He put me in control of his properties. I was listed as a partner, although I really had nothing to do with the business except to sign my name on contracts when he wanted me to."

Taking a drink, she straightens up her posture and continues, "You see, as a finance lawyer, Simon helped his friends in Venezuela set up their companies and create their trusts. Because they paid him so well, he decided to invest the money in real estate. That way he would have a financial backup when his political career kicked up. Politicians don't get paid as much as people think. That's why he needed backup."

"You didn't get concerned when he had you signing contracts?"

"I did work for him you know. The residents in his condo in Coconut Grove and in New York had my contact information. If they needed anything, I followed up with the building's maintenance. He gave me a nice salary for that. Separate from his campaign funds. He used one of his accounts out of the Cayman Islands to pay me. Guess it was another way for his wife to not find out. But it helped me as well. I didn't have to pay taxes, which was great since Violet didn't have a social security number and I couldn't use Gerri's. Wyatt would find me if I did."

"And this was the life you wanted?"

Violet looks at him for a moment, then at the lady barfly, and back at him. She listens to the sounds coming from the casino and tries to focus on the ceiling, but her scattered mind does not allow her attention to remain on one thing. When she does speak, it's off topic.

"You know, the nightlife in Miami is phenomenal. I could go out and dance all night and everyone thought I was beautiful. Sometimes I would go out with Simon and his friends, and we would club hop like young adults. It was glamorous."

"Did you eventually move there?"

"No, Simon made it clear that he wanted me based out of New York because I was essential in managing his office in the ninth district. It did begin to feel as though I lived part time in Florida. He used to go with me when I went, but eventually, he trusted me to handle the business on my own."

"But earlier you described your job as someone who mainly signed contracts."

"Well, that's right, but I had to be around for aesthetic purposes. Make tenants feel secure that the property was being taken care of. Meet with clients when they would come to town, make sure that deposits were made into the different accounts he set up."

"The Cayman accounts?"

"Among many. Sometimes the payments that were made by his finance clients were deposited into the condo accounts as if it was rent payments, and then other times payments were deposited into the foreign accounts."

"To evade taxes?"

Violet's voice becomes solemn. "I never understood those type of matters. I just knew that money had to be placed in the different accounts. He never wanted one account to have more than a hundred thousand in it. He said that would raise red flags for tax audits. Possibly hurt his political career. To him, that was where the power came. By being a politician."

"Doesn't sound like you were accomplishing your dream as a writer or a broadcast journalist."

"Oh, but you are wrong. I met this one lady named Helen Hatcher who worked as an investigative journalist. She had an assignment on an expose on what she referred to as the curiously rich and prestigious. When I told her of my interests, she offered to meet me for coffee and talk about the business. She had connections. Connections that could help me."

"How did you meet her?"

Violet begins to answer but the drink in her hand starts to warm, and the lime funnel once again appears. She looks down in it and sees herself happily talking to Helen.

"Isn't that odd? She turned on her phone recorder. I don't recall her doing that when this happened." Looking up with knitted brows, she asks in a cross tone, "Are you altering the images?"

"My good lady, I do not have the ability to alter a memory. I do know that sometimes we alter them in our minds and often need a refresher. Keep looking."

"So just how many buildings does your boss have?" Helen is heard asking Violet in a friendly tone.

"Oh, I don't know. I only handle the Miami and New York properties. I don't really consider myself a business associate. More of a condo manager. So, tell me about your expose."

Violet bleakly stares down, mumbling to herself, "How could I be so naïve?"

"Well, I'm interested in the congressman's business acquisitions. I think it is important to show the American people that anybody can be successful if they put their mind to it."

"Well, if you like, I can set up a meeting with him. I'm sure he would be happy to talk to you. He is always looking for positive publicity. How difficult was it for you to get into this career? Do you have a degree in journalism?"

"I would much rather talk to you, Violet. Your insight is valuable."

Violet looks down, embarrassed by how enamored she was by the whole situation.

"He began with all of his subsidiary companies back in 1972. It was much more difficult then as technology wasn't as common. He found a way though to make his contacts. He has very prominent friends you know."

"Really? Tell me about them."

"Well," Violet rattled, "he knows all these people from Venezuela, some even attached to the government."

"And is he their lawyer or just their financial conservator?"

"I'm not sure, but I know that when he had me sign documents, there is always one of their people witnessing it."

"Violet," Helen said excitedly, "do you have copies of everything you signed?"

"God no. Simon has all of that stuff. You really should let me set up a meeting with him for you."

"Oh, in due time. But, Violet, you should never sign anything that you don't keep a copy of. Does Simon have any file cabinets in here?"

Violet jerks her head up. "I'm so stupid! I didn't even see it. I was looking for my big break and here I was hers."

With a tone of sympathy in his voice, Gary asks, "Was she really an investigative journalist?"

"More like investigative journalist for the government. I didn't know it, but they were on to him way before I even got in the picture. He was pulling illegal profits from around the globe and here I was trusting him. Who would have thought that a US congressman would be involved in so many corrupt deals?"

Gary gave the lady barfly a harsh look when she let out a sputter of laugher.

"Excuse me," she says, "I got something caught in my throat." She then nuzzles her face close to Kitty Kat's face to receive her fair share of cat kisses.

After a cross look, Violet continues defensively, "The Simon that I know was kind and generous. He provided jobs in Florida to foreigners, helping them when they were escaping economic destruction. He was planning on doing the same in Texas as well." Raising her eyebrows, she states, "That's why he was traveling there. He wanted to secure buildings in Houston. One day, when I was back in New York, he pulled me into his office and put me on all these bank roll statements in Switzerland and Holland. Why, I have never even been to those places." She turns her attention back down at her glass. "Didn't even get to travel out of the country. Guess my transformation from Geraldine to Violet was a bust."

Violet grimaces when the twirling funnel cloud again changes scenes. This time she was in an office with Simon, and he was pushing papers in front of her. "What's all this?"

"Nothing to worry about. I'm going to use accounts to make a small loan that will double my investment in just a few short months."

"I didn't really follow the details, but I felt so important, and so appreciated to be trusted to sign off on so much money. This wasn't the first time, but I remember this time clearly. It was a lot of money." She looks over at the lady barfly. "Six million dollars," she whispers in an urgent voice.

The sound of the cackling demons in the background crept closer.

"How much time had gone by since you saw your children?"

"A few years, I guess. I tried hard not to think about it. The more time that went by, the easier it was to forget. Well … I can't actually say that I forgot them, but it became easier to convince myself that they were better off without me. I have heard the phrase that was a lifetime ago, but I guess that can come true. It was definitely a different life. It was like the married life wasn't mine. I was meant to be in the one I created. The only thing I kept was my skin. Even my appearance changed drastically."

Her mood goes solemn again, and Gary takes the cue to give her some space. When her drink is almost empty, he nudges on her hand and directs her to look up at the beveled mirror ceiling.

"You know, the gold isn't as tacky as I thought it was when I first got here." Suddenly, she notices the images begin to take shape. In the center, she sees a grown-up Giselle.

"Wait!" Violet says in shock. "No, she wouldn't be that old. Giselle would be only … wait, let me think. Giselle would just be …" She lets out a low gasp. "Oh my God, she would have already graduated high school. She would be in college now. And Virgil … why, he would be a senior I think." Noticing that her margarita is successfully filled up again, she grabs it, drinks it much faster than the others and waits impatiently as the glass begins to fill again.

"I know what you are doing, but don't get your hopes up," Gary says with a hearty laugh. "You ain't getting no buzz down here. The man upstairs wants everyone completely sober when they go to processing things such as life."

Tears fill Violet's eyes. "My God! I'm a horrible person!" she wails.

Gary rummages behind the bar, looking for a Kleenex.

"You fucker! You tricked me. This is all a façade to make me feel bad about myself, but I don't. I never hurt anyone. I never killed anyone or stole things. I'm a good person."

"I knew I'd get her. There's usually at least one blubberer a week," Gary says toward the lady barfly's direction.

Violet ignores him, sniffling on her jacket sleeve. "I left my husband and kids and for what?" Her cries get louder. "I never got to stardom. All my fancy stuff was paid for by Simon. My BMW isn't even in my name. He put it under one of his companies' names. The feds confiscated it along with all his other stuff. A few houses, the family yacht. All of it. I didn't see if coming either. But it wasn't my fault. I didn't steal."

Gary hands her a box of Kleenex with cupids on it. She grabs a handful, mascara smeared under her eyes and the sleeves of her jacket. "He hides his assets, and I have to pay for it." She puts her hands around her drink, about to take another swallow when she sees the funnel cloud again. She is in a conference room, the table made from cheap laminate. Not like the sleek tables in Simon's upscale New York office with framed campaign posters diligently displayed along with pictures of him with his family. One of the kids in the pictures, the girl is what he jokingly refers to as a rent-a-daughter. She is his niece, but voters appreciate an authentic family man, and since he is the model of one, he added a kid to make his image more impressionable.

In the conference room, two men in cheap business suits are questioning her … or badgering her was more like it.

"Miss Price, are you aware that you will be charged as well?"

"I don't know what you mean," she replies in a nervous but stern voice.

Her face only flinched when the older man was heard saying, "Seems like you don't even know your own name. It's Walters, isn't it? Geraldine Walters. What … you didn't think we would find out? That stuff isn't hard to come by. You know you were reported as a missing person back in 1982. Course you don't seem to be missing to me."

Violet's face turned pale, and she panicked. "Are you going to tell Wyatt that I am here?"

"Lady, you got a lot more to worry about than Wyatt. You have money laundering and tax evasion problems to worry about."

Violet looked up and said in a whisper, "I don't even know what that means." She looked back down.

Another man entered the room, introduced himself as Barrio Cantu, her lawyer.

The men left in the image as Violet watched on and is heard saying in a whimpering voice, "I didn't hire a lawyer."

"No need. The court appointed one to you."

"Why? I did nothing wrong."

"No, you did, but it seems to me that you weren't aware of it." He pulled some papers out of a soft leather briefcase. "At least that is what I intend to convince the judge tomorrow at your arraignment."

"Wait, am I under arrest?"

"You mean to tell me that you weren't read your rights and booked yet? Son of a bitch."

"I don't understand. What for?"

"I need to see the arrest report first, but from what I can tell the main charge will be money laundering through wire fraud and racketeering."

"Sir, I swear, I have no clue what you are talking about. I run an office and some buildings."

"Are you not the signee on twenty of Simon Barrator's off-shore accounts?"

Violet looked at him in confusion.

"Bank accounts that he has in other countries."

"Why yes, I guess. I wasn't aware there were so many, but those accounts are strictly for business purposes. I never withdrew for my own expenses. I swear."

Mr. Cantu looked at her with concerned eyes. "I need you to be honest with me."

Violet nodded, fumbling with the cuff on her jacket.

"What is your name? Your real name."

"Geraldine Walters, but I changed it a few years ago to

Violet Price."

"Not legally though."

"No, sir."

"What did you do with the money that Mr. Barrator gave you to run the properties?"

"I'd deposit it into the bank and use it to pay the maintenance crew and the bills of the properties."

"And the money Mr. Barrator gave you to live off of?"

"I'd withdraw cash for most of my personal expenses, and living bills was paid off another account in the Cayman Islands that Simon set up for me."

"Where did Mr. Barrator get the money to pay for his properties?"

"From the money he earned by helping the Venezuelans with their contracts and finances?"

"What kind of contracts were they?"

"I don't know."

"Who were these men from Venezuela?"

"I don't know," Violet said again, this time in a louder whimper.

"So why did you sign the contracts?"

"Because Simon asked me to."

"And if he told you to jump off a cliff, would you?" Gary asks as a sarcastic response.

"Stop it!" the lady barfly snaps harshly.

Violent doesn't pay any attention. She is too busy watching herself putting up a defense in the scene.

"I don't see how I can be considered guilty of any kind of money crime. I never touched the money. I never even met these people unless they were present when I signed something. Even then, I didn't talk to them. Hell, I didn't even know the language, so how could I possibly have done anything wrong?"

Mr. Cantu leaned back in his chair, rubbing his temples. Taking a breath, he ran his hands through his hair. "Gerri—"

"Violet, I go by Violet."

"Violet, regardless of your knowledge, you signed a contract entering into an agreement to handle the money. Your role in the activity is small but it is still a crime. A felony for that matter. And … well, if the feds want something from you and you don't cooperate, they can make this small part become huge."

Violet watches herself cry in the scene and plead with her lawyer. "But I don't know anything about it. Violet Price isn't even my real name. How can it be accepted as a contract if my real legal name isn't on it?"

"Oh, I am going to use that." Mr. Cantu sat forward. "But they are going to try and prove that you did know everything. However, there is something that you can do."

"What's that? Please tell me, I'll do anything."

"You can flip on Simon."

Violet gets quiet in the scene, looking around desperately at the grey walls and then down the table. She whispered, despite them being alone, "Simon is powerful. He has friends in high places. He'll get off. He gets away with everything."

"Like what?"

"Like hiding money and drugs in the storage houses by the docks. Like helping illegals cross the borders in Texas through big eighteen-wheeler trucks, charging them outrageous fees to falsify documents. The list goes on, but I'm sure nobody will believe me."

"So, you had to be aware of the good politician's criminal activity or you wouldn't be able to tell me about it now. Did you help with any of the things that you knew were illegal?"

"No, sir. I tried to talk to him about it once, but he said if I said a word that I would go to jail for a minimum of twenty years."

"So, think about this carefully because the prosecutor will come up with this. If you knew he was involved in illegal activities, why did you agree to sign the contracts and deposit funds? Think carefully about this, the prosecution is going to try and prove that you had knowledge of this as well as the human trafficking that you are speaking of."

"I don't know. Really. I wanted to please him. The position he put me in made me feel important. Surrounded by politicians from all over the world. Entertaining them, it all felt so glamorous." Wiping a tear from her face, she shook her head. "Besides the campaign funds, I really don't know anything about how he handled money."

"What about the campaign funds?"

"Nothing really. He took the donations flagged for the free clinic in his district and told me to take a portion of it and put it into one of the properties' accounts. I thought it was weird, but he said it was okay that the banks would flag him if the deposits were too big."

"Okay, listen to me carefully. I think I can get you released on bond, but when you stand before the judge tomorrow, I want you to remain silent. I am also going to go to the feds and tell them that you will cooperate with their investigation."

"What do you mean?"

Violet looks up at Gary as Mr. Cantu's voice echoes into the air, "They don't want you. They want Simon. It's an election year and they want to take him down."

"That was one of the last conversations that I remember before I came here. I was so scared but. I didn't tell Simon anything about what I had talked about with him. Mr. Cantu told me that I was not to have any contact with him, but I had no place to go, and all my funds are through him. I couldn't even pay for a hotel." Violet gets quiet. "I didn't tell him I was going to take a plea in exchange for information. Somehow, I feel as if he knew. He's a polititician. Politicians have connections."

She drinks another margarita, looks scornfully over her shoulder at three laughing demons on the shores, splashing water at a woman on the backs of the Styx sobbing hysterically. She turns back to Gary. "I'm a fraud. Flat out fraud. I wanted to be the adoring journalist, but instead I am a socialite wannabe, and I got mixed up with a man who sent me here."

"What do you mean?" Gary asks.

Violet looks down at her drink and blinks as she is commanding it to create another scene. Another memory. The funnel begins, quicker this time, and inside is a scene of Mr. Cantu walking her out to a white BMW.

"Thought this was confiscated?" the lawyer remarked, admiring the expensive car.

"Simon was able to borrow this for me," she is heard saying as she reached over and opened the door.

His expression turned to one of panic. "You didn't tell him anything about our conversations, did you? The investigation is going strong. You promised information. They will come and pick you up tonight if they think you have changed your mind about the testimony and—"

Violet held up her hand and shook her head back and forth. "Don't worry, I haven't changed my mind about anything. I just needed some wheels and a place to stay. Simon took care of that for me."

"We got you a place to stay at the Extended Stay, you don't have to—"

"It's all good. Trust me," Violet said with a smile as she turned her car engine on. "Simon would just be more suspicious if I didn't go back to the condo. I'll see you soon and thank you so much for everything."

Mr. Cantu watched as Violet pulled away and exited the parking lot onto a feeder road. She turned up the radio as she entered the New York State Thruway. The traffic was much slower than she was used to. The day was beautiful, the music was loud. She hummed her way until she saw, in the distance, a stalled tour bus on the Thruway. *Must be going to Niagara Falls,* she thought as she tapped her brake to slow down … but her brake did not work.

"Shit!" she yelled out loud, staring at the speedometer.

Seventy. I'm going fucking seventy, she thought.

"I had no idea why I was going that fast or why I couldn't slow down. The traffic was slow. How could I have gotten up to such a high speed?" She watches herself desperately stepping on her brakes, back and forth repeatedly, looks down and then looks up. Violet's shoulders scrunch and her eyes close in a tight grimace as Gary watches her gorgeous BMW fly and swerve, avoiding the back of an eighteen-wheeler but slamming hard into the side rails, sending the car to its side.

Violet's eyes remain closed for minutes after the scene reveals the fiery crash.

"I guess I'll die a fraud. I'll never know my children. Wyatt will never know that I still love him."

"That's not my call," Gary says, wiping down the bar. "Your glass isn't filling back up. I guess you've had your fill."

"I guess I have." She pulls out two gold coins, the shine reflecting off the mirror on the ceiling. She looks up but is unable to focus on anything. She then looks at Gary. "So what do I do now?"

Gary points to the slot machine, the lights glistening off it in an inviting way.

Violet looks down at the ground, concerned for her stepping, but the violent earth tents are gone. Her foot lands on a bubbled, cobbled ground. She's surprised but says nothing. Her hand hangs on the bar as she walks her way around to stand in front of the great slot machine.

She smiles. "My daddy used to call these spin sinners. Said that they were just as addictive as booze." Turning to face him, she shrugs. "Maybe he was right." She then inserts the coins and listen for the clunk, clunk sound.

"Don't look, Daddy," she whispers as she grabs hold of the arm of the machine and pulls down with all her might.

A chorus of honking horns from traffic jams sound, then the laughter of children screeching. "I've found it, Mama. I've found the last Easter egg," the child shouts, church bells ring through, a school bell, Harry Chapin's "Cat in the Cradle" begins to play. "I'm gonna be like you, Dad" sings out loud as the eyes of the machine spins at top rate speed, then it slows, a soft chug sounds out and then a plip.

The barfly is nervous on her seat, Gary fixated, as Violet says out loud, "*Arbitrium.*"

"I don't understand," Violet says quietly.

"Choose," Gary states sternly. "You get to choose life or death. The choice is in your hands. The most important choice you will ever make, and the one you will never remember."

"But why?"

"Sometimes we get a gift, but we don't really like it. We don't appreciate its value, so we return it in hopes to get our money back and get something better. But sometimes we keep that gift. Perhaps we don't like it, but we don't want to hurt the feelings of the person who gave it to us, and then we find that it grows on us, and we learn to appreciate it. No particular reason, we just do. What do you want to do, Geraldine? What do you want to do with your gift?"

A large tear plops out of her eye. "I want to see my children again."

"Then you shall." As Gary speaks, the waters of the Acheron calm as a pristine, white bridge forms over it.

Gary bows. "Allow me to escort you, Ms. Price."

Violent gives him a coy smile. "Well, sir, it's actually Mrs. Walters."

She then loops her arm around his and they walk quietly side by side down the bridge.

The crowd across the Cocytus throws out a friendly greeting as the two walk by with a few shoutouts, "Good luck, ma'am. Godspeed."

"Keep throwing those bones," Gary hollers. "There are no door prizes here."

As they reach the bridge over the Styx, Gary stops and turns to the hysterical woman still sobbing from earlier.

"Lady, ya gonna 'cause my banks to overflow. Go join the party." He pulls the woman up with an it's-gonna-be-okay nod and a gesture to the casino, and she steps on the bridge to the Cocytus.

"Here's your ride," Gary says as they approach the elevator.

Herman, the tall, Lurch-like creature, nods and press the emerald button.

"Good-bye, Violet."

"You forgot. It's Gerri now. Like the Jerry can. My daddy once told me I was gonna light a fire in my town one day. Guess he wouldn't believe this."

She then turns to Herman. "Wouldn't suppose this lift got some disco music?"

"Wouldn't know, ma'am. Not really my thing," Herman says in a deep drawl.

"Wow, dude. Didn't think you ever spoke."

Gerrie lets out a bark of laughter and waves good-bye as the elevator doors close. Gary stands there a moment and then turns right to view the Mare Lacrimarum.

"You just keep filling up, don't you?" he whispers as he bends down and plucks an elegant, yellow rose from a bush fed by the waters. At that moment, the waters of the Mare Lacrimarum tremble, then the waves grow stronger as a surge of water rushes through, sprays landing on Gary's face as he closes his eyes. "What is it now? School shooting? No … wait … plane crash? Nope, a bus crashed into a crowd. Forty-three dead. Yup, that'll feed the Sea of Tears for sure. God be with those families."

He then makes the sign of the cross, walks to the corner of the sea and the Lethe River, and listens.

An angel opens the door ever so slightly to release a few chords of "Family Tradition" by Hank Jr.

Gary laughs, breathes in the cool air, and then walks across the Acheron to his bar. His lady barfly friend smiles as he hands her the yellow rose.

"My favorite," she says as she smells it.

Gary smiles. "I know."

Then in loud, echoing voice he lets out another holler, "Last call."

Geovanni

Gary swerves around to step back and glance down at the Phlegethon River with a curious gaze. He spots six marked men with tattoos of serpents, flailing their arms, attempting to crawl up a steep slope that narrows away from the fiery water. They release cries of agonizing fear as the leaden weights strapped to their ankles tug down on them yanking on the frail thin layer of skin they had remaining and make them bleed but not enough to make their withered feet break away. Monk-shaped forms lend an occasional boney limb for them to grasp, gently offering an olive branch of refuge. But right as one of the desperate men touch the boney tip of the index finger, the evil monks yank their hands away, heckling shrills of laughter, mocking their victims, elated with themselves over their deceit.

"Poor bastards," Gary mumbles as he walks forward, avoiding any eye contact with the lurking demons. His position did not make him untouchable from their foul pranks. They would love to grab him by his shoulders and dangle him over the lava pit waters. He stops mid-point where the Acheron and the Styx meet. Three large stakes protrude while a tall, gaunt man with a shaggy beard and coal-like eyes tiptoes through his passage. His steps are elongated and careful as he weaves his way through the ominous maze, quietly hoping to avoid falling in the large snake pits that form with each lift of his legs.

"Coming my way?" Gary asks, a touch of pity in his voice.

The man gives a breathless nod and takes a small leap to cross to the Acheron side when a sudden rumble in the ground shakes him to his core. He takes hold of another group of three stakes, holding them with all his might to avoid falling into a gruesome pit, only to bloody up the palms of his hands as the spike's decorations of metal thorns pierce his skin. The shaken man lets loose of one and allows his hand to form a fist while hurling a vulgar obscenity at God.

"Wouldn't be doing that if I were you," Gary advises.

"What the hell? What more can they do to me?" As he speaks, the spikes begin to move slowly, rippling in his other hand. Suddenly, he is violently struck in his jugular vein by a thirsty cobra.

Gary watches as black-red blood spurts out of his neck, his face turning crimson red, lips whitening. Gary has no affect at all.

"Apologize. Ask for forgiveness." Gary scratches his head. "Look, dude, you're not going to die like this. You will just be tortured with unexplainable pain and riddled by all of your worst nightmares. The ones stuck inside of you. You know, the ones you didn't even know existed until now."

The man gurgles something inaudible, filled with remorse. Gary can't make out what he's saying, but he must have muttered the right words. His terrified apology is heard by the right entity, and he is immediately released. He slumps down to the fragmented ground. A sullen cobra slithers away, followed by two of its mates into the rapacious waves of the broiling waters.

"Rules say I can't help you up, but I can stay here until you are ready to walk with me," Gary says firmly.

The man looks up and tries to speak, but his gullet is not healed yet, so he whimpers.

"Take your time. It seems you've got a hard road to climb.

The man looks up and realizes that his steps on the bridge have once again begun to form. Although not as treacherous as the ones before, he can still see that the shattered rocks that pave his bridge are sharp and slippery, and that passage will be slow. He glances back. The snakes have disappeared into the water. His buddies, which he left at the casino, forgot him the moment he took the dare to walk the bridge. The doors of the Lethe were not within his sights and the doors on the side of the Phlegethon were shielded by the shadows of dancing flames entertaining guardian demons.

Looking up at Gary, he understands that his only hope is the man before him. Not very tall in stature and not particularly kind. But it is him who will serve him his last drink. The drink that has become legend in the land shielded by the Cocytus. And although grand tales of his magical abilities have been embellished in the sin city, the façade had lifted, and standing before him is a man. Just a man who is trapped in this godforsaken place just as he is. Yet somehow, he holds the upper hand. Here he is, a man like him. A man that lived once and probably sinned like him; maybe more than once. After all, why bring a man of great altruism down to hell where he is privy to the torture of lost souls? He lifts himself up. Terror fills his body. Afraid of the monstrous reptiles lingering at his feet, the dancing demons swooping down and lashing at him from the ceiling, the echoes of laughter bouncing off the rocked walls in disembodied voices. He is not afraid of Gary though. He knows he means no harm, and like the cop giving a speeding ticket or the waitress serving the undercooked food, a job has to be done and it is this man's fate that he does it to the best of his ability. His face softens at the sight of Gary, who stares upon him, not offering assistance or words of comfort. Just an indifferent gaze.

"The walk may seem long, but I can tell you the rocks are cold at the bar." He then turns around, waiting as the man limps after him. He was never more than a pace away, despite his fragile shuffle.

The waves of the Acheron soften as they cross it. Gary grabs a towel from underneath the bar and wipes the already shiny surface. The man carefully eases himself into a bar stool directly before him, the bottom cracked as he unloads his weight onto it. He notices that the floor underneath him is caked with ice.

"Guess you were right about the rocks being cold," he says wearily.

"I meant the ice, but I guess in this case I can speak for the stool. What can I get for you?"

"Do you have Crown Royale?"

"Geovanni, I have everything."

The man lets out a crooked smile. "So you know who I am?"

"Only what I'm privy to, and I suppose that I am privy enough to know that you want your Crown with a splash of Coke."

"You got it, uhm … sorry, I didn't catch your name."

"What do they call me down there?"

"Besides fearless asshole?"

Gary lets out a laugh. "Don't think I've heard that one before."

"Well, you have been described as some sort of centaur, but that is clearly wrong, and then there is cicerone, chaperone through hell, Sherpa … but the most common one is The Ferryman."

Gary nods in agreement. "Yeah, those all sound familiar." He turns to make the man his drink, and as he passes it to him, he adds, "I'm not exactly what you expected, am I?"

"Can't say that I knew what to expect. Then again, I can't say that I ever expected to end up in a place like this."

"Travels don't always come with an expectation list." Gary gives the bottle a whiff before he pours his own Crown and Coke and takes his perch across from him, his eyes checking to see where his cat is, a little disappointed that she is comfortably sleeping in the cradle of the barfly's arms. sighing, he turns and takes the time to focus on his new patron. He notices that he has Matthew 5:17 tattooed on his right forearm.

"Didn't take you to be a religious man."

"What?" Seeing Gary's gaze directed toward the fading words on his arms, he replies, "Oh, this. I'm not, I guess. Hell, for a while, in my youth I didn't even believe in God. I started dabbling in that Scientology crap if you can picture that. Gave them a shitload of money before I realized that the whole damn thing was based on science fiction. If only I could have that money back." Geovanni was quiet for a bit, studying Gary. "You got any smokes around here?"

Gary immediately pulls out a new pack of Marlboros and offers him a light.

"You take one, too. I don't like to smoke alone."

"Nah, you go ahead. I don't touch the things. Snuffed a can of Copenhagen a day, … well, up until cancer took hold of my mouth. Rotted it pretty good, too." He winks at the barfly. "That sure as hell wasn't a pretty sight. I will keep enjoying the drink with you though."

Geovanni holds up his class high. "Well, I'll toast to that."

The two glasses clang together. Gary brings his to his lips, sips, closes his eyes to let the liquor seep in, opens them again, and looks up at the mirrored ceiling. "Ah, good stuff." He then reaches his hand out. "I'm Gary."

Geovanni extends his hand. "Pleasure, I'm sure."

"So, Scientology you say? Heard some crazy shit about them. Even heard of them being thought of as a cult."

"Yeah, well," shaking his head, "they caught me when I was down on my luck. And oh, they paint a real pretty picture when they are recruiting. Indoctrinating you into their beliefs."

"I'm curious, Geovanni, do they believe in God?"

Geovanni lets out a chuckle while bringing his glass up to his lips. "Funny you say that. I never got a straight answer myself. All I got was these pretty words about how man is good, and his salvation depends on how he conducts himself in all facets of life."

Gary swallows a gulp of his own drink and then thoughtfully says, "Well, that sounds cool. I mean, man needs to take responsibility for his own actions."

Holding his class up to see it through the light, Geovanni chuckles, "Oh, you don't know the half of it. Friend, let me tell you, they spin a perfect world with their words. Although I didn't see it at the time, when I think back, it was like being locked up in a box with a bunch of politicians. You get internet down here?"

"Nah, half the people I deal with don't even know what internet is. They are slow to come up here. So, anyone from the eighties or before, forget it. They don't even really know what dial-up is."

"I was going to say, check out their website. It is a prime example. They state that they help you to help yourselves and the people are around you. Well ..." Geovanni pauses.

"Well, what?"

Geovanni holds up his hand again. "Hang on. I'm trying to think of an analogy to get my point across." He takes the last swallow of his drink. "What the fu—"

"Yeah, bottomless drinks here."

"Well, I'll be damned."

"Scientology?"

"Oh yeah. It's like those old timey music boxes that you wind up with a key. It sings real pretty music and then stops mid-tune. To keep hearing it, you have to throw in a dollar into the pot to wind up the music again."

"It seems to me that all churches ask for money. Hell, I'm Catholic and we were giving a dollar every mass. Sometimes there were two collections."

"Yes, but the Catholics let everyone in. I know. When I was down on my luck in Florida, I stumbled across a soup kitchen run by Catholic Charities. Yes, they had preaching going on when you ate in a separate room, but to receive the food, it wasn't a requirement that you listen or convert. Not like those big television churches with their preachers with egos as big as their wife's ass. These people, the pastors, and the volunteers. They focused on you. What you needed. If you needed food, you got food. If you needed a hot shower, clean clothes, a place to sleep …" he pauses, "they did everything they could to help you. It didn't matter who you were or where you came from." Geovanni looks down at his drink. "That's what I should've done. Stayed with them. Not carrying it on down the street."

Geovanni feels a chill run up and down him. He looks around to see where the cold winds are coming from, but the only visible movement is from the unaffected gamblers he sees in the distant casino and the sloshing of the burning waters. He turns to Gary, who is completely unaffected by the temperature. He then looks down again at his half-drunk drink. The ice cubes that never shrink with each sip even when he slurps it up in his mouth and then spits it back into his glass. A light dances across one of the cubes. He studies it for a minute, thinking he sees his reflection, but when he peers at it closer, he notices a purple swirl manifesting in the cube … and then a pink one, and then it opens a tiny scene in the glass that explodes in his mind. He sees himself, young, mid-twenties. He is sitting at a long, white, plastic table like the ones used in school cafeterias, but he is not at a school. He is in a barn-shaped building.

As he sat down, a young priest walked up and sat down with him.

"Hello, I'm Father Michael," he said with a gentle smile, reaching out to grip his hand. His perfectly manicured nails, and silk-like hands firmly grasped Geovanni's dirty hand poking out of a badly stained jacket cuff.

After the handshake, he pulls it back quickly, embarrassed about his appearance and undeserving of kindness. "Sorry, sir, I've haven't had any time to clean up."

"No worries," Michael said pleasantly, "we've got a place here where you can clean up if you like. We can get you a place to stay, too, if you need. We have many services."

"Father, I ain't got no money."

Michael smiled again, and in a smoothing voice, stated, "You don't need any here." Then he got up. "I didn't catch your name."

"Geovanni, sir. My name is Geovanni Rossi."

"Fine name. I'm pleased to meet you, Geovanni. There is an office over there." Michael points to the corner of the room where a newly built addition was added, housing a small desk with an old, white lady with a grainy, high-pitched voice answering the phones.

"Go see Jackie when you are done eating. She'll get you hooked up with some services. Work too if needed. Honest day's pay can do wonders to build confidence."

Geovanni looks up from the scene and says to Gary, "I worked in their food bank and resale shop for four months. Most steady employment I had ever experienced. I didn't get paid much, but they got me in a little efficiency apartment at a transitional center and paid for my food and gave me clothes. I was walking distance to work so I didn't need nothing. When it was time to move on, they helped me get a better paying job at a warehouse stocking orders for the big companies that went around and cleaned up oil spills and stuff. That was the highest paying job I had ever had up to that point. Well, at least that was honest work." Looking back down at his drink, he nods. "I had a lot to be thankful for. They changed my life. Got kicked out of my house for getting a girl pregnant in high school, ran away right after the birth of my son, and ended up on the streets of Florida, blending in with the Cuban immigrants sneaking over. Hell, one of the shoes that I was wearing was one I found that washed up on the shores of the beach. Imagine that me and my mismatched shoes. Father Michael or that old lady Jackie didn't say a word about it." He lets out a loud laugh, gulps down a bit of his drink, puffs on his cigarette, and mumbles to himself, "Me and my mismatched shoes. God, I was a pathetic sight."

Gary remains quiet, dropping a few cat treats close to him, initiating Kitty Kat's transition to his side. The lady barfly rolls her eyes at him in irritation.

Geovanni looks down at his drink again. Watches the interaction between him and Jackie. The scene jumps forward to him packing food boxes before saying out loud, "I was doing a good thing then. Didn't know it at the time but I was."

"But you eventually left to work at a warehouse?" Gary asks, breaking Geovanni's thought process.

"Uh, yeah. I worked at the warehouse for a while, but after a year or so, I was able to buy me a car and I went to work for a grocery store chain. I impressed them, so they sent me to management school. I found me a nice girl along the way until I got her pregnant and married her."

"What happened to your other child?"

Geovanni lets out a disgruntled snarl. "Don't know. I didn't leave a forwarding address."

"Regrets?"

Geovanni drops his gaze down to his hands wrapped around his glass. "I did a lot of bad things. Things that I am not proud of. I thought I was immortal I guess you can say." Looking up at Gary, he explains, "You see, right before I went to work at the warehouse, I got stopped by the Scientologists one day on my way down to the beach. I was used to them passing out their pamphlets and such. I was never one to pay any mind to propaganda, but this one girl, boy was she hot. So, I took her pamphlet and started to talk to her." He licks his lips after a swallow. "I was thinking I'd be able to tap that, if you know what I mean."

Gary shifts his position and nods, self-conscious of the barfly listening.

"Anyway," Geovanni continues, "I started chatting her up, so she invited me to one of their services. I thought what the hell? I hadn't really committed to the Catholics, and it wasn't like I ever paid attention when I did bother to go to services. Anyway, I go there, and some dude starts talking about some garbled gock about making positive choices in your life and the lives of others."

"Any talk of God?"

"Well, no, but it still seemed on the up and up. I mean, they believed in equal rights and that men had rights to lead their lives the way they choose. It sounded great to me. There didn't seem to be any reason to not buy into it. Hell, I felt immortal. That's where I met Rose."

"Rose, the girl that got you involved."

"Oh, no, that bitch led me on. Turned out she had a husband. Rose came later when I was studying the books. You see, the Catholics accept you for who you are, but the Scientologists put you through a series of tests. When my results were in, I was informed that I had a weak character but that was okay because they were going to make me better. Apparently, according to them it wasn't my fault because I was being punished for things in my past life." He laughed. "In a past life I was a grasshopper or some bullshit like that. Anyway, they could help me through it and make my life better and successful. Of course, that came with a hefty price tag. Money that I didn't have."

"So why not go back to the Catholics?"

"Because the Catholics preached about God and Jesus' salvation and being good Christians. I didn't want that stuff. I didn't want to be preached to. I didn't even care if I became a better man. I just wanted a better life, and it seemed that following the cult would get me there."

"Sounds like you wanted an easy way out. The cure all without having to deal with your conscience?"

"Kind of like that. With God, your soul and your life are a gift. With man, to each its own."

"So, in other words, with man you can get away with treating someone like garbage as long as it promotes yourself."

"Yup." He sighs. "But every time you turned around, they wanted you to buy more books, do more counseling. Hook you up to machines that looked like they were made from empty bean cans and string, yet it could tell you what a screw up you are by a single touch."

"And for this, you turned against God."

"At the time, I didn't see it that way. But I did take the Scientologist creed to heart. Even after Rose became clinically depressed. She started neglecting herself, the kids, and me." Geovanni looks down again at his drink. The ice cubes shimmered in the bright lights and moved slightly on their own in the beveled glass.

Then lights shot up, the cubes swirled, and a scene opened of a red-haired woman in her early thirties slumped over the kitchen table, a baby crying in Geovanni's arms and a toddler pulling on the motionless woman. "What's wrong with Mama?" she asked, looking up at Geovanni, wide-eyed.

"I should have gotten her help. I knew better. People at the church tried to convince me that mental illness wasn't real that she would snap out of it, or they could send her to Clearwater for a few weeks. I listened."

His right-hand balls up in a fist. "I'm so fucking stupid." He pounds on the bar. "My aunt …" he lets out a breath before continuing, "my Aunt Gene, she was bi-polar. She lived with us for a while. I knew this stuff was real. I'd seen it. We were miserable when she lived with us. Especially my mom who was always pissed at her because she had to be the one to make excuses for her all the time. She would tell us kids that it wasn't her fault that it was the disease talking. The Scientologists … hell, they think they can talk it out or work it out with manual labor. They believed that if they isolated or did some weirdo vitamin therapy or some stupid shit like that the ideal of depression would float out of their heads. Fucking bullshit! Mind sickness, it's real and I saw it in my Rose, and I didn't do anything about it. Hell, I made it worse."

"By not getting her help?"

Geovanni pauses for a few minutes. He drinks another Crown and Coke in silence, his dark, beady eyes darting back and forth. "Let's just say that my actions didn't help out much."

"What do you mean your actions?"

"I cheated on her. More than once too. I'd had started working in the grocery store business and I'd take on another cashier almost every other night. Some were even underaged. But I didn't care, or at least my dick didn't. I just wanted to live for myself. I figured if something came up, I'd get one of those fancy Scientologist lawyers to help me out. They were always helping people get out of jams. Bad people, too." Sipping from his glass, he shook his head. "Got one of them pregnant."

"One of the bad people."

"Hell no, smartass. One of the cashiers. You know, from the store I managed."

"Sounds like you fathered kids everywhere you went."

"Hey, I took care of my kids."

"Really? What about the one you abandoned when you left home."

Letting out a huff, he raises his voice defensively. "Okay, almost all of them, but that cashier bitch, she got pregnant on purpose. I know it as sure as I am sitting here."

"What did Rose do when she found out?"

Geovanni looks back down at the image. Rose slumped over, his daughter, Alicia, tugging at her, his son, barely five months old screeching while he frantically talks to the 911 operator.

"No, ma'am, I can't find a pulse. Alicia, go to your room please. Daddy will be in there in a minute."

"But what's wrong with Mommy? Why won't she wake up?"

"Alicia, please!"

Geovanni mumbles, "Kids can be such a pain in the ass. Especially when there is a crisis going on."

"Did she die?"

"The paramedics came. They were able to revive her. She survived, but she was banished from the church. They wanted me to disconnect from her. They said she was a suppressive person, and it was best for me and the kids to stay away from her. I think that is when I snapped to it."

"Snapped to it?"

"Yeah. Who in their right mind would tell somebody to shun the person they love because they were depressed? That's ludicrous." After taking a sip, he continued with a softened voice, "Now that I think of it, everything they said and did was ludicrous when I look at it under a microscope."

"I've heard horror stories about how they will not let you leave. They stalk you and talk bad about you … even go as far as to destroy a person's reputation and screw up their lives so bad that they go to huge lengths to disappear and all that shit. Did they do that to you?"

He takes another sip and smiles at Gary. "Nah, I'm not important enough for that. Didn't have enough coin to make their dirt digging scavenger hunt worthy. Besides, I don't think

I was ever really invested into the whole survival depends on yourself and the people you have around you type of thing."

"Doesn't sound too bad to me"

"Again, everything sounds good until you can't find the key to the music box."

"Did you stop cheating on Rose?"

"For a few months."

Taking a gulp from his own drink and leaning on the back bar, Gary waits for Geovanni to look up before commenting, "Only for four months? You don't seem very remorseful for your philandering. Were you?"

"Yeah, well, sex addiction is real. Besides, after Rose's failed suicide attempt, I had to do whatever I could to keep Tamara quiet."

"Tamara?"

"The little bitch that got pregnant. She ended up keeping the slimy little thing and demanded money or she was gonna to tell my wife. Hardly think Rose could handle that. Do you?"

"Guess not." Gary's voice softens but he doesn't lose his firm stance. "But you do know that all your whoring around fucked with your girl's head, don't you?"

"Yeah, well, the deed was done. So, I had to take care of it."

Looking back down at the glass, Geovanni sees he had grown a mustache, a beginning of a beer gut, and his hair looked greasy, sleeked back with a distinct gold chain peeking through his shirt that was not buttoned up all the way, revealing the flash and few black chest hairs. A slender, dark-skinned girl with a swollen belly is leaning over him, listening to his words.

"I've added a few extra hours to get you some more money. Almost a hundred dollars' worth."

"That's stealing. You'll get caught."

"Nah, if something is said, they'll think it's Terry. He's the one listed as doing payroll."

"All this over a broken condom. You must be proud."

"Hey, you could've aborted the thing. You could still give it up. My friend, Hector, and his wife desperately want a kid. They could take her off your hands."

"Fuck you. I know he offered to pay you for her. You're sick."

"Hey, you keep complaining about money, I'm just offering a solution."

Tamara walked out, slamming the door behind her. Geovanni kept looking at a computer screen, opening up another window playing a porn video.

"Terry got fired." Geovanni lifts his gaze to meet Gary's. "Not for the stolen money either. They got him on the porn." As he talks, he feels another shiver go up his spine. Ice cracks beneath him as he shifts in his seat. "Brr," he says, shaking his shoulders. "How long have I've been down here?"

"Couldn't tell you. Time is parallel here, so it depends on how long you've been sleeping." Gary points up as he talks.

"All I know is it was a Sunday."

"Sunday?"

"Yeah, the lord's day. Although, I didn't keep it holy. That's for sure."

"Looks like there were a lot of things that you didn't keep holy."

Geovanni smirks. "Yeah, well, the good lord didn't make man perfect."

A thunderous bolt of lightning streaks through the sky while a sheet of ice rain falls on the shores of the Acheron, waves spurting up so high they hit him in the back. Geovanni shrinks in his shoulders and looks at Gary who is not affected.

"How is it …" he begins, but then shakes his head. "Never mind." He then looks back into his glass.

The Crown and Coke refills itself, the ice glistening, inviting him to take another gulp. A scene unfolds in a purple, pink, and then gold twirl. A sixteen-year-old Geovanni emerges along with the sight of his father yelling at him.

"How dare you disrespect your mother like that? You snuck out and then lied to her. Worrying her to death and for what, so you can get a piece of ass?"

"I didn't mean to disrespect her, it's just—"

Before the child could finish his sentence, the old man slapped him across his face, knocking him toward the wall papered with orange flowers on a yellow background. A lamp fell over onto the woodstove. He could hear the paneling behind the wallpaper crack as he fell. His father backed up, hitting an end table holding a lit candle. It knocked over and the red wax and faint flame hit the thin carpet.

Geovanni's dad quickly stepped on the lit flame, then on the melted wax, embedding it deeper into the carpet. "Now look what you've gone and done!"

"I didn't do that. You did—" Geovanni was stammering his words but before he could get his statement out, he took another strong slap to the face, stinging him.

"You little fucker, don't be disrespecting your Daddy like that. I fuckin' made ya, I have no problem killing ya."

Geovanni looks up and immediately begins an outburst of defense for his ole man. "He's not always like that ya see. It's just when he is drinking. I loved my mama, I never meant to disrespect her."

"What about your father?" Gary asks solemnly.

"I ain't gonna lie." With a chuckle, he shakes his head. "Afraid if I do your boss will send the snakes after me again." Then in a more serious tone, he answers, "There were times I'd like to kill him myself. My dad that is. Especially when he got to beatin' on my mama. Fucking bastard. He got what he deserved."

"What did he deserve?"

"'Bout ten years ago he got in a bar brawl down in Jasper. He pissed them off so good that after they beat him, they hogtied him to the bumper of their truck and hauled him down a back county road. Guess they were so damn drunk that they didn't know how fast they were going. Killed his racist ass. Oh yeah, he was hollering out slurs, offending anyone in sight. That man liked nobody that was not like him. Too stupid to realize that he was the minority, being Cuban and all. The people that done killed him got life in prison. What they done though …" He takes a sip of his drink. "Well what they done was a kindness toward my mama. She don't have to put up with his shit no more even though she didn't see it that way." Geovanni takes another gulp of his drink. "Set us free they did. Set us free."

"You and your mom?"

"Yeah, and my brother, Francis. Francis, hmmm …" Geovanni shakes his glass, and it instantly fills up with Crown and Coke. "Man can get used to this," he says, laughing as he brings the glass to his lips. "Francis, he was such a puny wuss. Smart though. Could have gone to college if Daddy didn't make him stay home. He went to junior college instead of going away. Done real good in his classes but Daddy was always making excuses." Taking a deep breath, he holds it for a moment before releasing it. "I guess I'm partially to blame. I took off so he must have felt obligated to stay behind. Patsy! He should have just gone on."

"Guess college wasn't in the cards for you?"

"Nope. Didn't have the brains, and once I got that whore pregnant, my number was up. That's how I ended up at the shelter in Florida."

"Seems like for the most part it worked out for you."

"Yeah, well, guess I don't see things the way you do." Playing with his ice cubes, he shakes his head. "Nothing was ever good enough for me. Nothing." As Geovanni speaks, the cubes in his glass begin to rattle, toying with him to get his attention. He looks down and sees Rose talking in the backyard of his old house.

She was leaning over, conversing with the neighbors. "Look, honey, The Jeffersons got a new camper. They're gonna take the kids all the way to Colorado. Check it out, it's like an apartment on wheels."

Geovanni shielded his eyes, and hollered out, "Not now. We've got to get the kids their bath."

"I was making excuses you know. Anything to get her inside. Away from Fiona Jefferson."

"What was wrong with Fiona Jefferson?"

"Oh, nothin' if you can handle being around a stuck-up-know-it-all bitch who likes to shove all of what she's got in other people's faces. Her husband was a white-collar insurance salesman. He played off the concerns and misfortunes of others to get his money. He didn't give a shit about the people that he was selling to. All he saw when someone sat in the chair in front of his office desk was dollar signs. Nothing but dollar signs."

"Well, a man's got to make a living."

"Yeah, but off of other people's misery?"

"Embellishing, are we? Sounds to me that you are jealous."

"Well damn it! How'd you like it if every time you walked out your front door you were hearing and seeing about something new they got? Rose was always wanting what Fiona had. And believe me she had it all. Can't tell you how much I enjoyed letting her know that nurturing husband was screwing some receptionist at a car dealership."

Kitty Kat nuzzles Gary's hand. He scratches the bottom of her chin without taking his eyes off of Geovanni. Geovanni sits drinking, shivering when occasional sprays of water slap his back.

"How the hell is fire water so cold?" He looks back down at his drink. The ice magically clinks together as it settles, the brown liquid sloshing, quietly weaving between the cool cubes, a scene again forming. This time, Geovanni on his porch, smoking his cigarettes, laughing. As the scene became clearer, he is seen rubbing his fingers through his hair, rubbed his chin, and then ran his fingers again through his hair. He lit another cigarette without taking his eyes away from the story telling image or seeming to realize he already had one lit sitting in the ashtray next to his drink. In the scene he was kicked back in a lawn chair listening to screaming going on from his neighbor's house. Fiona telling Frank to get out. Pack his bags and go.

"She'd believed it," Geovanni says slowly.

"Believed what?"

"She believed me when I told her Frank was running around on her. I saw him talking to Kate, the young receptionist at the Ford dealer. She liked him. I could tell. She was swinging her heel, letting her toes hang on to the tip of her pumps, like women sometimes do, and then putting her foot completely back into the pump, making her calf's pop out. She laughed at every stupid thing he said. He ate up the attention, too. Like any man would. I mean, our wives stop noticing us after a while. They stop dressing sexy and doing sweet things for us. Their lives become entangled in soccer games and carpooling and lunches with the ladies. Just like Rose did. After a while they, Rose included, forget. They forget to put on a darker shade of lipstick. Some lace panties. They forget to tell us that they are still attracted to us after age has stomped all over our face, pulled our hair out as beer bloats our stomach. And they just stop."

The barfly, who had been quiet this whole time, speaks up. "And you?"

"Ma'am?"

"When was last time you told Rose that she was pretty? Brought her flowers for no particular reason? When was the last time that you asked her out on a date night?"

"Well, ma'am, I have taken her out to dinner to—"

"I don't mean to the local Cracker Barrel where you share an entree to save a dollar. When was the last time you asked her to go to a nice restaurant or a concert or a show? Something you initiated. It doesn't mean as much if she has to be the one to set it up. Make the reservation, plan the babysitter, and make sure the car has gas to get you to your romantic night out that she arranged all on her own and you don't even bother to see the importance of wearing a tie or even a nice shirt. A wife wants to be treated like a woman and not as a dependent that provides the occasional blow job when the mood strikes."

Gary lets out an embarrassed chuckle. "Don't mind her, she's been listening for a while, and she may be itching to move."

"Don't you make excuses for me. Men may want to play

this poor old me tune. My wife doesn't pay attention to me. She doesn't appreciate me. She won't do me anymore, and blah, blah, blah, but that crap is a two-way street. Appreciation is needed on all sides of the gender spectrum. A man can't expect to rub a woman's tit to get them all hot and bothered. Women want to feel beautiful and appreciated and safe. Romance shouldn't disappear after the five-year anniversary. It should be a lifetime goal so that couples stay passionately in love with each other instead of socially comfortable."

"Okay, I get it," Geovanni says condescendingly. "No need to get your panties in a wad."

Gary takes a large swallow of his drink. "Yep, sounds a bit utopian to me. Not likely to happen."

"Well, it should." Her voice has a combined tone of anger and sadness. She looks down at her own hands. "A woman feels ugly and pathetic when they have to ask for attention all the time. Especially sexual." When she lifts her head, her eyes flash, her voice harsher now. "You know, that is exactly why women do erratic things like spend money on useless items or pick up hobbies to keep them away from home. Maybe even fantasize about a neighbor's life. Thinking it is so much better than her own."

Gary shrugs his shoulders and pours himself another drink, but Geovanni goads her with interest. "You say so. You think my Rose needed more of my attention."

The lady barfly cocks her head to the side as if studying him and speaks slowly with thought. "Well, I don't quite know. I mean, it's not like I was there, but …" She pauses for a minute. "It does seem to me that women need more from their man as time goes on. When they age, they begin to feel old and unattractive."

"Well maybe they got fat and stopped caring for herself."

"Is that why you cheated on Rose?"

"I beg your pardon?"

"I heard you. You admitted to running around on her. Why? Was she fat? Did she stop taking care of herself? Stop wearing makeup or taking care of the house? Neglecting the kids even. Did she stop meeting your expectations?"

Geovanni gets silent for a moment. He sips his drink and then glances up at the dancing lights. He starts to speak after a time but then the ice in his drink begins to rattle. He looks down at the twirling kaleidoscope of colors.

"Don't worry, ole boy," he said, slapping Frank Jefferson on the back. "I'm sure it will blow over. You know how women are when they get those ideas in their head."

Frank was bent over a beer in the Twisted Sister, a dark, dank bar filled with vape smoke and sticky floors. He shrugged and said in a whisper, "I don't get it. I mean, I come home to her every night. Hell, my sister babysat that girl she thinks I'm running around with. How she got this in her head is beyond me."

"Women, they're so foolish." The scene darkens, but Geovanni keeps staring. "I wish I could have changed that."

"Changed what?" Gary asks patiently.

"My lies. I told so many lies. I damn near broke up that marriage and for what? Because I was jealous because he had a few too many toys. More than I did." He takes a drink. "I was always wanting more. Even when it came to Rose." He then turns to the barfly. "Ma'am, you're right. Wait. What's your name?"

"Joan. My name is Joan."

"Well, Joan, you are right. I am an ass, and I didn't appreciate my Rose. I was always wanting something better. No matter what in life. Even going as far as to spread the rumor that Frank was cheating on Fiona."

"You told her that?" Joan's brows knit together. "How could you?"

"Not directly. Not really. But I put the idea in her head, and when that didn't seem to seal the deal, I made hints around Rose. I knew Rose would tell her about it."

Turning to Gary, he tells him, "Rose could never keep a secret. Besides, Fiona was her best friend. I mean, she really didn't like her sometimes. She also always felt that the Jeffersons' wealth was getting rubbed in her face, but the truth was, Rose didn't have many friends. Her life was surrounded by the kids and me. She had to make friends in the neighborhood because there was no other place to go and get them. Hell, to her, excitement was when she got a text from the neighborhood watch warning her there was a stranger driving in the neighborhood. So, she talked to Fiona. Over the fence. Morning coffee. That type of thing because she really had nobody else to talk to. Not enough strangers came driving through the neighborhood."

Joan and Gary got quiet. Kitty Kat lets out a meow as she stretches and then flops over, showing her belly. The sounds of the rippling waves provide ambience as Geovanni continues to drink.

"I'm so sorry," he whimpers.

"About cheating on Rose?"

"About everything. I am a horrible person. I've cheated, I've lied and stole, but mostly—" Geovanni heaves a little, choking back tears. "Michael … I'm so sorry, Michael." He cries harder. "I want to take it back, I do. I would do anything to take it back!"

Gary stays quiet as he is allowed an occasional glance into the visions or his customer. The ice shines in Geovanni's glass. He lifts his head to stare into it, a clear vison appears in Gary's mind. Geovanni dressed in black, nervously sitting on a bench near the beach, watching crowds of homeless people go in and out of the barn-shaped soup kitchen. A mass is happening at the church adjacent to it. Bells are ringing, the night is beautiful, and the stars are bright.

"The congregation was especially big on summer nights. During the off season was when people come back from vacation and go back to attending church regularly. That meant lots of offerings." He looks up. "You know, the money they got. You said it yourself. Many nights they would have two collections." Geovanni's voice quickens. "I was desperate. Tamara was threatening to go to a lawyer if I didn't give her money. I didn't want Rose to find out. She was already so fragile and depressed.

I had to do something to shut Tamara up. I figured that the church would get the diocese to bail them out if they couldn't make their bills, so I went there. No security, lots of rich donors who wanted to help the church and the poor. Hell, I'm the poor. Tamara is trashy poor. So, I waited."

Geovanni gulps back tears and looks back down at the scene. He is still on the bench, watching people fall out of the church, shaking hands with the pastor. Getting into their cars and pulling away. The soup kitchen's light turns off. People are leaving. The lot is almost empty. Just the pastor who gives one final wave to a car pulling away. He then turns, carrying the night's donation. In a box. Not a lock box or a safe. A small, brown box. Not much bigger than a cigar box. Something you would expect a child to hide their baseball cards and other pre-adolescent treasures. Not for a grown man, a pastor, to carry the night's offering in. The same container that a five-year-old boy would carry their Matchbox cars in.

Geovanni ran up to him. He didn't know who the priest was at first. He could barely see a slit of a white collar under a windbreaker. "Hand it over!" he hollered in a shaky voice.

The pastor turned in surprise to see the barrel of Geovanni's gun.

His voice lowered and trembled when he said, "Hand it over, Father, and there will be no reason for me to use this."

"Geovanni? Geovanni, is that you?"

The recognition startled Geovanni so bad that he squeezed the trigger of the gun. There was no way to take it back. Not when he heard the smoothing voice. Not when he recognized the kindness in the priest's eyes. The soft, silk hands, the giving heart. It was gone in a moment's notice. The trigger was squeezed. The bullet spiraled into the forehead of the man. The man who offered him food, shelter, clothing, work, and dignity. The man who gave him hope for life when there was not hope in him. The man who he shot down just as quickly as he let out those last words, "Geovanni, is that you?"

The man fell backward before him.

"I'm so sorry, Michael. I'm so sorry." Geovanni is crying hard. His thin, gaunt body shaking. The ice on his stool and the floor beneath him cracking, lights flashing on him.

"I didn't mean to do it."

As he speaks, the vision melts into another scene. Rose at the kitchen table, Geovanni stumbling in.

"Did you see what happened to that priest last night down at St. Mary's? Isn't that the church that helped you all those years ago?"

Geovanni nodded as he sunk down into a chair. Rose placed a cup of coffee in front of him. "Are you okay? You look like you are coming down with something."

"I'm fine," he grumbled as two children, Alicia and Vincent, came flying into the room.

"Mom, Vincent took my—"

"Can you be quiet please?" Geovanni snapped in a harsh tone to his daughter.

"But Dad—"

"Now, you listen to your father. He's not feeling well."

Geovanni looks up. "Nobody knew. The cops figured it was one of the dope addicts that hung out on the beach. Nobody ever thought it was me. Never even considered a suspect." He takes a drink. "I wanted to go to the funeral. I drove there, but I couldn't bring myself to get out of the car. I was a stain on humanity. And not just any kind of stain. A shit stain. I killed a man. And not just any man. A good man who dedicated his life to helping others. He never asked for anything from anyone. He gave my life back, and in return I took his."

Gary and Joan stay quiet; Gary pours himself another drink, and Joan is too shocked to move.

Geovanni looks back into his glass. He is on a boat this time. Vincent is older and he is teaching him to drive it.

He heard a crack in the engine. "I'll check it out!" he told his son. He stood on the end as three other boats rushed by. He lost his balance and grabbed onto a rope, but it was no use. He fell into the turbulent water. The water was deep, and the rope snagged onto something on the bottom. He tried to pull himself up but hit the bottom of the boat with his head. He vaguely heard his boy. His youngest called for him.

"Dad!" he screeched, followed with hollers out to other random boaters for help.

Or at least he thought he heard it. Maybe it was imagination. He opened his eyes under the water but all he could see was a muddy blue. Not the cool drowning images like seen in the movies where the victim looked up and saw a bright light piercing through the vibrant blue waters. Instead, his eyes burned, his head panged, and he felt as if his whole body was being ripped from his groin to his chin. His insides dangled out, and he saw a bright red strand lifting over him. Blood maybe. Or perhaps a hallucination.

"How long was I in the water?"

"Don't know, but since you are in a coma, it must have been several minutes."

He lets out a chuckle. "Hell of a way to get baptized, isn't it? It was Holy Saturday, too." After drinking a bit, he puffs at his cigarette.

"Pissed off Rose to boot. Wanted us all to go to some non-denominational church she'd found so that we could celebrate the Easter holiday as a family." Releasing smoke, he shook his head. "What did I do? I took the boy out on the boat. Didn't want nothing to do with her new holy roller friends. Look what it got me."

Geovanni pauses for a bit, smoking his cigarette. "Gary, have you ever felt stuck?"

"What do you mean?"

"Like from the waist up, you can see the whole world around you. You know it is a great place and there is a way to do better with what you are given, but the lower half of your body is stuck in cement. You can't move. You want to reach for the gold, and to have the holy spirit accompany you, but instead …" Geovanni shifts a bit in his stool. Cracking is heard around him. He looks down and sees a piece of ice from his stool fall to the ground. He lifts his gaze. "I love Rose. I do. I love my kids."

Shaking his head, he puts it down in his hands. "But I'm no good. I've done nothing but cause misery every place that I went." As he speaks, another piece of ice falls off his stool. A splash of water hits Geovanni's back, but it is softer and warmer.

"I'm not deserving of the life that has been offered to me." Large, salty tears fall from Geovanni's eyes. "My kids are so great. Rose is wonderful, and all I do is fuck things up. She left Scientology for me. Everything she ever knew or has known. Even her family excommunicated her from the family. But she did it for me. She loves me. She never stopped loving me."

Geovanni coughs and wipes his nose on his sleeve. His tears are more noticeable. "I'm so sorry." Shaking his head, he puts it back in his hands again, in attempts to muffle his voice, and yet it is clearly audible. "Rose, Alicia, Vincent … oh my God … Michael. I'm so sorry, Michael."

"You're tormenting yourself," Joan blurts out in a passionate tone.

Gary looks at her and then slowly turns to Geovanni. "She's not very good at keeping silent and only being an observer, but she's not wrong."

Geovanni shuffles a bit in his seat, puts his hand on the bar, and opens it up. Two shiny, gold coins dance in the light. "From what I understand, I am to get a spin at your special wheel over there."

"Yes, you do. Feel strong enough to come around?"

Geovanni nods. Using the bar to keep him sturdy, he pulls himself down and feels suddenly alleviated. All the scars from his journey have dissolved. He walks up to the grand slot machine. "I must say, I have been curious about this beast ever since I came up here to rattle on about my misfortunes." He puts the coins in the slots one by one. He smiles at Gary and then pulls down the handle.

Screams echo from the casino. Geovanni looks back.

"Don't worry about them," Gary says gently. "Someone's got a jackpot and they haven't figured out yet that they can't take it with them."

Geovanni lets out another chuckle and then turns back to his own machine. The wheels spin quickly, a cool breeze swooshes into his face, and the sounds of bells tickle the air. "Here it comes," he whispers as the eyes of the machine begin to slow. One by one they stop. Each one landing on the word Arbitrium.

"Arbitrium! What in the world is that?"

"Huh!" Gary says. "Well, ain't that a plot twist." Then, he looks at Geovanni. "You, my friend, have landed on choice. Which means you get to decide if you want to go back to the realm of the living or move on to a new spiritual life."

"You mean, do I want to go to hell. Don't pass go, don't collect two hundred dollars. Just move on to the fiery pits."

"Not my decision on where you go."

Geovanni pauses. "I have life insurance. If I go, Rose and the kids will be taken care of. They are getting older; they will help her." He looks around. "I don't want to live on knowing and waiting on the inevitable. Let me go now where maybe my death will actually do some good."

"You know, regardless of your destination, there are no do-overs once you have made your choice."

"Gary, I've made a lot of bad decisions. I do love my family, though, and want what is best for them. Even if they don't see it right away. It is time for me to face my sins and take my punishment."

"Well, it seems to me that you have spent quite a bit of time punishing yourself."

The waves of the Acheron soften and steps form on the bridge. This time smooth. Geovanni is able to make it with great ease. He looks over to the hissing laugh of the Phlegethon River. "Wish me luck," he says with a hesitant whisper.

"Good sir, you don't need luck where you are going."

A violent wave hurls from the left as the two turns to the right. The waters shine, inviting the men in shades of gold and pink. A chorus of angels began to sing as the pair step toward the Lethe River.

"I don't understand," Geovanni says in confusion. "I've broken them all. The commandments, I've broke them all. I shouldn't be here. I'm a liar, a cheat, a murderer."

The mahogany doors open, and a gentle breeze welcomes them.

"Geovanni, my old friend." A kind, middle-aged man steps just beyond the gate. "Come join us. It's beautiful. Come see the city."

Tears fall down Geovanni's face. "But Michael … how can you? You can't possibly forgive me. From what I did. What I took from you—"

Geovanni falls to his knees and hides his face with his hands. "This is wrong. This is wrong," he wails in rapid repetition. "I'm not deserving of forgiveness from anyone. I am bad. I was born bad, and I will always be bad. That is who I am. Who I was born to be!"

Gary kneels by the man, placing his hand on his shoulders, but before he can whisper his thoughts, Michael holds his hand up to Gary.

"I've got this," he says with a friendly smile.

"My dear friend. The impulse of the living is not who you are. You did something in a moment. A horrible moment that you have spent the rest of your entire life regretting." Michael gently nudges Geovanni's hands away from his face and makes eye contact. "Life is not just one moment. It is a menagerie of many. Some are beautiful, some are sad, and in the case of our last one together, that moment was tragic. But, my dear friend, one moment does not define who you are, and at this one, you are my dear friend."

Geovanni looks at him, his eyes open in a confused wonder as Michael helps him to his feet. "Please come. Come to the city of God. Leave your sorrows and fears behind. You asked for forgiveness, and you have received it. Besides, it was my life you took. Not my soul. Let's go and rejoice in that."

Geovanni embraces Michael. As they do, Gary watches the splendor of the gates opening, and the warm lights silhouette the two men. Smells of delicious foods waft out and the sounds of religious hymns trickle out of the gate. Without turning, the two-walk in.

Gary watches as they disappear farther and farther into the light until they were completely gone and the golden gates slowly close, clanging shut as a flutter of angel wings sound.

Gary turns around and slowly walks back over the bridge, stopping only momentarily to let out a bellowed, "Last call."

Joan

Gary takes his place behind the bar and then pulls up his stool to get closer to the lady barfly and begins to pet Kitty Kat who is still in her arms.

"You know that Geovanni, he wasn't really a bad guy. He just did bad things."

"Aren't we all? Sinners that is."

"Yeah, well we don't all commit murder."

"Maybe not. But I can see you have come a long way during your time at the Last Chance Casino. Your judgement has turned to empathy and your punishments have turned to mercy."

"Well, I guess that I have learned a lot here. I know now that although I thought the world surrounded me while I was on earth, I was merely a speck on the universe. Regardless of our positions in life, we had one, and that means something to someone and well it should mean something to me."

The two get quiet for a moment as they gaze up at the beveled mirrored ceiling. This time they both see the same scene play out. An old cemetery filled with large oak trees and magnificent memorial markers. A young, tanned boy is laughing as he runs through the maze of buried love. A tall, slightly curvy woman with dark eyes and long, dark hair laughs as she catches him.

"You little goblin!" she said while she nestled her face in his dark hair. The boy turned to her, placed his hand on her face, and dropped to rest his head on her swollen belly.

"When will my baby sister be here?" he asked, looking at his mother intently.

"In about six weeks I suppose." She put her index finger under his chin and lifted his head up to gaze in her eyes. "You know, newborns can't count very good, so she will show up in due time I suppose."

"Happy Mother's Day," he said with a giggle. "Next year, you will have two kids to get gifts from. Hopefully Daddy won't be so sad then."

"Little ones grow so fast. Look how smart he is," the lady barfly says while still staring into the scene.

"Just like his daddy, who was just like his mama," Gary replies. His eyes shift to a tall man with thick, blond hair, a slight mustache, and deep blue green eyes. He sees the gold band on his left hand as the man pushes his hair back and wipes away a tear. The voices come in stronger through the vision. The woman talking to her son.

"I wouldn't say that your daddy is exactly sad. He knows that Grams is in a better place. He knows that her back hurt and that her pancreas quit functioning all together and she was miserable. He just wishes he could taste her cookies one last time. Sing with her all the times she asked him to sing and didn't. He just wishes he could go to church one last time with her because he regrets all the times, she asked him to go, and he didn't go. He just wants one more ten-minute talk with his mom. It's normal, Norbert. It is normal to think back and have regrets when someone is gone and to wish they did more while someone was still here."

"But she is not gone," the child said excitedly. "Daddy, Daddy, come here. I have to tell you something."

The boy slipped away from his mother's embrace and scampered across the cemetery again, finding his daddy on a marble bench placed the day the stone was updated. Written across the back was:

Pop a squat. We have lots to talk about!

"God, your mother had a strange since of humor," the lady said after catching up to her son who had plopped himself on his dad's lap.

"Yeah, I know."

He then pointed to the words that were updated on his mother's gravestone. "Look underneath the dates."

His wife bent down, arranging a bouquet of yellow roses so she could see the printing better.

Awoooooooooooooooooo.

"I don't get it."

"When I was small and my mother would wake me up for

school, she would yell out as loud as she could, 'Cock-a-doodle-doo.' Sometimes it was so loud that it would wake up my daddy. God, he would get so pissed at her. At night, after she would tell me some ridiculous bedtime story, that she usually made up by the way, me and her would howl to the moon as loud as we could. Sometimes we were so loud that even the dogs that were outside would get on it." The man started laughing as he spoke. "She was crazy but that was what made her who she was."

"Daddy, Daddy, I gotta tell you something."

The man looked down at his son who was bundled in his lap.

"Grams is still here sometimes. She comes to visit me all the time in my dreams."

Gary stops looking at the scene for a moment and glares at the lady barfly who defensively remarks, "Well, what do you expect me to do when you are escorting your demons? I've got to have something to do. A lady gets bored."

Gary nods his head and looks back up. "Do you think he is happy?"

"As happy as he knows how to be."

"Do you think he will be okay?"

"My grandfather told me once, in a dream by the way, that parents shouldn't be so hard on themselves. You have to take what you are given and do the best that you know how to do. In this case, what was given was the lottery of kids and now he is a magnificent man."

"I suppose so." Gary looks around at the bar and then stares longingly into the casino. "I suppose nobody is up for a last drink." Then he looks at her. "Guess it will be a while before you get another story."

"No need. I am all storied out."

"I would have never thought I would hear that from you."

"Well yes, but I am just here for a visit and now I am tired. I think I would like to go on to my final destination. Besides, I am privy to a little information, too, and I think I want to take advantage of that."

Gary smiles. "Well if you must go. I know you are past the need to take a spin," he says, nodding to the slot machine.

"Aw, no. I have no need to tempt fate." She gets up, holding the cat.

"Uh, no. She stays with me."

"I know that, but …" she nuzzles the cat's neck, "let me hold her while we walk."

Gary smiles while placing his arm around her. "We will be turning right."

"Well, I shall hope so. I mean, I know I messed up some, but I did have a conversation or two with your boss during Sunday masses."

The waves on the river slosh a refreshing cool sprinkle on them as a white wooded bridge with fresh green ivy and honeysuckles form their path. As they walk, the woman's hip becomes stronger and her long, gray braid releases itself and turns into long, dark curls that circle her face, dissolving her frown lines, and brightening her smile.

When they approach the gates, Kitty Kat purring between them, the lady barfly looks up into Gary's eyes.

He looks down and asks, "So, what information are you privy to?"

"Oh, that little baby is not waiting six weeks. She is coming out in a few hours, and I will be darned if I don't get to hold her before she is released to the universe."

"Well, you make sure you give her an extra hug and kiss from her grandpa, too."

"Will do." They both turn to the opening gold gates; the smell of yellow roses and honeysuckles fill the air, and light Lorretta Lynn music in the background begins to play. She quickly looks up at Gary and asks, "When will you be joining me? Soon I hope."

"I don't know. My shift isn't over yet."

As she places Kitty Kat into his arms, she steps up and kisses his cheek. "I'll be waiting for you, my love."

Gary forces back tears as he watches the now much younger woman, the woman he remembers from so many years ago, wave. He waves back, looks up at the ceiling, and chuckles as he hears the man, the woman, and the boy in unison let out a bellowing, "Awooooooooooooooooooooooo,"

He hears her laugh, too, and he quickly looks back to catch one last glance of her before Joan disappears behind the mahogany doors.

He stays there for a minute, then slowly starts walking over the bridge, only stopping to glare out t the casino.

In a deep southern drawl he hollers out, "Last call!"

THE END

ALSO BY GINA LYNELLE SCHAEFER

Tenaha

"Evil lurks everywhere. In woods, in churches, and sanctuaries. In words such as manipulation, trust, and devout. It is the trickery that harms the soul as it sneaks up on someone disguised in shepherd's clothing." Sixteen-year-old Tiffany has gone missing in the small town of Tenaha, Texas, and it is up to a handful of misfits to unravel the mystery behind her disappearance. As the devil dances through the small community only Joseph holds the secret in his mind while Tilly holds it in her soul, and it is up to them to weave through the crossroads between the living and the dead to battle evil with the only weapons available to them: truth and faith.

Thirteenth Hour

Life is a gift, not an obligation. The stuff that you endure, the torture of childish bullies, divorces that are no fault of your own, and all the other squabbles you have complained about are a mere nuisance in the universe. There are much more horrible things and occurrences that people must endure. Even yourself, in past lives."

These are the first words spoken to Merritt by her quirky spirit guide, Alma Chaser, before she journeys through the lost hour of the time-change dimension, where she uncovers worlds where serial killers play, where evil spirits dance, and where she uncovers the triggers that ignite her own unmotivated anger and the hidden evils buried within her soul as she takes on other lives in parallel worlds and times.

Alma looks up. "Oh, that's the tunnel, ready to take you to your first destination. Don't worry. It doesn't hurt. It's quite fun, actually." But before she can finish her sentence, Merritt's soul is gone to dance through time through the portal of the thirteenth hour.

About Gina Lynelle Schaefer

Gina Lynelle Schaefer was born in Lafayette Louisiana in 1970 where she spent the first five years of life dancing to Cajun music and eating beignets. Although she does not have many memories of the swamp, dreams of the amazing cemeteries sprouted throughout the cities mesmerize her mind and igniting a flourishing imagination. To this day she enjoys reminiscing about field trips visiting the historic cemeteries that pepper the landscape where they decorated the graves with flowers and coins in remembrance of the dead.

At the age of six, she picked up her Texas twang when she moved to Spring, Texas, a small suburb outside of Houston where she spent most of her childhood except for a brief stint in London. This is when her eyes opened to a much larger world outside of southern hospitality and a love for all things Victorian grew.

Although these places seem very different in geography, one thing they all had in common was ghosts. Paranormal activity was a bigger part of her life than Barbie Dolls and Easy Bake Ovens. When making vacation plans, she scopes out haunted sites with an interesting back story. When contacted regarding all thing's ghosts, she is there to help with paranormal consultation and investigations and assurance that not all things are evil and when there is, it can be fought with good. Many of her experiences are documented on her social media accounts.

After meeting and marrying an amazing man, she sought out a degree in Psychology, gave birth to her wonderful son Joseph and became a teacher. Now she focuses on her passion of writing paranormal thrillers and investigating haunted sites.

www.ingramcontent.com/pod-product-compliance
Lightning Source LLC
Chambersburg PA
CBHW051301210726
48287CB00002B/616